Deborah Alcock

By Far Euphrates

A Tale

Deborah Alcock

By Far Euphrates
A Tale

ISBN/EAN: 9783337080846

Printed in Europe, USA, Canada, Australia, Japan

Cover: Foto ©Andreas Hilbeck / pixelio.de

More available books at **www.hansebooks.com**

BY

D. ALCOCK

*Author of " The Spanish Brothers" " Crushed, yet Conquering"
" Dr. Adrian" etc*

London

HODDER AND STOUGHTON

27 PATERNOSTER ROW

MDCCCXCVII

BUTLER & TANNER,
THE SELWOOD PRINTING WORKS,
FROME, AND LONDON.

BUTLER & TANNER,
THE SELWOOD PRINTING WORKS,
FROME, AND LONDON.

PREFACE

MANY a tale of blood and tears has come to us
of late from far Euphrates, and from the regions
round about. It is not so much the aim of the
following pages to tell these over again as to show
the light that, even there, shines through the darkness. "I do set My bow in the cloud" is true of
the densest, most awful cloud of human misery.
As in the early ages of Christianity, "what little
child, what tender woman" was there

"Who did not clasp the cross with a light laugh,
 Or wrap the burning robe round, thanking God"?

As in later times, of no less fervent faith, "men
took each other's hands and walked into the fire,
and women sang a song of triumph while the grave-
digger was shovelling the earth over their living
faces," so now, in our own days, there still walks in

the furnace, with His faithful servants, " One like unto the Son of God."

Every instance of faith or heroism given in these pages is not only true in itself, but typical of a hundred others. The tale is told, however feebly and inadequately, to strengthen our own faith and quicken our own love. It is told also to stir our own hearts to help and save the remnant that is left. The past is past, and we cannot change it now ; but we CAN still save from death, or from fates worse than death, the children of Christian parents, who are helpless and desolate orphans because their parents *were* Christians, and true to the Faith they professed and the Name they loved.

D. ALCOCK.

CONTENTS

CHAPTER I

PAGE

THE DARK RIVER 1

CHAPTER II

FATHER AND SON 9

CHAPTER III

FIRST IMPRESSIONS 17

CHAPTER IV

A NEW LIFE 26

CHAPTER V

BARON MUGGURDITCH THOMASSIAN . . . 44

CHAPTER VI

ROSES AND BATH TOWELS 59

CHAPTER VII

GATHERING STORMS 66

CHAPTER VIII

A PROPOSAL 73

CHAPTER IX

PEACE AND STRIFE 91

CHAPTER X

AN ARMENIAN WEDDING 113

CHAPTER XI

AN ADVENTUROUS RIDE 125

CHAPTER XII

THE USE OF A REVOLVER 143

CHAPTER XIII
WHAT PASTOR STEPANIAN THOUGHT . . . 155

CHAPTER XIV
A MODERN THERMOPYLÆ 173

CHAPTER XV
DARK HOURS 194

CHAPTER XVI
"THE DARK RIVER TURNS TO LIGHT" . . 214

CHAPTER XVII
A GREAT CRIME 229

CHAPTER XVIII
EVIL TIDINGS 241

CHAPTER XIX
A GREAT CRIME CONSUMMATED 256

CHAPTER XX
BY ABRAHAM'S POOL, AND ELSEWHERE . . 271

CHAPTER XXI
"GOD-SATISFIED AND EARTH-UNDONE" . . 287

CHAPTER XXII
GIVEN BACK FROM THE DEAD 301

CHAPTER XXIII
BETROTHAL 315

CHAPTER XXIV
UNDER THE FLAG OF ENGLAND . . . 323

CHAPTER XXV
AT HOME 341

CHAPTER XXVI
A SERMON 351

APPENDIX 367

PAGE

Chapter I

THE DARK RIVER

> " A thousand streams of lovelier flow
> Bathed his own native land."

THE Eastern sun was near its setting. Everywhere beneath its beams stretched out a vast, dreary campaign—pale yellowish brown — with low rolling hills, bare of vegetation. There was scarcely anything upon which the eye of man could rest with interest or satisfaction, except one little clump of plane trees, beside which a party of travellers had spread their tents. They had spent the day in repose, for they intended to spend the night in travelling ; since, although summer was past and autumn had come, the heat was still great.

The tent in the centre of the little encampment was occupied by an Englishman and his son, to whom all the rest were but guides, or servants, or guards. The Syrians, the Arabs, and the Turkish zaptiehs who filled these offices were resting from their labours, having tethered their horses under the trees.

It was about time for them to be stirring now, to attend to the animals, to make the coffee, and to do other needful things in preparation for the journey. But they were used to wait for a signal from their master for the time being—Mr. Grayson, or Grayson Effendi, as they generally called him. Pending this, they saw no reason to shorten their repose, though a few of them sat up, yawned, and began to take out their tobacco pouches, and to employ themselves in making cigarettes.

Presently, from the Effendi's own tent, a slight boyish form emerged, and trod softly through the rest. "Hohannes Effendi"—so the Turks and Arabs called him, as a kind of working equivalent for "Master John"—was a bright, fair-faced, blue-eyed English lad in his sixteenth year. He was dressed in a well-worn suit of white drill, and his head protected by a kind of helmet, with flaps to cover the cheeks and neck, since the glare reflected from the ground was almost as trying as the scorching heat above.

Once beyond the encampment, he quickened his pace, and, fast and straight as an arrow flies, dashed on over the little hills due eastwards. For there, the Arabs had told him, "a bow shot off," "two stones' throw," "the length a man might ride while he said his 'La ilaha ill Allah!'"—ran the great river. Waking some two hours before from the profound sleep of boyhood, he had not been able to close his eyes again for the longing that came over him to look upon it. For this was "that ancient river," last of the mystic Four that watered the flowers of Eden, witness of ruined civilizations, survivor of dead empires, the old historic Euphrates. Not that all this was present to the mind of young John Grayson; but he had caught from his father, whose constant companion he was, a reflected interest in "places where things happened," which was transfigured by the glamour of a young imagination.

On and on he went, for the wide, featureless, monotonous landscape deceived his eye, and the river was really much farther than he thought. He got amongst tall reeds, which sometimes hindered his view, though often he could see over them well enough—if there had been anything to see, except more reeds, mixed with a little rank grass—more low hills, and over all a cloudless, purple sky. The one point of relief was the dark spot in the distance, that meant, as he knew, the trees from which he had started.

He thought two or three times of turning back, not from weariness, and certainly not from fear, except the fear that his father might wonder what had become of him. But, being a young Englishman, he did not choose to be beaten, and so he went on.

At last there reached his ears what seemed a dull, low murmur, but what was in fact the never-ceasing sound of a great river on its way to the sea ; while at the same time—

> "The scent of water far away
> Upon the breeze was flung."

He hurried on, now over a grassy place, now through tall, thick reeds, until at last, emerging from a mass of them, he found himself on the edge of a steep precipitous bank, and lo ! the Euphrates rolled beneath him.

He could have cried aloud in his surprise and disappointment. Was this indeed the great Euphrates—the grand, beautiful river he had come to see ? Had this indeed flowed through Paradise? —this dull, muddy, most unlovely stream ? Dark, dark it looked, as he stood and gazed down into its turbid waters. "Dark ? " he said to himself, "no, it is not dark, it is *black*." And the longer he gazed the blacker and the drearier it grew.

Why stay any longer by "this ugly old stream"? —for so he called it. There was nothing to do, nothing to see. He turned to go back, and then the whole scene in its loneliness and desolation

took a sudden grip of his young soul. The awe
and wonder of the great, silent, solitary space
overcame him. The river, instead of being a voice
amidst the stillness, a living thing amidst the
death around, was only another death. It seemed
to flow from some—

"Waste land where no man comes,
Or hath come, since the making of the world."

Then all at once, by a very common trick of
fancy, young John Grayson found himself at home
—at home really—in happy England. His mother,
dead a year ago, was there still. He saw her
room : the table with her books and work, and her
favourite clock upon it ; a shawl she used to wear
of some blue, shimmering stuff like silk ;—he saw
her face. And then, as suddenly, all was gone.
He knew that she was dead. And he stood alone
with the silent sky, the desolate earth, the gloomy
river—an atom of life in the midst of a vast, dead
world. Before he knew it the tears were on his
cheek.

This would never do. He was ashamed of himself, though there was no one there to see. Dashing the disgraceful drops aside, he started at a run
to go back.

After a time he stopped, in a space fairly clear
of reeds, to look about him. He could see in

the distance the clump of trees that marked the camping place, but it looked very far off. The low hills confused him ; it would not be such an easy matter as he thought to return. He sat down to rest a little, for disappointment and discouragement made him feel suddenly very tired.

But he soon sprang to his feet again with a shout. A familiar sound reached his ear, the long Australian "Coo-ee-en!" which his father had adopted as the most penetrating kind of call. He gave back the cry with all the strength of his lungs, and waved his handkerchief high in air.

Presently he saw his father coming towards him through the reeds, followed by two of the Arabs. He ran to him in high delight, his sad reflections gone into the vast limbo that engulfs boyish sorrows. "Father! father! I have found Euphrates."

"Yes, my boy, but *I* had some trouble to find *you*."

They stood together, son and father, in that great solitude, as in a sense they did also in the greater solitude of the world. The father was one of those men of whom it is impossible to say he belongs to such and such a type, or, he is cast in such and such a mould. Rather was he hand-hewn, as by the Great Artist's own chisel. He was tall, spare, wiry, with a cheek as brown as southern skies could make it, dark hair and beard showing early threads of grey, dark eyes full of fire, and a mouth as sensitive as a woman's. The boy had inherited his mother's blue eyes and fair hair, but he was very like his father, both in expression and in the cast of his features, especially the shape of his forehead and the moulding of his fine mouth and chin. Slight as was the shadow of rebuke conveyed by his father's words, he felt it—it was so rare.

He said simply, " I am sorry."

"Did you think Euphrates worth the trouble when you found it?" asked his father, who had seen the far-famed and disappointing river long ago.

" Very much the reverse, father. An uglier, muddier, blacker kind of a river I never saw."

" I suppose we are quite close to it? I will go on and have a look, as there is no hurry about our start. Stay here, if you are tired, with one of the Arabs."

" I will come back with you. I should like it."

" Come along, then."

A short walk brought them to the bank, the two Arabs following at a respectful distance stately and indifferent.

The sun was setting now, and, behold ! a wonder met their eyes. The dark stream was transfigured, as if by the wand of an angel.   It poured rejoicing on its way, a torrent of liquid gold; for it had taken to its heart of hearts all the glory of the setting sun, and gave it back to the beholder in a marvel of radiance.   So might look to mortal eyes the river of God, the river of the water of life, that runs through the shining streets of the New Jerusalem.   The boy uttered a cry of wonder and delight.   The father gazed in silence.   At last he said, "*So the dark river turns to gold.*"

"But come, my boy," he added presently, "before the sun sets.   Let us take away with us in memory this look of the Euphrates."

Chapter II

FATHER AND SON

" I cannot rest from travel, I will drink
Life to the lees."
—Tennyson.

WHILE the travellers go back to their encampment, now in full preparation for the start, it may be well to introduce them formally by name. In this respect they were exactly alike; the father's name in full was John Frederick Pangbourne Grayson, and so was the son's. His friends, however, generally called him John, Johnnie, or Jack, by preference the latter, which was his father's custom also.

John Frederick Pangbourne had made himself remarkable in early life as a bold, adventurous traveller, going into places and amongst peoples little known to the rest of the world. He was in perils of many kinds, often great, sometimes desperate, but he always came through, thanks to his cool courage, his quickness of resource, his tact in dealing with men, and last, but not least, his abounding sympathy and kindness. So other

men said ; he himself said simply, if any one spoke
of his dangers and deliverances, " I got out of it," or
" they went away," or " they did me no harm," as
the case might be,—"*thank God.*" For he feared
God ; and though he did not go out of his way
to tell it to the world, he was quite willing for
the world to know it.

Beside the travel-hunger of the Englishman,
which is as strong or stronger than the earth-
hunger of the Celt, Pangbourne had another
motive in his wanderings. He was smitten to
the heart with love and longing for " brown Greek
MSS.," or MSS. in any other ancient tongue.
He had already made a find or two, chiefly of
early copies, or part copies, of the old Christian
Apologists. But these only whetted his appetite
for more. He had heard of MSS. to be found in
the neighbourhood of Mount Ararat, and was pur-
posing to go in search of them, when two events
changed his plans—he got a fortune, and he
married a wife.

As he was a younger son, the family acres had
gone of course to his elder brother, Ralph Pangbourne, a squire in one of the Midland counties.
Not that they brought him any great wealth ; for
he suffered like others from the economic changes
of the time, there was a heavy mortgage on his
property, and his family was large and expensive.

Therefore he was not particularly rejoiced when Miss Matilda Grayson, a distant connection of the family, left her large fortune to his younger brother instead of to himself. However, as there was the condition attached of assuming the name of Grayson, she may well have thought that the representative of the Pangbourne family would not choose to comply. "But I wish she had given the chance to one of my boys," thought Ralph Pangbourne.

Frederick, as he was usually called by his kinsfolk, behaved with great liberality. He cleared off the mortgage, and virtually adopted one of his brother's children, his god-son and namesake. Still, the fortune was his.

But it would not have kept him in England if he had not about the same time met his fate, while visiting one of the universities, in the daughter of a learned Professor who was interested in his archæological researches. The course of true love in this instance falsified the proverb. He bought a pleasant country seat in the south of England, and settled down to the life of an English gentleman. Quiet years followed; and if even in his happy home he sometimes felt the stings of a longing for wider horizons and more stirring scenes, at least he told of them to none. One son, and only one, was born to him.

After some fifteen happy years his wife died, very suddenly. No man ever mourned his dead more truly; but it was inevitable that when the first pangs of bereavement died into a dull aching, he should long to resume his wandering life. Some special studies, which he had been making when the great calamity overtook him, gave definiteness to his plans. His fancy had been caught by the old legend of Agbar, King of Edessa, of his letter to our Lord, and the answer, fabrications though they manifestly are. An idea possessed him that in the neighbourhood of the ancient Edessa, Agbar's " fair little city," so early Christianized, MSS. might be found, dating perhaps from the first century. The thought gave an object to his proposed wanderings in the East, for to the East his heart was ever drawn by strong, mystic yearning. And if his dreams should prove only dreams, there was no duty now which forbade him to pursue them.

One duty indeed he had—the care of his boy. Always much attached, in the days of their bereavement son and father drew very close together. Everybody advised him to leave Jack at school, but everybody spoke to deaf ears; for Jack entreated him to take him with him, and his own heart echoed the plea. After all, why not? He was a strong, healthy lad, very manly, and full of bright intelligence. Might not foreign travel be the best of schools for him? To Jack the prospect seemed the most delightful ever unfolded before mortal eyes.

Grayson could well afford every luxury of travel that might ensure safety and preserve health. Had he been alone, he would have cheerfully faced many risks and inconveniences to which he did not care to expose his son. So far they had journeyed in great comfort, keenly enjoying the adventure. They expected next morning to reach a little town on the Euphrates called Biridjik, where they proposed to rest for a day or two, arranging, as they always did in such circumstances, for the use of a room or rooms in some comfortable house.

The journey by night, in that land where night never means darkness, was delicious. The moon was at the full, and bathed in beauty even the desolate, monotonous landscape. Its light was quite enough for all travelling purposes; it seemed indeed only a softer, cooler, and more genial day.

Early morning found them on the stretch of road leading to the river. At the other side was a sort of natural amphitheatre. A picturesque hill rose in terraces from the river, near its summit the ruins of a castle. A semi-circular wall, which had once belonged to the castle, formed a bow, of which the river was the string, and which enclosed the little town with its houses, orchards, and gardens.

On each side of their road, as they drew near the river, was a large Turkish burying-ground, full of upright tombstones, all very narrow, and some of them very high. Then came a solitary plane-tree, and a small rude khan. Around it, and down to the river's brink, gathered a noisy, shouting, vociferous crowd. "Oh, such a crowd!" Jack thought. There were camels from Aleppo, with their heavy burdens, and their swearing, screaming drivers; khartijes or muleteers, with their laden mules; stately Arabs; zaptiehs in gold-laced uniforms, stolid and indifferent amidst the turmoil; Kourds with horses and donkeys, and dresses of every colour of the rainbow. Jack was especially amused with a Kourdish woman who joined the throng with two little donkeys, which she be-laboured vigorously with a short club, her lord and master sitting the while upon one of them, content and passive. But even this sight lost its interest when he thought he discovered in the distance some one on horseback in a European dress, and beside him—wonderful vision!—what looked like a European lady. He could scarcely believe his eyes.

But now, every eye was fixed upon the river. Floating swiftly down stream, with only a stroke

or two from the paddles of the ferry-men, came
two enormous wooden boats, each in shape
like a woman's shoe. Then began a regular
stampede, the whole disorderly crowd wanting
to get in at once, and fearing to be left behind.
As soon as the boats touched the land the rush
became frantic. It was like Bedlam ; the men
pushing, swearing, shouting,—the animals, who
objected strongly to the whole proceeding, being
urged on by their furious or frightened drivers,
to the peril of all within reach of them. Jack got
separated from his father, and carried nearly off
his feet, but he found himself at last in one of
the boats, which was swaying horribly from side
to side. The terrified horses, jammed together
in a narrow space, were kicking, biting, and
squealing, and the shrieks and curses of their
drivers were not likely to soothe them. Some of
these had dismounted, others kept their seats.
Jack saw one of their own zaptiehs pushed against
the side of the boat, and thought he would be
killed. But he called on Allah, and used his fists
manfully, and in a minute or two had extricated
himself, and was sitting safely on the bulwark.
Jack climbed up beside him, anxious to see where
his father was, and soon discovered him, near
the other end of the boat, helping to keep
the frightened animals under control. It was

impossible, however, to reach him through the throng.

Looking back, he saw the other boat quite close. There, amidst the crowd of men and horses, stood the English lady (as Jack supposed her), a tall, slight figure, holding the bridle of her horse. He saw the look of terror in the creature's face, the ears laid back, the nostrils quivering, and red as fire. He was going mad; he would bite or trample her! No; she had snatched off her veil, and, quick as thought, tied it over his eyes. The situation was saved. And Jack was gratified by a moment's vision of a girlish face, very fair, very young, and crowned with clustering golden hair. Then the boats changed position, and he lost it.

After half an hour's swaying and joggling, they all got safe to the other side. Then there was more noise and confusion, and then they found themselves slowly ascending the steep, irregular flights of stone steps that formed the streets of Biridjik. Here Jack caught a last glimpse of his lady of the golden hair, now decorously veiled, and seated on her horse—very unsafely, as he feared, for she looked in danger of falling off over his tail, at every step he took in the perilous ascent. But the party to which she belonged went on at once upon their journey, while the Graysons remained in Biridjik.

Chapter III

FIRST IMPRESSIONS

" Manners are not idle, but the fruit
Of loyal nature, and of noble mind."
—*Tennyson.*

YOUNG John Grayson stood alone in the large
upper room which had been assigned to him
and to his father.   Mr. Grayson had gone out to
reward and dismiss the zaptiehs and the Arabs,
and to make arrangements about the Syrian
servants, whom he meant to keep with him ; but
Jack was looking for his return every moment, to
partake of the breakfast which had been just
brought in.   First, a stool had been placed in the
middle of the room, and then a metal tray, much
larger, set upon it.   Handsome embroidered
cushions, placed beside, showed where and how
the guests were expected to sit.   Except these
cushions, and a few rugs or small carpets, the only
furniture the room contained was a divan running
along the side, covered with Turkey red, and
adorned with white embroidered cloths.   There

werc also some beds, or mattrasses, folded up in
a niche in the wall ; and a few articles belonging
to the travellers had been brought and left in the
room.

There were several windows, large, and very
close together. Jack stood at one of them, and
looked out on the courtyard round which the house
was built in the form of a hollow square. There
must be a great many rooms, he thought, and
wondered if one family occupied them all. The
court looked gay and pleasant, with late crocuses,
a few fruit trees, and, best of all, a little stream
of living water flowing right through it, and filling
the air with its cheery murmuring.

But the eyes of the hungry boy soon turned
back to the well-spread table, where they rested
approvingly upon a remarkably good breakfast.
There was a dish of pillav, made of a preparation
of wheat called *bulghour*, with boiling butter
poured over it, and upon the pillav a well-cooked
fowl lay in state, as the best part of the banquet.
There was queer-looking bread in large cakes thin
as wafers, and folded together like napkins ; there
was a great copper vessel lined with something
that looked like silver, and filled with *madzoun*, a
kind of cold, sour, boiled milk, and there was a
pitcher of tempting pink sherbet, with glasses
to drink it from. Jack gave a little sigh of satis-

faction, and ejaculated, " Wish father would come before the fowl gets cold."

Grayson came, looking white and weary, a thing unusual with him.

" Let us have our breakfast, father," Jack said. " I am sure you are starving,—I am."

His exploits on the fowl went far to prove it. But his father gave him little assistance.

" You don't eat, father," he said.

" I am not hungry. Though the sun is up such a little while, it has contrived to give me a headache. I shall sleep it off. *You* want a sleep too, as your eyes are crying out."

" Not a bit of them, father. I could not sleep now ; I want to go out and see this queer old place. I'll sleep all the better when I come back."

" Well, do so ; but take care of the sun, and get one of the servants to go with you. You will find them about somewhere."

Grayson spoke with a dull, listless air, quite foreign to his brisk, energetic nature.

" He is very sleepy," Jack thought, as he put on his protective head-dress, and ran cheerfully down into the court.

He looked about for the servants, but could not see either of them. As he was standing there, an open door attracted his eye, and he could not help looking in. A woman was baking bread, in an oven consisting of a large round hole in the clay floor of the middle of the room. She was taking small pieces of dough from a lump beside her, slapping them on the inside of the oven, and promptly removing those already baked suffici- ently. Two dark-eyed little boys were playing quietly at some game on the ground, and an older lad was standing beside her, talking, apparently about a bundle of cotton in a cloth which he held by the four corners.

Raising her eyes for a moment from her oven and her dough, the woman saw the stranger at the door. He did not know a word of Armenian, nor she a word of English, but she saluted him with great courtesy, bowing almost to the ground ; then, as she rose slowly, touching her heart, her lips, and her forehead. The children did the same ; the youngest acting his little part so prettily that Jack fell in love with him on the spot. As the woman, by signs, invited him to enter, he did so, and the children placed a cushion for him in the corner farthest from the door. The older boy brought him sherbet, flavoured and tinted with rosewater.

"This is all very nice," thought Jack. "Still, when one pays a visit one is expected to talk. And how can I talk to people who don't know a word of my language, nor I a word of theirs ? "

He tried to solve the difficulty by introducing himself, patting his own breast and forehead, and repeating, " John—John Grayson," an experiment attended with only partial success, his new friends learning to call him " Yon Effendi."   Then he pulled out his schoolboy silver watch for their edification.   The two little boys, who stood gazing at him with their great black eyes, evidently thought he was a far greater wonder himself ; but the elder looked at it intelligently, as one who perfectly knew its use.

He tried next to get at their names, pointing to each in turn with a look of inquiry.   As well as he could make out the unfamiliar sounds, he thought the eldest boy called himself something like Kevork, the second was certainly Gabriel, the youngest probably Hagop.   He took Gabriel's little brown hand in his own large one, whereupon the child stooped down, kissed the hand that held his, and touched it with his forehead.

Fearing that he was interrupting the baking operations, he soon rose to go.   He happened to notice a picture on the wall ; or rather a coloured daub in staring blue, red, and green, representing an impossible warrior, running an impossible sword through the heart of a monster three or four times as large as himself.   Seeing him look at it, the woman and the eldest boy began an explanation in which he could only distinguish one of the names he had just heard—"Kevork." He thought they meant that it belonged to Kevork; and did not find out until long afterwards that "Kevork" is one of the Armenian forms of "George," and that he had lighted upon a picture of the patron saint of his own land, slaying the traditional dragon.

He left his new friends after a silent exchange of courtesies; and, forgetting all about the servants he ought to have looked for, began to descend the crooked, winding steps, or streets, that led down to the river. Presently he heard a patter of feet behind him, and, looking back, saw Gabriel trotting after him. The child came up, and held out to him a little roll of something yellow, with what looked like the kernels of nuts in it. It was evidently to be eaten, for Gabriel, smiling, pointed to his mouth; so Jack sat down on one of the steps and made his first acquaintance with the Armenian delicacy called *bastuc*, a preparation of grape sugar, into which the kernels of nuts are sometimes put. He liked it at first; but it soon palled, and he began to fancy it was making him sick. Whatever was the cause, a strange faintness and dizziness came over him as he sat there by the river. "It is too hot here," he thought. "I must go back." He got up, but found it a hard matter to keep his feet. Twice or thrice, as he toiled up the steps, he was obliged to sit down and rest. Little Gabriel had stayed beside him, and he was very glad of it, as without a guide he would almost certainly have missed the gate of the house where their quarters were, since all the houses, built in the same way about their court-yards, looked so exactly alike. Feeling worse every minute, he stumbled up the stairs, threw the door open, and got into the room just in time to fall down in a faint.

When he came to himself, he was lying on one of the beds; and his father, stooping anxiously over him, put a glass to his lips, from which he drank obediently.

"How do you feel now, my son?" he asked.

"Oh! all right," Jack said. "I don't know what came over me down there by the river. I suppose it was the sun. But I am better. I can get up."

"Don't. Lie still and give me your hand. I want to feel your pulse."

Jack gave it.

"Father," he said, looking up, "your own hand is shaking. Is there anything wrong?"

"Not much, I hope. You are a little hot and feverish. A dose of quinine will do you no harm."

"Hot!" said Jack. "No; I am shivering with cold. I can't keep still."

The dose was administered; and Jack, following his father's movements with his eyes, noticed that he took one himself also.

"Now, my boy," he said, "you have not slept for nearly four and twenty hours, and you spent all last night in the saddle. Unless you take a good rest, you may be ill. Lie as quiet as you can, and try to sleep."

"I will, father; but—I'm so thirsty!"

His father gave him some sherbet, and covered him up comfortably with a silk rug. Then he sat down, and took out his note-book and pencil; but he wrote only a few words in a faint, irregular hand, difficult to decipher: "Have heard from Jacob, my Syrian, that the plain we have just traversed is noted for its deadly malaria—is, in fact, a perfect hotbed of fever. I fear John has it."

After some time Jack dropped off into a troubled doze. Strange dreams came to him, ending usually in some catastrophe that made him start up in sudden fright. Once he thought he was walking by the river, and somehow lost his footing and fell in. He woke up with a cry, "The water is so cold—so dark!" His father was at his side and soothed him.

"Don't you remember," he said, "the dark river turns to light?"

But as soon as the boy was quiet and at rest again, John Grayson added one more to the records in his note-book, and it was almost illegible: "We have both caught the fever. God help us! If I can, I will arrange——"

Chapter IV

A NEW LIFE

"Among new men, strange faces, other minds."
—*Tennyson.*

AFTER that, for young John Grayson, life was a blank. Dim shadows came and went like reflections in a mirror, having no continuity and leaving no impression. In a passing way, as a dumb creature might, he felt burning heat and freezing cold, pain and weariness, and nameless, indescribable distress. So too he saw forms around him — kind, dark - complexioned people, who gave him things to drink, and spoke to him in words he could not understand. Sometimes he was conscious of a sort of dull relief, or pleasure, when they cooled his burning brow with snow, which had been brought from the mountains packed in straw, and carefully preserved. But throughout all he missed something—some one. At first he knew that he wanted his father, and used to call for him piteously. But this passed at length; he grew too weak even for the pain of longing.   With the very ill, as with the very old, " desire fails."

Yet, in spite of all, he crept slowly back to life.   One day he felt himself carried somewhere, and then became suddenly conscious of a delicious coolness after what seemed a lifetime of burning heat.   Looking up presently, when the sense of fatigue had somewhat passed, he saw that he was lying on a large bedstead, like one of our old " four-posters," in the open air. There were white curtains all around him, which were being softly stirred by a refreshing breeze ; while over his head—no roof between, not even the canvas of a tent—glowed the deep, rich blue of the Eastern sky.   He was on the house-top.

For a while after that he recovered more quickly.   But the hot weather, coming early that year, brought on a sore relapse, and again for many days his life was despaired of.   More than once the watchers thought he was actually gone, and often they thought the question was one of hours.   Yet in the end the long conflict of death and life ended in the victory—the slow, uncertain victory—of the latter.

He came back to life like a little child only just beginning it.   For the time, his past was completely blotted out.   Too weak in mind and body for connected thought, he accepted the things about him without question. He seemed to have been always there, amongst those dark-eyed people, who sat upon the ground, ate rice and bulghour, and wore striped "zebouns" of cotton cloth, and many-coloured jackets. He picked up their speech very quickly, as a child picks up his mother tongue; and at this stage did not remember his own. He came to know those about him, and to call them by their names. Between twenty and thirty persons dwelt in the large house in which he was a guest. But they were all one family—the sons and sons-in-law, the daughters and daughters-in-law, and a whole tribe of the grandchildren of a grey-haired patriarch called Hohannes Meneshian. The whole household were Jack's familiar friends. But he loved best the three boys who had been his first acquaintances, and their mother Mariam Hanum, who throughout his illness had been his devoted nurse. He liked the gentle touch of her hand, and the tenderness in her eyes as she looked at him. Sometimes he called her Mya—"Mother," as the boys did.

Of the three—Kevork, Gabriel, and little Hagop—Gabriel was his favourite. Indeed the child was like his shadow, waiting on him continually, and often bringing him beautiful flowers—gorgeous pomegranate blossoms, or roses of many kinds and of most exquisite perfume. Or he would bring him fruit—delicious grapes, pears, plums, and peaches. Or sometimes he would just steal silently up to kiss his hand, and touch it with his forehead, or stand or sit quietly beside him.

There was one thing that soothed him inexpressibly; though, like all else, it was accepted without question or comprehension. When Mariam and the other women went about the household tasks that, as he grew better, he liked to watch, they would say, "Hesoos ockña menk"— "Jesus, help us." When they finished, they would say, "Park Derocha"—"Praise the Lord." In everything there was devout acknowledgment of God; and the sweetest of all names that are named in heaven or upon earth was often on their lips, spoken with reverence and love. Something that for John Grayson still lived on,

"In the purple twilight under the sea"

of conscious thought, made this very grateful to him, and joined it with what were like the first heavenward thoughts and prayers of a little child.

So time passed on. But, as he grew stronger, there awoke again within him a vague sense of want and longing. He had no power to express his feelings, but he felt something was wrong with him—he was not in his proper place. Or was it, rather, that there was something wrong with all the people about him? They were very kind; but they and their ways had a queer, distorted, unnatural look in his eyes, like the things one sees reflected in the bowl of a spoon. He longed continually, longed inexpressibly, for something he could not get, for some one who was not there; yet he could not tell who it was he wanted.

He grew silent and melancholy, and his friends thought him in danger of another relapse, which would certainly have been fatal. Happily, it was now autumn again, the sultriest months of the year being over. So one day they wrapped him up carefully, seated him comfortably on cushions upon a donkey, and brought him with them, to a vineyard which Hohannes possessed on a slope of one of the hills above Biridjik. He was a man of some property, having flocks and herds also. The great, luscious grapes, "as large as plums," purple, green, and amber, hung in ripe profusion, nearly breaking down the low bushes they grew upon. Jack ate of them to his heart's content, and lay in the pleasant shade of a fig-tree, watching the other young people as they gathered them for their various uses. Tents had been brought, and it gave him a kind of dreamy satisfaction to sleep in one of these; it seemed somehow to bring him nearer to the things he had lost, and was vaguely feeling after. Often hints of them seemed to flash on him unbidden, but when he tried to grasp them vanished as they came, leaving him confused and faint, with a fluttering heart and an aching head.

However, his strength improved in the cooler air and amidst the new surroundings. He had soon an opportunity of testing it. One day he happened to be by himself, resting under his favourite fig-tree, when he heard a noise as of something trampling and tearing the vines. Looking up, he saw that a flock of goats had got in among them, and were doing terrible damage, not only to the ripe fruit but even to the trees. He got up and called for help, but no one heeded, and he supposed no one heard. It was dreadful to see all this harm done; in fact, he could not endure it. Taking heart, he went to the rescue himself, or rather, for the first time since his illness, he *ran*. His steps were unsteady, his limbs shook under him; once indeed he fell, but he was up and on again in a moment. The exercise seemed to give back strength to his muscles and vigour to his brain. He shouted aloud; he took up stones and flung them at the trespassers, sending them flying over the low stone wall. Then, the Englishman's joy of battle waking in him, he gave chase as fast, or faster, than his limbs would carry him.

He heard the others crying out to him ; but he thought they were encouraging his efforts. Even when they came running up with evident intent to stop him, he thought they were only afraid he would do himself harm. But at last the youngest son of Hohannes caught him bodily in his arms, shook the stones out of his hand, and cried breathlessly, "You must *not!* You must *not!*"

Jack had a good deal of Armenian by this time. "*Inchu? Inchu?*—Why? why?" he gasped ; "they were destroying your vines."

The young man, by name Avedis, or "good tidings," looked sadly at the injured trees, but only said, "Those goats belong to the Kourds."

Jack stammered in his eagerness to find the words he wanted. "What has that to do with it?" he got out at last. "What right have the Kourds to spoil your vines?"

"Don't you know, Yon Effendi, that if we dare to stop them doing it, or even to drive their sheep and goats out of our fields and vineyards, they think a great deal less of stabbing or shooting one of us than you would of killing a cat?"

"But then they would be hanged for it!" cried Jack. "Have you no—oh, what is the word for it ?—have you no—*police ?*" He said the word in English, and a rush of old, new thoughts and impressions came crowding into his brain.

" *Police ?*"

" The men who keep order, and take people to prison."

" Do you mean the zaptiehs? They are worse than the Kourds. The Turk and the Kourd are the upper and the nether millstone, grinding us to powder. If one of us is fool enough to complain of a Kourd or a Turk, the Kamaikan—the governor, I mean—says he will enquire into the matter. And he does. He sends for the man who has complained, throws him into a dungeon, and keeps him there till he confesses all the wrong is on his own side ; or perhaps until his people pay a sum of money. Or perhaps he may be never heard of again at all."

Avedis did not say this with fierce looks and indignant gestures, but in a calm, matter-of-fact way, as if such things were part of the everlasting order of nature, which has been from the beginning and will be until the end. Jack did not follow every word ; but one thing he understood very clearly : they must all stand still and see their beautiful vines destroyed. There was no remedy—why? Because this was not England. *England !* Now he knew everything. He was an English boy, left alone here in this strange land. And his father—where was his father? "Where is my father?" he cried aloud in English.

"What is that you say?" asked Avedis.

Jack repeated his question in Armenian.

"Come and sit down under the tree," said Avedis.

Jack obeyed, silent and trembling. Avedis stood, looking at him sadly. "Tell me, where is my father?" Jack repeated with pleading eyes, into which a new expression was dawning slowly.

"You know, Yon Effendi, you have been very ill," Avedis said. "Your father, a great English Effendi, very wise and good, was ill too. You recovered; your father did not recover. He is gone to God. Do you understand me, Yon Effendi?"

Jack understood so well that he flung himself face downwards on the ground, and burst into a passion of weeping. In vain Avedis tried to comfort him. "God forgive me," he thought, "I ought not to have told him. I fear I have killed him." And he certainly had not acted up to the meaning of his name. The rest of the family blamed him severely, when they heard what he had done. It was the custom of their country for the bearer of sad tidings to go about his task with great circumlocution, carefully "breaking" them, as we say in England.

Yet the shock, instead of killing John Grayson,

brought him back to his true life. Up to this there had been a serious danger that his brain would never wholly recover the shock of that long and terrible illness ; and that, if he lived, he might go through the future years as one whose mind had an important leaf left out of it. But that day's agony of weeping, and the days and nights of distress that followed it, meant that he would either die, or else recover wholly, and claim his intellectual inheritance in the present and the past. This full recovery, however, might well be an affair of time—perhaps of a long time.

Old Hohannes heard with the rest that the English youth knew now that his father was dead, and that he was weeping and refusing comfort, in a manner very likely to make him ill again. "We will take him back to the town," he said ; and so they did the next day.

The following morning Hohannes took him by the hand, led him into a low, dark room on the ground-floor, where bulghour and rice were stored, and shut and barred the door.

"Sit down," he said. Jack did so ; and looked on wonderingly while the old man dug a hole in the ground with some implement resembling a trowel.

At last he grew impatient, and asked, "Will you not tell me about my father?"

Hohannes looked up. "There is not much to tell," he said. "Feeling himself, no doubt, very ill, the English Effendi sent for me, and I came. He asked me to take care of you, and if you should recover to try and send you back to your friends in England. And he gave me, to use for you as I thought best, the things I have kept hidden here. He spoke somewhat also of certain papers, but before he could finish what he wanted to say, the fever increased upon him, and his mind began to wander. As to the papers, we never got them. They were stolen away, with his other baggage, by the two Syrian servants, who were brothers, and precious rascals. But these I have." He stooped and took out of the hole something wrapped in a skin and tied with cords. These he carefully unfastened, took off the skin, and revealed two books and a belt of chamois leather. The books he gave to Jack, who recognised, with a thrill of joy and a pang of sorrow, the pocket Bible his father always carried with him, and the notebook in which he used to see him write. "Keep these thyself," said Hohannes. "This," holding up the belt, "I must keep still. There is gold in it." Instinctively his voice dropped lower, though there was none to hear the dangerous word.

"I am very glad of it," Jack said frankly, as, for the first time, it occurred to him that these people, upon whom he had no claim, had been providing for all his wants. "Father Hohannes, you and yours have fed and tended me all this time like a child of your own. It ought to be all yours!"

"You have a generous heart, Yon Effendi. And, in fact, I have used it for you as far as was necessary and just. There were medicines and other things when you were ill, and there was the tax to pay for you."

"The tax for me?" Jack repeated. "What tax?"

"Know you not we have to pay, year by year, every man and boy among us, for breathing the air? Even for the new-born babe the Turk exacts it. So your tax had to be found along with our own, and will be next year also. Moreover I own, a piece or two went to the Kourds as backsheesh, that they might let our cattle alone."

"Indeed, father," Jack said again, "I wish you would take it all; it is yours by right."

Hohannes shook his head. "And what, then, if you should want to go home?" he said; "or if any way for your doing it should open? Moreover we dare not, for our lives, let any one know we have so much gold in the house. The Kourds would come down from the mountains and rob us, or the Turks would take it from us on pretence of arrears of taxes.   It is best for me to keep it here for you. You see where I put it?"

"Yes, Father Hohannes; it is all right," said Jack.

He was longing to go away somewhere by himself, and feast his eyes on his father's handwriting, and on the printed words he loved so well. But, as he was going, a thought came to him that made him turn again. Things which he had heard Kevork say as he began to get better, and which at the time he had scarcely noticed, came to his mind with a sudden inspiration.

"Father Hohannes," he said, "Kevork, your grandson, longs sore to go to Aintab, to the great school the Americans have set up there for your people. Kevork loves learning very much. May he not take some of this gold and go?"

Again Hohannes shook his head. "Kevork is a foolish boy," he said. "The cock that dreamed of grain fell from his perch trying to scratch for it. Let him stay at home, and mind the cattle; or take to the weaving, if it like him better."

Jack was sorry for Kevork, but the possession of the precious books drove everything else out of his head. He flew upon the spoil; nor was it with a passing joy alone, since during the time that followed the chief sustenance of his life, that which made it worth living, came from these books.

He was himself again, but only a childish, weak, discouraged self—a different being from the strong, active-minded, energetic lad who had come with his father to Biridjik. His illness and its consequences had thrown him back in his development of body, of mind, and still more of character, for at least a couple of years. He was quite unable at present to look his life in the face, or to take the initiative in any way.

Nor was there any one about him who could give him effectual help. How to go to England was a problem no one in Biridjik seemed able to solve. Even a letter was a difficult and doubtful undertaking. It is true the town possessed a Turkish post-office, but this, at all events for foreign letters, was a perfect "tomb." In answer to his questions, his friends told him of a certain "Cousin Muggurditch," a kinsman of Hohannes, who lived at "Yeatessa," but was a great traveller, going sometimes even as far as Constantinople;—he could send a letter safely to England. Jack thought Yeatessa was the place his father wanted to go to, and which was mentioned in his note-book as Edessa, the city of the legendary King Agbar. His friends assured him it was; that they knew all about it, and that the story of King Agbar was quite true, for his tomb was still to be seen just outside the city, which the Franks called Urfa, and which was only two days' journey from Biridjik.

"I shall go there some time," Jack said; but he said no more about it, and it seemed as if for the time all thought of change had passed out of his mind. He slipped into the life and the ways of those about him. Even his European clothes were out-worn or out-grown, and he adopted the striped zeboun, the gay jacket and the crimson fez of the Armenians. Mariam Hanum (Mrs. Mary) took care of his wardrobe, and he might be seen every Saturday going with the other men and youths to the bath, and carrying his clean clothes with him tied up in a towel.

One day he wanted a kerchief to put under his fez and keep off the sun, and he went by himself to the shop to buy it. He came back with one of bright green, which he thought very handsome; but, to his amazement, Kevork snatched it from his head and Avedis flung it into the fire, with the approval of all the rest.

"Don't you know that green is the Moslem colour?" they said to him.

"Then be sure I will never wear it," Jack answered; "I am a Christian."

He went with his friends to the Gregorian

Church on Sundays and feast days; often too in the early mornings before sunrise, or in the evenings at sunset. It is true he did not understand very much of the service; but the Armenians themselves were scarcely better off, as the ancient Armenian language is still used in the liturgy of the national Church. He was shown, in the adjoining graveyard, the resting-place of his father, marked like all the other graves with a flat stone. Then he printed carefully, in English capital letters, his father's full name, and gave it to the best stonecutter in the town, asking him to engrave it for him, with a cross.

"I should like it put upon another stone," he said; "one to stand up, as we have them in England."

The stonecutter explained that he could not have it here. It was unlawful. Mahometans had their tombstones erect, but a Christian might only mark the resting-place of his dead with a flat stone. "But," the man added with a smile, "that will not hinder our rising again at the last day."

Kevork and his brothers continued Jack's greatest friends. Kevork talked much with him, and told him many things. He said he should like to go to Yeatessa, or Urfa, because he had a sister there.

"A married sister, I suppose?" Jack said, rather wondering he had not heard of her before.

"*No*," said Kevork, lowering his voice mysteriously. "My grandfather had to send her away to our cousins, because the Kamaikan who was here before this one wanted to marry her; and we never talk of her, not even before Gabriel and Hagop, lest any word might slip out about where she is, and the Turks might overhear. But I had rather go to Aintab than even to Urfa, to learn English and Greek and Latin, and grammar and geography, and all kinds of science."

"And what then?" Jack asked with a smile.

"Then I would go, if I could, to America or to England, learn still more, and become at last a famous professor in some grand college in a Christian land."

Kevork had already learned from a friendly priest, Der Garabed, to read and write Armenian, and to read Turkish in the Arabic character. For the Turks, and it is a significant fact, have never reduced their own language to writing; their books are printed either in the Arabic or in the Armenian character. He was in raptures when Jack offered to teach him English, which he promptly began to do, using as a text-book his father's Bible, the only book he had, with the exception of a Tauchnitz "Westward Ho," which happened to be in his pocket when he came to Biridjik. In return, Kevork taught him to read and write Armenian, and these lessons were shared by Gabriel and Hagop. Gabriel was a remarkably quick, intelligent boy, all life and fire; Hagop was quiet and rather dull, more at home at his father's loom than at his brother's book. Both used to listen delightedly to Jack, when, chiefly as an exercise for himself, he would translate some simple Bible story aloud in Armenian.

Not that such were the only uses Jack made of his father's Bible. Outwardly his character still continued unformed, boyish, passive; inwardly it had begun silently to grow and to deepen. He did not act, but he thought a great deal. His mind was like a stream flowing underground, gathering volume as it flowed, and sure to emerge again to the light of the upper world. Its sources were fed by observation, memory, faith, and hope, and most of all by that matchless fount, not only of spiritual but of intellectual inspiration, the English Bible.

Chapter V

BARON MUGGURDITCH THOMASSIAN

NO doubt some subtle form of nervous weakness, the relic of his long and terrible illness, still held young John Grayson in its grasp. Moreover the loss of his father, so intensely loved, had entered like iron into his soul. His mother's death was still, when he left home, a recent bereavement, and he was an only child. He had no near relatives except in his uncle's family, and even amongst them there was only one he cared for much, his father's godson, a cousin five years his senior, whose fag he had been at school.

What had he, after all, to go back to in England? He excused his torpor with thoughts like these, whenever it occurred to him to ask himself if he meant to spend his life tending vines, teaching English, and studying Armenian, in a little out-of-the-way town on the banks of the Euphrates.

He spent many months there without taking much note of time. The Meneshians were his family; the whole Armenian community his friends. He entered more and more into their life, shared more and more their interests. He was especially interested in the culture of the vineyard, wanting to know the how and the why of everything. Once—but this was in early days—he proposed taking Kevork and a couple of other lads with him, and going to stay there long before the regular vintage time. "We could guard it a great deal better," he said, "than that lazy Turk, who does nothing but lie all day on his perch smoking cigarettes, and is always wanting back-sheesh." [1]

"You could not do it at all," answered Boghos, the eldest son of Hohannes, and the husband of Mariam Hanum, "just because you are not a Turk. Backsheesh is very well spent in setting the Turk to watch the Kourd, instead of both of them preying upon us. Do you not know that yet, Yon Effendi?"

[1] The "perch" upon which the Turkish guard reposed was a kind of booth, erected on the top of four poles, twelve or fifteen feet high, planted firmly in the ground.

They all continued to give him that name, which he had taught in the first instance to Kevork and his brothers. To them all he was a cross between a pet and plaything to be taken care of, and a superior person to be honoured. In both capacities he had every attention, and all his wants were liberally supplied. But he insisted that Hohannes should expend for that purpose some of his father's gold, and should give from time to time a small sum by way of compensation to Boghos and Mariam Hanum, with whom he lived. Money was so scarce in that region that a very small sum sufficed.

At last one day the whole Meneshian family, and indeed the whole Armenian quarter of Biridjik, was thrown into excitement by the news that Baron Muggurditch Thomassian (in English, Mr. Baptist Thomson), was about to honour them with a visit. He was travelling from Urfa to Aintab, and proposed staying a day or two on his way with his kinsfolk, the Meneshians.

Jack shared in the excitement. He was very curious to see this wealthy, travelled, educated Armenian, whom he expected to find of a very different type from the simple folk of Biridjik. And now, at last, he was sure to find through him the opportunity of communicating with his friends in England, which, however little eagerness he might feel in the matter, he knew he ought not to neglect.

What could the duteous and admiring kinsfolk of Baron Thomassian do on the occasion, except pay him the attention of riding "three hours dis- tance" to meet him on his way, even although it was midwinter, the rains heavy and the wretched road ankle-deep in mud?   Boghos led the party, and Jack went among the rest.   Old Hohannes had a few fine horses, of which he was very proud; and he had given one of them to Jack, to his immense delight and satisfaction.

In that district there is scarcely any snow, and the rain had happily cleared off, so it was only a splashed and muddy, and not a drenched and soaking company that drew up by the wayside in the shelter of a little hill, to await the coming of the travellers.

At last the jingling of mule bells announced the approach of the caravan.   There was a long string of khartijes, or muleteers, there were some servants on horseback, and a few zaptiehs to act as guards. These were fully armed of course, and the central figure of the whole, Baron Thomassian himself, rode a very fine horse, and actually carried a gun at his side, for which he must have got a special "permit" from the government.   He was a good- looking middle-aged man, dressed *à la Frank*, or in complete European costume, except that he wore a fez in place of a hat, which was amongst the things forbidden to an Armenian.

There was something else which gave all the Biridjik folk a great surprise. Beside him rode a slight young girl, closely wrapped in a long "ezhar" of striped silk, which was drawn as a veil over the greater part of her face, leaving very little of it visible except her large, beautiful, dark eyes. Veiled though she was, Boghos recognised his daughter, and Kevork at least guessed his sister. Scarce, for looking at her, could they give their kinsman the customary greeting, "Paré yejock" (your coming is a joy), or wait for the response, "Paré dessack" (we see you with joy). And Thomassian hastened to say, "I have rought your daughter back to you at the request of your cousin, Baron Vartonian. I will explain the reason afterwards." Then Boghos kissed his daughter on both cheeks, and she kissed his hand and asked for his blessing. Kevork kissed her also; and Jack, keeping modestly in the background, thought what a pleasant thing it must be to have a sister. He had already seen lovely faces among the girls and women of Biridjik, but never, as he thought, eyes quite so soft and dark, lips quite so rosy, and cheeks of such perfect form and hue.

All the rest, who were old acquaintances, came crowding round her ; and then Boghos turned his attention to Jack, and made him known to Thomassian, with much polite observance, as their English friend, John Grayson Effendi.

They rode back together to Biridjik, Boghos devoting himself to the entertainment of Thomassian. Jack could not help wondering that they all showed so little pleasure at the return of Shushan ; on the other hand, a sort of constraint and gloom seemed to brood over the whole party. Kevork would give him no explanation. Even when he said, " I am surprised to see your sister looking so young. She seems scarcely fourteen. I thought, of course, from what you told me, that she must be older than you," Kevork only answered, with a quick, guarded look around, " She was but ten years old when she left us."

After the festive supper in honour of the guest, Thomassian explained the matter in private to Hohannes and to Boghos.

" Your former Kamaikan, Mehmed Ibrahim," he said, " has come to Urfa. He has got some good office there in the Government. Somehow he found out that Shushan was there with the Vartonians, and—he has not forgotten. In short, she must go. There was no other way."

" Amaan ! " or " Oh dear ! " was all her father

said. But he looked perplexed and sorrowful, seeing trouble before them all.

Hohannes put the trouble into words. "He may find out, and send after her here."

"The Vartonians thought not. You must keep her as close as you can, or send her in disguise to one of the villages."

"How dare we—for the Kourds? A bride on her way from the church was carried off the other day from Korti, and the bridegroom and her father, who tried to defend her, were both killed. Our girls are not safe anywhere, except in their graves." Though they sat within closed doors, they all spoke in low tones, and with furtive glances around them.

"Our only possible protection," Thomassian said, "lies in the wealth our abilities and our industry enable us to gain. The Turks and Kourds consider our peace and safety marketable properties, which they are willing to sell us at a good price."

"Yes," said Hohannes sadly, "until they find we have nothing more to give, or until it suits them to take all together."

Thomassian, who probably did not much care to talk on these matters, said that he was weary with his journey, and expressed a wish to go early to rest.

Kevork had been hanging about watching for an opportunity of speaking with him, and now, as soon as the door was opened, he came forward, offering politely to attend him to his sleeping-place.

A little later he came quickly, and evidently in much excitement, into the room where Shushan was sitting, with her mother and several other women and girls of the household, who had come in to see her.

"Mother, I have done it!" he cried.

"Done what, my son?" asked his sad-faced mother.

She was sitting, as usual, behind her wheel, but its whirr was silent now. She had enough to do in looking in the face of Shushan, and holding her hand.

"I have made a conquest of old Cousin Muggurditch," said Kevork triumphantly. "He will take me with him to Aintab, and put me to the Foreigners' School."

A murmur of surprise ran round the room. But his mother asked, with some shrewdness,—

"What did you give him?"

"What you gave me, mother. I owe all to you. It was those gold coins that did it."

The other women looked significantly at Mariam. The strings of gold coins which she wears about her person are the Armenian woman's only absolute and indisputable possession. They stand to her instead of settlements and dowry. That must be precious indeed for which she will sacrifice them.

" He made little of the coins at first," said the quick-witted lad ; " but that was all in the way of business. I could see that he thought a good deal of them, and liked well to get them."

" How much did you sell them for ? " asked Mariam.

" I did not sell them. Not such a fool as that ! I mean you to have them again some day, mother. I only gave them in pledge to him—he promising to advance my school expenses—until I should be able to repay him."

" But that is for ever and ever," said one of the women.

" Nothing of the sort. After two years at Aintab I shall be a teacher, and able to earn money for myself."

Here Shushan looked up and spoke. She was very beautiful ; not only with the beauty characteristic of her race—soft dark eyes, black pencilled eyebrows almost meeting, long curling eyelashes, and olive-tinted, regular features—but with the rarer loveliness of a sweet, pure expression, that suited well her name, Shushan, the Lily. During her four years of absence the familiar surroundings of home had become strange to her, so she spoke with a certain timidity.

"My brother," she said, looking appealingly up to the tall youth whom she had left a mere child—"my brother, will you do something for me when you go to Aintab?"

Kevork protested his willingness, although somewhat surprised.

"My dearest friend," said Shushan, "the person I love best in the world, next after my father and mother and my brothers, is just now going to Aintab, to the school for girls. They hurried me away so quickly that I could not see her to say good-bye. And I shall not see her now; for, although she must pass by this on her way, she will not come into the town, but lodge in the khan outside. Will you salute her for me, and give her this as a gift from her poor little friend, Shushan Meneshian?" She drew from her bosom something resembling a necklace, made of amber beads, and held it out to Kevork.

He stooped down to take it, saying, "Well, then, my sister, what is the name of the girl?"

"Elmas Stepanian; she is the daughter of the Badvellie."

"Badvellie" means "full of honour"; and the Armenians usually speak of their priests and pastors by this respectful title.

"Stay, Kevork," said his mother. "You had better not take that *tebish*. Shushan is a child, and does not know the world. But do you think that it is possible the foreigners would allow the boys and the girls to speak to one another? They are very good people, else surely our cousins would not have let their own children, and Shushan, go to school to them."

This certainly was a difficulty, and even Shushan looked perplexed. But Kevork was equal to the occasion. "Yon Effendi tells me that the foreign Effendis, men and women, talk to each other just as much and as often as they like," he said. "Shushan, my sister, I will pray of the Effendi who teaches me to give thy token to the Effendi who teaches Oriort[1] Elmas Stepanian, and she will find some right way, I have no doubt, of giving it to her."

"Do so, Kevork, and I thank thee many times." She gave him the string of beads, and then her tongue waxed eloquent in praise of her friend. "She is so good, so clever," she said. "She knows, oh, so many things! She can speak and write English, not just a little as I do, but beautifully, like a real American! She knows grammar and geography, and the counting up of figures, and the story of the world. She does not want a

---

[1] Miss.

thought-string like that to help her." (Both Turks and Armenians are accustomed, when thinking or talking, to finger strings of beads, called *tebishes*, and to obtain some mysterious assistance from the process.) "Oh! no. She would never use one at school, nor indeed would most of us. But now she is going where she will have such *very* hard lessons to learn, that perhaps she may be glad of it. At least it will remind her of her poor little Shushan. Tell her, Kevork, that Shushan puts a prayer for her on every bead she sends her."

"I think it is a very foolish plan to teach all those things to girls," one of the old women observed. "They will be fit for nothing else in the world but reading books, and who will mind the babies? And what will become of cooking and washing and baking bread, not to talk of spinning and sewing?"

"The girls of the American school at Urfa cook and bake and spin and sew right well for their years," Shushan spoke up bravely. "And those who go to Aintab, like Elmas, learn those things even better there. Oh, I wish you could see Elmas in her home, working to help her mother, and taking care of her little brothers and sister; you would know what she was worth then."

This did not fall upon unheeding ears. Young

Kevork made a mental note of it ; then turned quickly to ask his mother what she could manage to give him in the way of clothing, as his cousin wished to set out on his journey the morning of the day after next.

Meanwhile Jack was busily employed writing to his uncle, and to his uncle's son. The former he told, briefly enough, of his father's death, his own long illness, and the care and kindness of the people amongst whom he had fallen. He asked him to write to him, and to send him money for his journey home, and also to recompense those who had been so good to him. He knew, of course, that he would have a considerable income of his own, so he felt no difficulty in making this request. He concluded with love to his relatives and enquiries after their welfare. To his cousin he wrote more freely, and gave more particulars. But even to him his words did not flow easily. He could not take up his life in his hand, and look at it from the outside, so as to describe it to another. He could only give details of his surroundings, and of this he soon tired, being unaccustomed to write in English, or indeed to write at all. He broke off abruptly, folded up the two letters in one, sealed the packet, directed it to his uncle, and brought it to Thomassian.

Baron Muggurditch Thomassian was emphatically the courteous, cultured, cosmopolitan Armenian. He had amassed a considerable fortune in his business, which was that of a merchant of drugs; and to which he joined some cautious and lucrative money-lending. Moreover, he had travelled far, and seen much. He could speak several languages quite well enough to make shrewd bargains in them; and he knew the art of spending as well as of making money. He could appreciate music, poetry, and painting, no less than luxuries of a more material kind. Yet Jack felt as if he could never love him, never trust him even, as he did his friends in Biridjik. "I don't know what it is," he said to himself; "for there is nothing amiss with his looks, except perhaps something a little shifty about his eyes."

Nothing, however, could have been more courteous than his response to Jack's request that he would take charge of his letter, and see it safe into some really reliable post-office.

"I am asking my friends to send money to bring me home," he added, by way of explanation.

"How did you tell them to send it, Mr. Grayson?" asked Thomassian.

"I never thought of telling them how. I thought they would know themselves," Jack answered simply.

" It is not so simple a matter as you think," said Thomassian.

" Then what must I do?   Stay, could it be managed this way?   You are going to Aleppo?"

" Yes, Effendi."

" The English Consul there was my father's friend, and very kind to us.   He would let my uncle send the money to him, and would know how to send it to me.   I daresay he would write to my uncle too.   You will ask him, will you not, Baron Thomassian ?"

" I will do it without fail."

" And I am very grateful to you," Jack said, giving him his hand in English fashion, though the courteous Eastern did not fail to bow low over it.

Next morning Muggurditch Thomassian· went his way, taking with him Jack's letter and Jack's chief friend Kevork, but leaving behind him what was destined to be of still more importance in the life of the English youth.

Chapter VI

ROSES AND BATH TOWELS

G OOD-MORNING, Mr. John, I give you my salvation."
Very softly and sweetly fell the English words from the pretty lips of Shushan. Jack stood before her (it was spring now) with a great basket of spring flowers—glorious red anenomes, fragrant wild roses, pink and yellow—wild heliotrope, wild hyacinths, and other flowers for which we have no name in England. They were not alone together, of course; Mariam Hanum was there at her wheel, and two or three other women or girls of the family, spinning or sewing. Shushan herself was bending over a piece of the beautiful silk embroidery she had learned in Urfa, when the en trance of the young Englishman with the flowers they all loved so well made all look up together. Only the men and boys of their own family might

"

come in thus freely to the room where the women sat ; for any others the younger ones would have withdrawn, or at least have veiled their faces modestly. Shushan, at her first home-coming, used to do so for Jack ; but the practice had gradually and insensibly fallen into disuse. She had been learning English in the school in Urfa, and at this time it was the greatest pleasure Jack had in life to hear her speak it. She was not un-willing to do so, being most anxious to remember all she had been taught.

"Is that right said, Mr. Yon?" she asked.

"It is very nice. And now, for my *salutation*, I give you my flowers. Here are enough for every-body."

He laid the basket down beside Mariam, having first taken out a fragrant nosegay of roses and heliotrope, carefully chosen and tied with grass.

"It is for saying a good lesson," he explained, as he offered it to Shushan.

Jack was now a tall, handsome youth of eigh-teen. Of late he had grown strong and active, and he took part as much as he could in outdoor life, especially in riding. In the saddle he was utterly fearless, and he began to be very helpful to Hohannes in the training of his young horses.

A month after the departure of Thomassian, he

began to look out for answers to his letters. But in vain he watched and waited; nothing came for him. Weeks passed away, and then months; still the silence was unbroken. Jack was astonished, disappointed; sometimes, by fits and starts, he was angry. It looked as if his English friends did not care for him any longer, as if they chose to forget him. If it were not so, why had they, all this time, made no effort to find out what had become of his father and himself? Very well; if so it were, he could do without them. He could not just then feel any pressing anxiety to leave Biridjik; although of course he always meant to go back to England some time or other. When he came of age, he would certainly go, for then he could claim his inheritance.

But it was pleasant here. How richly glowed the Eastern sky! how glorious the wealth of roses! how sweetly smelled the blossoming vines, as he rode past the vineyards on the hills!

At last the vintage time came round again.

One fine autumn morning a string of horses, mules, and donkeys stood at the door of the Meneshians' house. Upon them were packed two tents of coarse black cloth—that cloth of Cilicia which the tent-maker of Tarsus used to weave. Some thin mattrasses and rugs were thrown over the bright-coloured saddles, and in the saddlebags were provisions, cooking utensils, and a few changes of dress. Then the whole family, from old Hohannes down to the youngest child, seated themselves, or were seated, on the animals as best they could find a place; and the yearly visit to the vineyards—the great autumn holiday of the Armenians—began.

If ever they shook off the deep melancholy which ages of oppression had stamped upon their race, it was in the simple pleasures of those sweet vintage days. The days were all too short for them, so they began them very early, with the singing of a psalm or hymn together. Then they dispersed to the different kinds of work allotted to them. Some stripped the low trees of their wealth of clusters, others trod out the juice in wooden troughs; again, others made it into sherbet, or into a kind of sugar, or mixed it with starch and with the kernels of nuts for the pre-paration of bastuc. Again, a company of happy children plucked the large grapes singly from their stalks and laid them in the sun, on great white linen cloths, to turn themselves into raisins. Their labours were lightened with talk and song, and sometimes even with jests and laughter.

One morning John Grayson, gathering grapes apart from the rest, heard a piteous cry for help. The voice was Shushan's; she was in pain or danger. Dropping his basket on the ground, he tore along, leaping over the low vines, making a straight line for the spot whence came the cry, whence came also horrible sounds—the yelps, the snarls, the growls of savage dogs.

In a corner of the vineyard Shushan and little Hagop clung together, just keeping at bay, with loose stones from the low wall, five or six wild, half-famished, wolfish dogs. Their strength was nearly gone. Another minute and they would be torn to pieces.

Jack dashed in amongst the dogs, dealing frantic kicks and blows about him. No matter what came next, if only he saved Shushan.

"Run! make for the tent!" he cried to her and Hagop.

The brutes being for the moment occupied with him, the thing was possible, and they did it.

The sunshine flashed on something bright in the belt of his zeboun—the great scissors used for cutting grapes. He seized it, and drove it with all his might into the neck of the nearest dog. Yelping with pain, the creature ran off. But the stoop was nearly fatal ; two or three sprang on him at once ;—he felt fierce teeth meeting in his flesh.

"Done for!" he groaned, conscious only of agony and blackness.

But the next moment a tumult of cries and

shouts rang in his ears ; the dogs were flying in all directions before the sticks and stones of his friends, who had hurried in a body to his help. They had heard the yelping even before Shushan and Hagop, trembling and exhausted, were able to reach them. The creatures belonged to some Kourdish shepherds, who chanced to be passing that way, and the low wall of the vineyard was no protection against their attacks.

Jack was brought back to his tent amidst the praises and condolences of the whole company. Mariam Hanum bound up his wounds, weeping and blessing him, and saying many a hearty "Park Derocha" ("Praise to the Lord") for the deliverance of her children.

Shushan did not say much ; but, after they went home from the vineyard, she was observed to be very busy over some choice embroidery. She did not take the time for it from her ordinary work, or from any of her domestic tasks, but she worked diligently all her spare time, and sometimes far into the night.

At last, one day, she laid a parcel of considerable size at the feet of the astonished English youth, saying timidly, "Yon Effendi, you saved my life. I want to thank you."

The parcel contained what an Armenian lady considers the most graceful and most appropriate gift she can offer to a gentleman, especially if it be all her own work—a set of beautifully embroidered bath towels!

But a day was to come when John Grayson would have given all he possessed, nay, his very life, that he had *not* heard Shushan Meneshian's agonized cry for help in the vineyard, or had heard it too late.

Chapter VII

GATHERING STORMS

" If thou seest the oppression of the poor, and violent perverting of judgment and justice in a province, marvel not at the matter : for He that is higher than the highest regardeth ; and there be higher than they."—*Eccles.* v. 8.

AFTER this adventure Jack matured much more quickly. His manhood grew in him apace, and with it came courage and energy, and the spirit of enterprise. He thought often of England now, wondering at the silence and inaction of all his relatives. That, *before* he wrote to them, they made no sign, he would not have wondered at, if he had known all the truth. The Syrian servants of his father, who had abandoned him in his illness and stolen his baggage, brought back word to Aleppo that both father and son were dead of the fever. For obvious reasons they did not remain in the city ; but the story came to the ears of the Consul, and he had no reason to doubt its truth. He opened some letters which had been sent to him for Grayson, and having thus discovered his brother's address, wrote to tell him what had happened.

Ignorant of all this, Jack was sometimes tempted to unkind thoughts of his relatives in England. He even occasionally allowed himself to think, with a touch of bitterness, that they were finding the Grayson money very convenient, and that it might go hard with them to give it up if he should reappear. But the thought, like snow in a warm climate, did not *rest*. Jack's was essentially a generous nature. It was an added wonder, however, even greater than the first, that they never answered the letter sent them through Thomassian.

But wondering and watching was idle work; and Jack, now a man grown, began to ask himself why, if he really wanted to go to England, he did *not* go? It would be difficult, and it might be dangerous, but all the better for that! What hindered his borrowing a horse, asking Hohannes to give him whatever remained—if anything did remain—of his father's money, hiring a Turkish servant, and making a dash for Aleppo? Once there, the Consul would help him; and soon after his return to England he would be of age, and able to act for himself.

What hindered him? Certainly not the perils of the way, though these were very real. He had passed beyond that stage now, finally and

for ever. The thought of peril, far from daunt-
ing him, now made his blood tingle in his veins.
Then what hindered him? He was an Englishman, and he had his life to live, his inheritance
to claim, his birthright to recover. But still more
he was something else, and that something—
not yet expressed, not yet acknowledged even
in the depths of his own heart—held him fast
in the little town by far Euphrates.

At Shushan's first home-coming he had been
very shy of her. But in brotherly intercourse
that had worn off, and a pleasant " camaraderie "
had grown up between them. He read English
with her, using the two books he had, his father's
Bible and " Westward Ho "; and she had an
Armenian Bible which they used to compare
with the English. Well she loved its sweet
words of promise, and often she would point
them out to Jack and to Gabriel, who generally
shared the lessons. But their talks were not
all grave ; they had many a quiet laugh together
over her broken English, and sometimes Jack
would tell her stories of his own country, and
of things that happened there.

She in return would talk of Urfa : of the
dear American school, of her beloved Elmas
Stepanian, and her other friends. She would
describe the American ladies of the Mission :

tall, grave Miss Celandine, revered as a mother, and her bright young colleague Miss Fairchild; Jack's fair-haired lady of the ferry-boat, whom, however, he entirely failed to recognise from her description.

But since the battle with the dogs and the gift of the towels, his shyness had returned in full force. So much so that when, with great trouble, he caught in hunting, and brought back to her, one of the pretty little gazelles the Armenians love to keep as pets, it cost him more trouble still to present his offering. But he was rewarded by the light in Shushan's lovely face, and the smile with which she spoke her gentle "Much very thanks, Master John."

Yet the passion that began to grow in John Grayson's heart was two-fold. Love and burning indignation were so closely twined together, that he could not have severed them if he tried. As his whole development since his illness had been slow, so it was but slowly and gradually that he grew to understand the conditions under which Shushan and all the rest were living. But when he came to realize them fully, he wished at first to escape and fight his way to the coast, so as anyhow and on any terms to get out of that horrible country. But he wished afterwards to stay, and stand side by side and shoulder to shoulder with these, the desolate and oppressed, whom he so loved.

Never, perhaps, has oppression been at once so comprehensive and so minute. The iron entered into their souls ; and at the same time their fingers were vexed with innumerable pin pricks. Jack had seen a hundred times, without much notice, the rude wooden ploughs in use in the district—mere hurdles with pieces of iron stuck in the end ; but one day it occurred to him, on some provocation, to abuse them roundly, and to ask if there was not a smith in the country who could make a decent ploughshare.

" Our smiths could make anything yours could," said Avedis, with whom he was walking.

" Then why don't they ? "

" I thought you knew." He lowered his voice and whispered, " *Daajek* "—the Turk.

" You mean they won't allow you ? "

Avedis nodded. " Wait till we get home," he said.

The conversation was resumed, where alone such conversations were safe, though not always even there, within closed doors.

" I know," said Jack, " that the Turks hate machinery."

" They detest it, and they fear it. They think every machine the work of Shaytan—the Devil."

"I can't help thinking," said Jack, "of the Dark Ages, and of what I read of them before I came. Here are men of the twelfth century, with their feet on the necks of men of the nineteenth. It's bad for both. *They* must be puzzled with *you*, and afraid of you, as a Norman Baron would have been of his Saxon serfs if they had understood all about steam and electricity, while he thought those things mysterious works of the Devil. But I wonder how long he could have kept them serfs?"

"As long as he had arms, and they had none. More especially if he was backed up from outside," Avedis answered sadly. Then he sang softly, as if to himself, two lines of an old Armenian national song—

> "If I cannot have a Christian home,
> I will have a Christian grave."

"Yon Effendi," he resumed, "their hate of us is growing every day. And now, I think, they mean to make a full end of us."

For rumours of terrible and wholesale massacres were reaching them every day. Now it was about Sassoun, now about Zeitun, now about Marash and Trebizond, that these things were whispered from lip to lip. Such rumours kept them in a continual state of apprehension and panic; for they knew not what to believe, and had no means of learning the truth. It was easier to know in England what happened in any town of Armenia than to know it in another town of the same country. The Turks of Biridjik triumphed openly ; and some of them boasted to their Giaour neighbours that they would soon have all that belonged to them. Some of the Christians thought they were all sure to be murdered ; others remembered there had been just such a scare seventeen or eighteen years before, but that then it had come to no-thing ; so they thought that now also things would just go on as usual, neither better nor worse.   Others again thought anything between the two extremes that their fears or their fancies prompted.

John Grayson thought, for one, that certainly for the present he would stay where he was. " It is not in the hour of danger one rides away and leaves one's friends behind," he said to himself.

More than four years had passed now since his first coming to the country. He was twenty years of age, full six feet with his slippers off, with light brown hair and beard, fair complexion well tanned by the sun, English blue eyes, and frank, fearless English face.

Chapter VIII

A PROPOSAL

He either fears his fate too much,
Or his desert is small,
Who spares to put it to the touch
And gain or lose it all.
—Marquis of Montrose.

JACK often went to the service held daily, a little after sunrise, in the Gregorian Church.

So did many members of the household, Mariam, Shushan, and Gabriel especially being constant attendants.

One day the returning party was met at the door by Hagop, weeping bitterly.

Asked by every one what was wrong, he sobbed out, " The cattle !   The cattle ! "

" What is wrong with the cattle ? "

" They are not wrong—they are all gone.   The Kourds have taken them away—every one."

" Every one ?   The kine, and the sheep and goats as well ? "

" There's not a cow left to low nor a lamb to bleat of them all.   The shepherds have come in, wounded and beaten, to tell us. Grandfather says they did all they could. Amaan ! Amaan !"

By this time the women were all weeping. For them it meant ruin—almost starvation. But Gabriel touched his mother's hand caressingly, and whispered a word from the Psalm they had just sung in church : " His are the cattle upon a thousand hills."

"But that is unbearable ! " Jack burst out.

" It *has* to be borne," Mariam said sadly.

" We shall see ! I cannot believe such things are done—here even—and there is no remedy. A man's whole possessions swept away at a stroke. Hagop, where are the men ? "

" In the great front room."

" I will go to them. Come, Gabriel."

But Hagop pulled his brother back. " *You* won't be let in," he said. " I was not."

" I am two years older."

" But you are not a man. Father said, ' This is for men,' and took me by the shoulder and turned me out."

Jack rather wondered what had to be talked of which intelligent boys of twelve and fourteen ought not to hear, but he said nothing, and went in at once.

He found all the men of the household, with a few of their intimate friends, gathered in the large room of which Hagop had spoken. As he entered all were silent. They stood together in a dull stupor, like cattle before a thunderstorm. In their faces was profound sadness, mingled with fear. Jack looked around on them, and cried out impetuously, "Are we going to stand this outrageous robbery? Is there nothing to be done?"

There was no answer. Some bowed their heads despairingly; others put their hands on their hearts, and said, "Amaan!" Others, again, looked up and murmured, "God help us!"

Jack turned to Hohannes. The old man was weeping, his face buried in his cloak. The sight touched him.

"Father, do not weep," he said gently. "We will try to recover at least something."

Hohannes flung his cloak aside with a gesture of passionate pain. "Dost think I am weeping for sheep and oxen?" he said. "Friends, this young man is to me as a son, and to Shushan as a brother. Tell him—I cannot."

Pale with a new alarm, Jack turned to the rest, "What is *this?*" he cried. "Tell me, in God's name."

They looked at each other in silence. At last Avedis, who seemed fated to belie his name, found his voice. He said hoarsely, "Just after the shepherds came to tell about the flocks, my father was called aside. It was a private message from the Kamaikan, who is not so bad as some. He sent to warn us that Mehmed Ibrahim has found out Shushan is here. He will send to demand her for his harem, and we will have to give her up."

Jack groaned, and turned his face away. Silence fell upon them all—a silence that might be felt. After a while some one said, "He has not sent yet. The Kamaikan's warning was well meant."

"Yes," said Avedis, "we have given gold. He will get us a respite if he can."

"What use in a respite," Boghos, Shushan's father, moaned in his despair—"except to dress the bride?"

"The *bride!*" a younger man repeated,—rage, hate, and shame concentrated in the word.

There was another pause, and a long one. Then John Grayson strode out into the middle of the room and stood there, his form erect, his eyes flashing, his arm outstretched. "Listen!" he cried, in a voice like the sharp report of a rifle.

Every one turned towards him, but old Hohannes said hopelessly, "It is no use; yet speak on, Yon Effendi; thou dost ever speak wisely."

"There is one way of saving Shushan."

"Let me speak first," an old man, as old as Hohannes, broke in hastily. "Englishman, thou hast lived long among us, but thou art not of our race. Thou dost not yet understand that we are born to suffer, and have no defence except patience. I wot thou wouldst talk to us of fighting and resistance; for thou art young, and thy blood is hot. But I am old, and my head is grey. I have seen that tried often enough—ay, God knows, too often! Did not my son die in a Turkish prison, and my daughter, whom he struck those blows to save—— Well, she is dead now, and Shushan—as we hope —will die soon, for God is merciful. But let there be no word spoken of resistance here; for that means only anguish piled on anguish, wrong heaped on wrong."

Without change of voice or attitude, Jack repeated his words, "There is one way of saving Shushan."

Avedis spoke up boldly. "Let us hear what Yon Effendi has to say. He saved her once already from the wild dogs."

Jack looked round the room. "Do I not see a priest here? Yes, Der Garabed."

The priest had been ill, and had come out now for the first time, drawn by sympathy for the troubles of the Meneshians. He was sitting in a corner on some cushions, but when his name was spoken he rose, in his long black robe with large sleeves, like an English clergyman's gown.

"What do you want of me, Yon Effendi?" he asked.

"I want you to marry me to-morrow morning to Shushan Meneshian."

A murmur of astonishment ran round the room. Old Hohannes was the first to speak. "Dear son, thou art beside thyself. Forget thy foolish words. We will forget them also."

"I am not beside myself, and I speak words of truth and soberness," said Jack, to whom Bible diction came naturally now. "There is no other way."

"One cannot do things after that fashion," the priest said vaguely, being much perplexed, "nor in such haste. One must be careful not to profane a sacrament of the Church."

"Where is the profanation? I love her—more than my life." Crimson to the roots of his hair, and with the blood throbbing in every vein, John Grayson stood, in that supreme moment, revealed to his own heart, and flinging out the revelation as a challenge to all that company of sorrowful, despairing men.

"It is a strange thing, a very strange thing," said Hohannes, stroking his beard.

He expressed the sense of the whole assembly. The proposal was a breach of every convention of their race, amongst whom betrothal invariably precedes marriage. "It cannot be done in that way," was their feeling.

Jack knew their customs as well as they did; but, being an Englishman, he thought necessity should and must override custom. He spoke again, with that curious calmness which sometimes marks the very heart of an intense emotion, the spot of still water in the midst of the whirlpool. "As the wedded wife of an Englishman, no Turk will dare to molest her. I should like to see him try it! He would have England to reckon with, and England can keep her own."

Now, if any hope survived in the crushed hearts of these oppressed, downtrodden Armenians, it was hope in England. The English were Christians, so they would have the will to help them; they were mighty warriors and conquerors, so they would have the power. Themselves under the pressure of a malignant, irresistible power, they had perhaps an exaggerated idea of what power could accomplish, if combined with beneficence.

Certainly for a young man to marry a girl in that way, without preparation, without betrothal, without even time to make the wedding clothes, was a thing unheard of since the days of St. Gregory. Yet, what if it were the only way of saving Shushan?

Hohannes spoke at last. "Yon Effendi," he

asked, "have you the *right* to do this? Is there in your own land no head of your house, no kinsman, without whose leave this thing ought not to be done? Answer, as in the sight of God."

Jack held up his head proudly. "There is none," he said. "I am my own master."

"Then," Hohannes resumed, "it is my mind to say to you, do what is in your heart, and may God bless you."

"Then," said Jack, "with your leave, father, I will ask her."

"And I, the head of her house, give her to you in the name of God."

Jack looked around in perplexity. "But you know I have got to ask her," he repeated. Boy as he was when he left England, he knew that when a man wished to marry, the one indispensable preliminary was to "ask" the lady of his choice.

Then arose Boghos, who had been nearly silent hitherto in a sorrow too great for words or tears. "I too her father, I give her unto thee in the Name of God," he said solemnly.

"I have only, then, to ask her," Jack persisted.

"Thou *hast* asked, and we have given her." It was Hohannes who spoke now. "What yet remains to do?"

Jack pulled himself together, and tried to explain. "But if she—does not like me—I can't—

you know.—Don't you understand?—I must speak to her, and ask her if she will have me."

The men stood silent, looking at each other. Had they spoken their thoughts, they would have said, "Heard ever any man the like of that?" Scarcely would they have been more surprised had Jack, wishing to sell his horse, announced that he could not conclude the bargain without the creature's express consent.

At last Avedis threw out a modest suggestion. "This may be one of the customs of the English people, which we do not understand. No doubt they have their customs, as we have ours."

Jack turned to him gratefully. "You are right, Avedis. It *is* the custom of my country to take the 'yes' or 'no' only from the lady's lips.

"A very strange custom," muttered Boghos.

"But if it *is* the custom, we ought to conform to it, however strange or unsuitable it may appear to us," Der Garabed advised. "We should do all things in order; and moreover, should we fail in this, it might happen that in the English country the marriage would not be recognised. Therefore this is what I propose : let us send for the young maiden, and let the Englishman, in our presence, do after the manner of his country."

This was too appalling! Jack tingled all over at the thought of such an ordeal for Shushan, and for himself. "Oh, I can't! For Heaven's sake, let me go to her," he said.

"If that also is according to the custom, it shall be duly observed," said Hohannes, with the air of one who humours a sick person. "Let us all go."

Happily for Jack, some of those present had the sense to reflect that the women's apartment would not hold them all, and that therefore their assistance might be dispensed with. Still the grandfather and father of the maiden, two of her uncles, the priest, and three other persons thought it behoved them to go and witness the due performance of this ceremony of the English.

Jack was conducted by this solemn group to the room where Shushan sat with her mother. As with trembling footsteps he approached her, the rest fell back and stood in a grave half-circle, their ears and eyes intent upon his every word and motion. "Heaven help me!" thought Jack. "Had ever man to propose in such a way? What shall I say?" But no words would come to him; sense and speech seemed both to have departed from him.

The silence throbbed in his ears like a pulse of pain—the awful silence, which he knew he ought to break, which he *must* break, for his life, and more than his life—and yet he could not. Not a word could he utter.

Shushan, meanwhile, not knowing what all this might portend, hastily veiled her face, and clung to her mother. Mariam had a copper dish which she had been cleaning in her hand, and in her surprise and alarm she let it go. It slipped slowly down her dress, and fell at last with a slight sound upon the floor. In the strained silence every one started, and Shushan dropped her veil with a little frightened cry.

Jack saw her sweet face, pale with anguish, her soft, dark eyes, heavy with unshed tears. Every thought was lost in an unutterable longing to snatch her from the fate that threatened her. "Will you let me save you, Shushan?" he pleaded, coming close to her,—and his voice was the voice of a strong man's infinite tenderness.

Shushan stood up, looked around upon her father, her grandfather, and all the rest, then looked calmly and steadily in the face of the Englishman. "*Yes*," she said softly.

For she knew there was one way of escape for the Christian maiden in a strait like hers. There had been often in Armenia Christian fathers strong enough to say, like Virginius,—

> "And now, my own dear little girl, there is no way but this."

What more likely than that the brave, kind Englishman—whom it would not hurt so much, as he was not of her own blood—might do for her that which her kindred would find too hard? There was a strange fascination, a sort of rapture in the thought of dying by his hand. "I am not afraid," she said, with a firm sweet look,—"not afraid to die."

"*To die!*" Jack cried in horror. "Who talks of dying? No, you shall not die, but live. You shall live for me, my own true wife, in happy England. Say 'yes' to that, Shushan."

She looked at him in wonder. At last the colour mounted to her pale cheeks, her lips parted softly, and a low murmur came, "If God wills."

Hohannes turned gravely to the rest. "No doubt," he said, stroking his beard, "Yon Effendi has done after the manner of the English, when they would take their wives. If he is satisfied, we may go our way, thanking God, who has sent him to the help of our dear child in her peril."

Jack's heart beat thickly, as one by one they went, and he was left alone with Shushan and her mother. Hohannes had looked back to see if he were following; but no, he stood rooted to the spot. "The custom of his country," thought the old man, and passed on.

Jack stood looking on the ground, not daring to raise his eyes to Shushan's face. But when the last retreating footstep had died away, he looked up, and there was that in his face which she had never seen before. The question of his heart was this: "Does she care for *me*, or am I only better than a Turk?" It spoke in his eyes, and thrilled her with a sense of something strangely new and sweet. He had been kind and good to her for so long a time, but *this*—what was this?

Instinctively she turned from him to her mother. Mariam's tears of joy and thankfulness were falling drop by drop. She could have thrown herself at the feet of the deliverer of her child. But, true to the custom of her race when a maiden is in the presence of him who has chosen her, she drew the veil over her daughter's face.

"Ah!" Jack exclaimed involuntarily. But he had seen enough—enough at least to assure him that he could teach Shushan to love him as he loved her. "Dear mother," he said, "you have been a mother to me for so long; now I am going to be your son altogether, and take care of your Lily."

Scarcely had the men reached the court when the priest said gravely, "There is one thing we have left out of our account, which is serious, and may not be disregarded. An Englishman cannot marry a subject of the Sultan without a written permission from his own Consul—even if he can do it except in the Consul's presence. Under the circumstances, I dare not perform the ceremony;

terrible harm might come of it; and moreover it might not be valid in England."

Most of the party knew this already, but in their excitement they had disregarded or forgotten it. They stood just as they were in the court, and looked at one another; "all faces gathered blackness."

"Call forth Yon Effendi and tell him," said Hohannes.

Avedis called him, and he came, his face flushed and glowing with a shy, half-hidden rapture.

Der Garabed explained the difficulty. Jack tossed his head impatiently, like a young horse restrained unwillingly by bit and bridle. "What a plague!" he cried in boyish indignation. Then, his face changed and sobered as the man within him asserted himself; he seemed to grow years older all at once. "This is what we will do," he said: "Bring Shushan well disguised to one of the Christian villages near—you know them all, and which is best to choose—and hide her there for a few days. I will take horse this very hour and ride to Urfa. You know it is reported the Consul is there at present. If he is, I can see him; if not, I can go after him. I daresay he can give me some writing, or document, which will make everything straight for us. But if he cannot, and the thing must be done in his presence, I will bring

Shushan to him, were he at the end of the world. For I carry this thing through, or I die for it—so help me God!"

"Good. And before you go, we will betroth her to you," Hohannes answered.

Then he took him privately into the room where his father's things were hidden. He gave him all the gold that remained ; and then, with an air of mystery, took out another parcel, and having unwound its many wrappings, displayed to Jack's astonished eyes a small revolver and a belt of cartridges.

" I did not know you had these," he said.

" No ; I was afraid to tell you while you were but a boy ; lest some chance word to your companions might betray that we had firearms here, and ruin us all ; or else you might have been too eager to get hold of them, and unwilling to wait. But now you are a man, and have sense and understanding ; and on the way to Urfa, where there are robbers, they may be of use to you."

Jack took the revolver in great delight, and went off to examine it. In England he had been a good shot for a boy of his age, though only with an ordinary gun. But he had sometimes cleaned the revolver for his father, so he knew what to do. He found it in a terrible condition from rust and damp, and feared it would be quite useless. However, he managed with great difficulty to clean two barrels out of the six, and to load them ; more it would be useless to attempt.

As he was thus engaged some one knocked at the door. Knowing his occupation to be a very dangerous one, he did not say, "Come in," but went and opened it cautiously. Gabriel stood there. "Yon Effendi," he said, " the post is going to-night."

" Well ? "

"That means that you may get to Urfa in nine hours instead of in two days ; for you know they go the whole way at a hard gallop. It means safety too, for they have zaptiehs to guard them."

"Good, Gabriel. 'Tis *thou* shouldst be called Avedis (good tidings). I will go at once and settle to go along with them."

"You will hide *that thing*," said Gabriel, with a frightened glance at the revolver. "'Twould mean death. And oh, Yon Effendi, one word, please!" He stooped, kissed his hand, and pressed his forehead to it. "Tell them a boy comes with you. Take me, I pray of you, Yon Effendi!"

Jack hesitated. "There would be danger for you," he said.

" No more than here."

" But your father and mother, and your grandfather, Gabriel ? "

"They give me leave; nay, they wish it. They say it is for my sister you are doing all this; therefore if I can help you—and I can. I know Turkish well, and that will be very useful. I know the ways of the Turks too, much better than you do. And I love you, Yon Effendi."

There was reason in what he said, and in the end he had his way.

That evening all the Meneshian family met together in the largest room of their house, the men and boys sitting at one side of it, the women at the other. At an ordinary time they would have "called their neighbours and chief friends," but now they were afraid to do it; so Der Garabed was the only outsider, and his presence was official, for he read certain prayers of the Church and a passage of Scripture. Then Jack stood up, and walked over to the place where Shushan sat, beside her mother. In his hand was his father's Bible and another book—an Armenian hymn-book. Shushan rose and stood before him with bowed head and veiled face, as with a few low-breathed words he gave her the books. She took them from him, and laid them on the table. No word was spoken by her; in taking them she had done enough. The betrothal was sealed. Then, according to custom, the boys handed round bastuc and paclava, (a kind of paste made with honey,) and also coffee and sherbet.   But this was rather a sacrifice to use and wont than a genuine festivity.   The little gathering soon broke up, and Jack and Gabriel prepared for their journey.

At nightfall they said to their friends and kindred the usual " Paree menác " (remain with blessing), and were answered by the usual, and in this case most heartfelt " Paree yetac " (go with blessing).

Chapter IX

PEACE AND STRIFE

"They that have seen thy look in death
No more may fear to die."

JOHN GRAYSON and Gabriel Meneshian were threading their way through the narrow, un-savoury streets of Urfa, the gutters which ran down the middle often not leaving them room to walk side by side. They had left their horses at a khan, and were now seeking the dwelling of the Vartonians, to which they had been directed. Emerging at last into a wider thoroughfare, they saw a church, standing in the midst of its church-yard, of which the gate was open. "We must be in our own quarter," cried Gabriel, delighted, "for this is a Christian church."

Jack stepped inside the gate and looked at it with interest. The door of the church was open also; and Gabriel, seeing him look towards it, said, "You might go in there, Yon Effendi, and rest a little, for I see you are tired to death; I will run on and try and find the house. It cannot be far off now."

"But you are tired too."

"Not a bit. I would feel quite fresh this minute if I only had a drink. And, by good luck, there goes a fellow outside, a Turk too, with a bucket full of *iran* to sell."

The Turk, who had been crying his ware, stopped at the moment, for he saw an Armenian boy coming down the street with a large empty pitcher in his hand. "You want this?" said he, preparing to pour his sour milk into it.

The boy said he wanted nothing of the kind. He had been sent for water, and water he must bring. His people were waiting for it, and would be very angry. He tried to pass on, but the Turk laid hold on him, seized his pitcher, and emptied the bucket of *iran* into it, not without spilling ·a good deal in the street. "Now pay me my money," he said.

"But the thing is no use to me," the boy protested ruefully.

"What does that matter, dog of a Giaour? You got it; and, by the beard of the Prophet, you must pay for it."

As the boy, crying bitterly, searched for the few piastres he had about him, Jack's honest English face flushed with wrath, and Gabriel would have sprung to the rescue had he not laid his hand on him and whispered, "Wait."

They waited until the Turk had turned down a side street, then Jack hailed the lad, who was standing quite still, gazing dolefully at his useless pitcher of *iran*. "Will you give us a drink?" he asked, coming out of the gate. "We are dying of thirst."

The boy checked his sobs; and for answer held up his pitcher to the lips of the stranger. Jack took a long deep draught, then passed it on to Gabriel, while he made the boy happy with more piastres than the Turk had taken from him. His tears all gone, he blessed the strangers for good Christians, and thanked them in the Name of the Lord.

"What church is that?" asked Gabriel, giving back the pitcher.

"That? Oh, that is the church of the Protestants."

"Is it English then?" Jack asked, feeling a pull at his heart strings.

"No; it is Armenian. But it is of the religion of the foreigners, who talk English. They are good people, and very kind to the poor."

"Perhaps there is service going on, as the church is open," Jack said. "I will go and see."

"Do," said Gabriel; "meanwhile, this lad will help me to find the Vartonians, and I will come back for you."

Jack passed through the churchyard, and, leaving his shoes on the threshold, entered the church. The interior was very handsome, all of white stone, and adorned with fine pillars and beautiful carving. It was not unlike a Gregorian church, save for the absence of pictures. In the window, over what the Gregorians called the Altar and the Protestants the Table of the Lord, was a small red cross. There was a very low partition, separating the places where the men and the women sat, and the floor was covered with rushes.

Before the Holy Table, on a kind of couch, all draped in snowy white, and covered with flowers, something lay. Jack knew what it was, for he had seen the dead laid in the church at Biridjik, to await their final rest. With bowed head and reverent footsteps he drew near to look. Venturing gently to draw aside the face-cloth from the face, he saw it was that of a woman. Not, evidently, a young and lovely girl like Shushan, but one who had lived her life, had borne the burden and heat of the day, and, it well might be, was glad to rest. Perhaps yesterday there were wrinkles on the cheek and furrows on the brow; now death,—"kind, beautiful death,"—had smoothed them all away, and stamped instead his own signet there of which the legend is " Peace." The closed white lips had that look we have seen on the faces of our dead, as if they are of those " God whispers in the ear,"—and they *know*, though they cannot tell us, *yet*. English words, that he had heard long ago, came floating through the brain of John Grayson. " The peace of God that passeth all understanding." He found himself once more in the church of his childhood, while a solemn voice breathed over the hushed congregation those words of blessing. Then, coming back to the present, he thought, " It takes away the fear of death to see a dead face like that." He reverently replaced the veil, and withdrawing somewhat into the shadow, knelt down to pray.

As he knelt there, he heard the footsteps of one who came to look upon the dead. Rising noiselessly, he saw a tall, noble-looking man, dressed *à la Frank*, approach the bier. His bent head was streaked with grey, his face pale with intense, though quiet sorrow. As he knelt down silently beside his dead, John Grayson knew instinctively that the love of those two had been what his love and Shushan's might become, if God left them together for half a happy lifetime.

For a few minutes the silence lasted, then came that most sorrowful of all earth's sounds of sorrow, the sob of a strong man. Jack kept quiet in the shadow of his pillar, in reverence and awe; not for worlds would he have betrayed his presence there.

Afraid Gabriel might come in search of him, he looked round for some chance of escape. He saw, to his relief, a small side door, near where he was standing. He crept towards it noiselessly, found it unlocked, withdrew the little bolt, and going through the pastor's study, slipped out into the churchyard to wait for Gabriel. Yes, there he was, just coming in at the gate. He went to meet him.

"Did you think me long, Yon Effendi?" asked the boy. "I have found the Vartonians, and I am to bring you to them at once. Baron Vartonian himself is away from home, but one of his sons would have come with me to bid you welcome to their house, only they are in great trouble to-day, for Pastor Stepanian, their Badvellie, whom they love, has just lost his wife. Shushan will be very sorry, for Oriort Elmas Stepanian, the Badvellie's daughter, is her greatest friend."

"I know," Jack answered softly. "I have seen the face of the dead. Gabriel, I do not think *now* that it can be very hard to die."

"No," said Gabriel. "It would not be hard to die for Christ's sake, Yon Effendi."

" It reminds me," Jack went on, as if talking to himself, " of the last words I heard my father say, ' The dark river turns to light.' "

Jack was received with open arms by the whole Vartonian household. It was even a larger household than that of the Meneshians in Biridjik. Its head, a prosperous merchant, was absent in Aleppo, but there was his old infirm father, and there were his numerous sons and daughters, two or three of them married, with children of their own, but the youngest still a child. There were also many servants. Some of the family were Gregorians and some Protestants, but there was no friction or jealousy between the two. Being people of substance, their house, built as usual around a court, was large and very handsomely furnished, the wood-work carved elaborately, and the curtains, rugs, and carpets of rich materials, and beautifully embroidered.

The Vartonians considered Jack in the light of a hero. But they were uneasy at Shushan's being left, even for the present, in a village exposed to the attacks of the Kourds ; for much more was known at Urfa than at Biridjik about the disturbed state of the country, and the terrible massacres that had taken place in many towns and villages. Was not the Armenian quarter still full of the miserable refugees from Sassoun, who had come there during the past winter—diseased, starving, wounded, sometimes dying, and with horrible tales of the cruelties they and theirs had suffered?

It was agreed on all hands that the best thing Jack could do was to refer his case to the lady at the head of the American Mission, whose school Shushan had attended. We shall call this heroic lady, who is happily still living, Miss Celandine. She thought the best plan would be to bring Shushan, as soon as she was married, back to Urfa in disguise, since under her charge and in the mission premises she would be, for the time, absolutely safe. She believed the English Consul would be able to give permission for the marriage without being personally present. But she was not certain as to where the Consul was to be found. Very likely he was at the baths of Haran, the season being August, and very hot. She would find out as soon as possible, and put Mr. Grayson into communication with him.

Two or three days later, Jack was setting out, with one of the young Vartonians, to explore the hill that overhangs Urfa, and to visit the remains of the ancient citadel, and the other interesting ruins with which it is strewn,—when Kevork Meneshian walked in. As soon as they had got through the usual salutations, Barkev Vartonian and John Grayson asked him together, " What has brought you here?" And Barkev added, "It is not the time for vacation."

"True," answered the young man, smiling; "I did very wrong to come away. And I am very glad I came."

"You speak in a riddle," said Jack.

"It is easily read. When Pastor Stepanian's wife died, the news came by telegraph to Oriort Elmas in Aintab. It was in her heart to go home at once to her father and her young brothers, who must need her sorely. But what a journey for a girl, and a girl all alone, with only khartijes for companions and protectors! Only think of it, four long days on horseback, and three nights in the wayside khans! And then the perils of the road—wild Kourds everywhere, not to speak of other robbers, more treacherous, if less violent. I could not have it! So I told no one, but just wrote a note of apology, and left it for the Principal, slipped out without waiting for leave, put on a servant's dress, and became her shadow, from the moment her lady teacher bade farewell to her in Aintab until she fell fainting into her father's arms here in Urfa, last night."

"A proper person *you* were to act as a young lady's guardian!" said Barkev laughing.

"I did not say 'guardian,' I said 'shadow,'" Kevork returned coolly. "One's shadow is always before or behind. So I took care to keep ; only letting her know I *was* there, if I was wanted. There were many ways I could help her. That is how I came to be here ; and I suppose the Mission folk at Aintab will have no more of me, since I have broken all their rules. But I have got a good deal of their learning already," he added with some complacency. "Yon Effendi, how are my father and my mother, and all our house in Biridjik, for we did not stay there on our way ? And what in the world has brought *you* here ? "

Jack answered his questions, marvelling the while at the mixture in his character. Shrewd, practical, and almost selfish in the pursuit of his ambition as he used to think him, he had served Elmas Stepanian with a delicate, self-sacrificing chivalry of which any lover might have been proud.

"I think," said Barkev, "you would do well to go to the Badvellie. He is very learned, and might give you the lessons you have missed."

"I will not trouble the Pastor *yet*," answered Kevork with decision—"not until I can go to him for something else. No ; I shall beg of Miss Celandine to give me work, teaching the boys that come to her school, and study for myself in the evenings."

"You'll get on," said Barkev approvingly. "For

you know what you want. 'A polished stone is not left on the ground.'"

"I might, in any other country. But," lowering his voice, "what is this I hear of fresh massacres?"

"Oh, rumours, rumours! There are always rumours. I would not think too much of them—not until we hear more."

"You may well talk of rumours," Kevork returned. "Some of the things people say are past thinking for foolishness. Do you know I heard in Aintab that some people say in Europe it is *we* who are massacring the Turks? As if we *could*, even suppose we would! Without firearms, or weapons of any kind, so much as to defend ourselves from the Kourdish robbers—good for *us* to think of killing Turks! 'Twould be striking the point of a goad with one's fist."

"The wolf eats the lamb, and cries out that the lamb is eating him," said Barkev. "But," he added, glancing round apprehensively, "is there any talk of the English coming to help us?"

"Much talk there is of the Sultan's having consented, moved thereto no doubt by the English and the other Christians, to grant us certain privileges."

"We do not want privileges," said Barkev; "we want *justice*. We want security for our lives and properties, and, above all, for our women."

"Well, that is what these reforms are intended to give us."

"I'll believe in them, when I see a Moslem punished for a crime against one of *us*. And that is what my grandfather, in his seven and eighty years, has never seen, nor I think will little Nerses, who is not weaned yet, live to see it."

"Where is the use of that kind of talk, true though it be?" said Kevork; "it only brings trouble."

The heart of Kevork Meneshian was not just then attuned to trouble. The deepest gorges of the Alps have every day their gleam of sunshine, though it be but for one short hour; so even in the most shadowed lives there is usually some brief, golden moment, when the light in a soft eye or the smile on a dear lip is more than the fate of nations or of empires. It was such a moment now with Kevork; and it ought to have been such a moment with John Grayson, only, for him, it was love itself that hung suspended in the balance of fate.

Fate, for the time, seemed to have turned against him. The ride from Biridjik to Urfa had been done at headlong speed, and he had not reached his destination until it was almost noon, and the sun's heat absolutely overpowering. He thought his miserable sensations afterwards were only the result of fatigue, and kept up bravely until the coming of Kevork, when he had to own to overpowering headache, and feverish alternations of heat and cold. He just managed somehow to write a letter to the Consul, which he asked the Vartonians to get Miss Celandine to forward for him, if she could. Then he yielded to destiny. For eight days he tossed in fever, with Kevork as his special nurse, his kind hosts also giving him every care and attention in their power.

Once the fever left him however, he recovered rapidly, his good constitution, strengthened by a simple and healthy life, coming to his aid. As soon as he was able to be about again, he said he would go to the Mission House, and ask Miss Celandine if she had any tidings for him. As he spoke, he was standing near one of the few windows of the Vartonian House which looked out upon the street. Something he saw there made him break off suddenly, pause a moment, then utter an exclamation of pity and horror.

"What is it?" asked Kevork, coming to the window, followed by Barkev, and two of the ladies of the house, who chanced to be present.

Along the street passed slowly, by twos and threes, in a straggling procession, some of the most miserable creatures the eye of man has ever looked upon. Gaunt, half famished, with limbs reduced to skin and bone, or else swollen out of all shape by disease, they walked on with uneven, tottering footsteps. All were in filthy, ragged garments ; some had rags clotted with blood tied about their heads or their arms, others limped along with the aid of sticks. Just under the window a woman dropped in the street, and lay as one dead. The man who was walking beside her stood and looked, without doing anything to help. How could he? Both his hands were gone.

The three young men ran to the street together. Jack proved the quickest, and was already kneeling on the ground and trying to raise the poor woman when the others came up. "It is no use," said the man beside her in a dreary, almost indifferent, tone. "She is dead."

"I don't know that," said Jack. "Give her air, for heaven's sake. Kevork, keep back the others. Barkev, you could fetch us some cordial."

It was not so easy to obey him ; for those before had stopped, while those behind came crowding up, and with the strangers a few Armenians of he town. One of these pushed through the rest with an air of authority. "Make way, good people," he said ; "I am a doctor."

He did not seem a very prosperous member of the fraternity, to judge by his dress ; but then he was young, and had the world before him. He felt the woman's pulse and her heart, and said presently, "She is not dead; but she soon will be unless she gets proper care and nourishment. Who will help me to carry her into my dispensary close by?"

Jack volunteered, quite forgetting his recent illness; but Barkev raised an objection. "Better bring her to the Mission House," he said. "Miss Celandine has food and medicine, and will take good care of her."

"Miss Celandine will have her hands full. Besides, my place is near. Yes, sir, take her feet,"—he nodded to Jack. "I'll manage the rest. This way, please."

"You are a good fellow, Melkon Effendi, and I believe you are right," said Barkev, his attention claimed by another of the miserable group, who was begging in God's name for a bit of bread, as they had eaten nothing for several days but grass and roots.

Jack helped Melkon to lay his patient on the surgery table, and watched his efforts to restore animation. "Who are they?" he asked.

The young doctor answered in broken phrases without stopping his work. "From one of the villages—Rhoumkali—fugitives—there has been a massacre—wholesale—of our people—by Turks and Kourds."

" Horrible ! "

" Horrible ?   If you had seen the Sassoun refugees when they came here last winter, you might talk of horror.   I believe the young Mission lady, Miss Fairchild, sacrificed her life to them."

Miss Fairchild, Shushan's friend !   " Is she dead then ? " Jack asked anxiously.

" They sent her away still hanging between life and death, and we know not yet which will conquer.   But, as for massacres—to-day there, to-morrow here."

" Not *here*, in a great city like this—not here surely," Jack said.   " But the villages, the little towns like Biridjik, for them one's heart trembles," he added, his thoughts flying to Shushan.

" She is coming to," said Melkon cheerfully, the duty of the moment shutting out the terrors of the future.

" Well, my lad, what do *you* want ? "—this to a youth who appeared in the doorway.   " Oh, I see ; you are one of Baron Thomassian's people, and come just in time to fetch what I want.   I am out of these drugs," and he handed him a list.

" You shall have them, Melkon Effendi," said the young man.   " But my business now is with the other gentleman.   I have just met Baron Barkev Vartonian, who told me I should find him here."

" With *me* ? " said Jack, a little excited ; for

what possible business could Thomassian have with him, except to give him a letter from England; or, at least, a letter or a message from the Consul?

"With you, sir. My master salutes you with all respect, and begs of you to honour his poor dwelling with a visit, and to drink his black coffee."

Still under the same impression, and with bright visions floating before him of bringing his young bride in triumph to England, Jack only waited to see the poor woman fully restored to consciousness, and to give Melkon a little money to supply her immediate necessities. He then accompanied the youth to the house of Thomassian, leaving a message on his way for the Vartonians, to say whither he had gone.

He was rewarded with the first specimen of genuine Oriental wealth and splendour he had seen in Armenia. He had thought the house of the Vartonians a model of luxury, but this was a fairy palace! Muggurditch Thomassian himself, in a faultless European costume, met him at the door. He had heard nothing of his illness, which was not surprising, as he seldom saw his kinsfolk the Vartonians. He explained that he had taken the freedom of asking him to visit him at the earnest request of his wife, who had a great desire to see an Englishman once more. "She is from

Constantinople," he said a little proudly. " There she used to have much intercourse with the Franks, and especially with the English, whom she greatly esteems." Then he led his visitor across the spacious marble court, with its beautiful fountain in the midst, its bushes laden with fragrant roses, its flowers of many kinds and hues. Some of them, which were rare and newly brought to the country, he pointed out to the Englishman.

Jack admired them duly, and expressed the satisfaction he would have in waiting on " the Madam "; but, the claims of courtesy thus fulfilled, he could not help adding, " I hoped you might have a letter to give me from my friends in England, or at least a communication from the Consul."

" Have you had, yourself, no answer to your letter, Effendi ? " Thomassian asked, as he stopped to gather for his guest some roses he had particularly admired.

" None whatever."

" Djanum ! " (my soul ! a common exclamation) " Then I fear it must have gone astray in the post. You know how often, unfortunately, that happens here."

" But the Consul ? " Jack asked eagerly ; " you spoke to him, did you not ? "

" He was absent when I went to Aleppo,"

Thomassian answered. "I wrote to him about your matters ; but I fear that letter may have miscarried, like the other one."

"That Consul is always *somewhere else*," Jack thought despairingly, as he took off his shoes at the beautifully carved and polished door that led to the apartment of the ladies. He found himself, on entering, in a large room heavy with perfume. Silken hangings, richly embroidered, adorned the walls. Silk and satin cushions of all colours, often heavy with gold and silver, lay about in profusion. The only other furniture the room contained was the long satin-covered divan which occupied one side of it, and upon which there half sat and half reclined a very handsome lady. Her dress was of the costliest materials, and of a fashion partly Eastern and partly European. Jack made the usual compliments in his best style ; and was invited to sit upon luxurious cushions, and by-and-by to partake of choice coffee, sherbet and sweetmeats, which were handed to him on silver trays by pretty, dark-eyed girls in silk zebouns and jackets. Meanwhile his host entertained him with what he could not help calling, in his disappointed soul, vapid and uninteresting commonplaces, the lady putting in now and then a languid but courteous word or two. His heart full of his own perplexities and of what he had just seen of the wretched fugitives from Rhoumkali, he began a question about the massacres there, but his host, with a warning glance directed towards his wife, turned the conversation immediately. Jack could understand his not wishing to alarm her, or to wring her heart with terrible details; especially as she did not look very strong.

But the time seemed long to him; and as soon as he thought it consistent with good manners, he rose to take his leave.

The lady called one of her attendants, and gave her a brief direction. The girl left the room, and speedily returned, bearing a pretty card-board box about a foot square, covered with coloured straw wrought in patterns. "Will you do me a kindness, Mr. Grayson?" said "the Madam." "Will you take charge of this box of Turkish sweetmeats from Constantinople, and present it, with my salutations, to the little Vartonians, the cousins of my husband? But, I pray you, take toll of it in passing. Open the box, and eat the first sweetmeat yourself." As she said this her dark eyes, for one instant, met and *fixed* the English blue eyes of Jack Grayson; the next, she was bidding him good-bye with perfect Eastern courtesy, just touched with the dignified nonchalance of the typical fine lady.

When Jack was once more alone with Thomassian, he spoke again of the horrors of Rhoumkali. Thomassian shrugged his shoulders. " It is very dreadful," he said.

" Can nothing be done ? "

" *Nothing*, Mr. Grayson. Foolish people, who run about talking of things they do not understand, only get themselves and other men into trouble. Here is what happens many a time— there is some wild talk going of help from England, or some such nonsense, and on the strength of it some hot-headed fellow kills a Kourd, or resists a zaptieh, and then all hell is let loose upon us."

" But if the zaptieh is torturing his father for not paying a tax he does not owe, or giving up a rifle he has not got? Or, if the Kourd is taking— well, you know what I mean ; the word chokes me," said Jack, thinking of Shushan.

" Let be ! let be ! ' Speech is silver, silence is golden.' ' The heart of the fool is in his tongue, the tongue of the wise man is in his heart.'—Mr. Grayson, I thank you for honouring me with a visit. I beg of you to salute my cousins in my name. I hope old Father Hagop's cough is not so troublesome now ? And how is the little one ? Does he begin to walk yet ? I hope to have the pleasure of visiting them very shortly, but business is pressing just now." With such talk as this he led Jack once more to the outer door ; and he, as he took his final leave, remembered an English word which he had hardly thought of since he left the shores of his native land. He confessed himself decidedly " bored."

As soon as he got home, he opened the box of sweetmeats and looked anxiously for what the giver might mean by the " first." Each of the dainty morsels was wrapped up separately in thin paper ; but one of them looked, on close inspection, as if the paper had been removed, and then carefully replaced. He took it off, and found—traced upon it in very fine, faint handwriting—the following words :

" MR. JOHN GRAYSON.—Shushan is in danger. The chief wife of Mehmed Ibrahim is my friend. She does not wish Shushan to be found. She tells me Mehmed has discovered the name of the village where she is, and will set on the Kourds to attack it, and to make her a prisoner. There is no safe place for her, except the house of the American missionaries here—if only you can bring her to it secretly, in some disguise—for the Turks do not dare to enter it. I may not write to the Mission ladies myself, as my husband forbids me to have any communication with them, therefore I write to you. You will know what to do. God bless you.—YEVNEGA THOMASSIAN."

Chapter X

AN ARMENIAN WEDDING

AT Biridjik, in the house of Hohannes Mene-shian, and in the very room where John Grayson had caught his first glimpse of Armenian domestic life, two women sat at work. Mariam, looking old and careworn, was behind her wheel as usual ; Shushan was bending over her beautiful embroidery. The room looked much barer than in the olden days, most of the curtains and rugs had disappeared, and there was no sign of any cooking in progress. This mattered the less however since grapes were in season now, and a basket of great, luscious clusters lay in the corner, destined to form, with rye bread, the evening meal of the family.

The villagers with whom Shushan had been staying had brought her home the day before. She was no longer safe with them. A Kourd, who had shown them a little friendliness, and to whom they had given backsheesh, had called to one of their men over the wall of the vineyard where he was working, " Take care ! you have got a lily our sheikh wants to gather." So they acted on the hint. Shushan was once more with her kindred, and in the place of her birth. But little joy had she, or they, in the meeting.

Her presence was a danger to her friends. She was hunted from place to place, like a partridge the dogs start from its cover that it may fall by the gun of the sportsman. Happy partridge, that would fall at once, gasp its little life out on the grass, and rest ! No such rest for the Moslem's victim !

More than once indeed, across the sad texture of Shushan's life, there had shot a gleam of gold. She had been a happy girl in Urfa, when she went with her cousins to the Mission school, and learned beautiful things from the dear foreign ladies there. Afterwards in Biridjik, for a little while, she had been still happier, though with a different kind of happiness. The brave, strong, splendid English youth had come into her life and transfigured it. He had saved her from the savage dogs ; he had done a still more wonderful thing than that. He had come to her help in her direst need, choosing her, claiming her for his own. Her heart throbbed yet with the fearful rapture of that day, the wonder-day of her short life—the day of her betrothal.

But now Yon Effendi was gone from her. All her joy seemed to have melted from her like the snow on the mountains, like the dreams of the night. It had left instead a yearning, painful in its sweetness, an "aching, unsatisfied longing," for him who was its core and its centre. Yon Effendi was gone; but Mehmed Ibrahim, whom she had never seen, yet regarded with unutterable dread and loathing, seemed by his agents and instruments to be ever present, all around her, pressing her in on every side. She feared death far less than she feared him; but she was not yet quite sixteen, and since she had known Yon Effendi, she would have liked to live.

The well-taught pupil of the Mission school thought more clearly and felt more keenly than her simple-hearted mother, who had never had her chances; but the more capacious vessel only held in larger measure the bitter wine of pain. She had once or twice to turn her head aside, lest her tears should fall upon the work she was doing and spoil it.

"Mother," she said at last, "I think, if God willed it, it were better I should die. There seems no place in the world for me."

"Child, it is wrong to speak so," Mariam answered. We must live in the world as long as God pleases. To go out of it by our own act were a sin."

"Except it were to avoid a sin," said Shushan gravely, raising her sad eyes to her mother's.

Both were silent for a moment. Then the mother spoke again.

"Daughter, before you went away you used to tell me the good words you learned in the school. I liked them, and they often came back to me when I was anxious and frightened. You remember how sore afraid I was that day the zaptiehs came for the taxes? Thy father had Gabriel's tax and Hagop's all right, but he thought Kevork's would be paid in Aintab, and never thought of getting ready to pay it here. But they demanded it all the same, and I thought—'Now surely they will beat or torture him or your grandfather, because we have it not.' But I remembered that word you told me from the letter of the holy St. Peter, 'Casting all your care upon Him, for He careth for you.' So I said, 'Jesus, help us!' with all my heart,—and He did. For though they found and took away all our rice, they never saw the barley, or the bulghour, so we have that to live upon. And they went away content."

Shushan put a few stitches in her embroidery

before she answered. She was working, with crimson silk, the deep red heart of a rose. Richly the colours glowed beneath the skilful touch of her slight brown fingers, but out of her own life all the colour seemed to have gone. And now it was the strong that failed, and leaned upon the weaker for support ; it was the better taught that turned wistfully to the simpler for words of cheer.

"Oh, my mother," she said, " my heart is weary, my heart is sad ! Sometimes even it asks of me, and gets no answer : ' Does He care for us Armenians ? "

Does He care for Armenians? Not only from the trampled land herself has that cry gone up in the ears of the Lord of Sabaoth,—from many a quiet home in countries far away, wherever the tale of her woes has come, it has echoed and re-echoed. " Strong spirits have wrestled over it with God " in the silent watches of the night, even until the breaking of the day ; " tender spirits have borne it as a terrible and undefined secret anguish." Is there any answer, *yet*, except this one, " What I do thou knowest not now, but thou shalt know hereafter " ?

Mariam had no wise words of comfort to give her child ; but she had the mother's secret of love, which so often is better than wisdom. She folded

Shushan tenderly in her arms and kissed her. Then the girl recovered a little.

"I ought not to talk so to you, mother," she said. "We know He does care."

"Amaan! God is good," Mariam said. "He cares for every one; even, I suppose, for the Turks."

There was a silence during which Mariam resumed her spinning, and Shushan her embroidery.

"I am not easy about the grandfather," Mariam said presently. "I wish we could get him to eat a little more. Since the fright about thee, and the loss of his flocks and herds, he has scarcely been his own man. And that last visit of the zaptiehs did him no good——What is that noise in the court? Some one has come."

The whirr of the spinning wheel ceased, and Shushan dropped her work, growing very pale. Neither thought of going forth to see, for neither expected any good thing to come to them. Shushan would have hidden herself, but there did not seem time; so they sat in silence, listening to a confused Babel of sounds outside. But presently both cried at once,—

"The voice of Kevork, my son."

"The voice of Yon Effendi, my betrothed."

"Cover yourself, my daughter," said Mariam hastily. And Shushan veiled her face, and sat still where she was, while the mother went forth to welcome her son, whom she had not seen for more than eighteen months.

That night, for once, the voice of joy and thankfulness was heard in the house of Hohannes Meneshian.

Jack had taken Kevork into council over the communication made to him by the wife of Thomassian. The two young men had agreed that no time was to be lost in returning to Biridjik and bringing Shushan back with them to Urfa, even if they had to disguise her for the purpose as a boy. Thinking the knowledge of their plan might imperil the Vartonians, they did not tell them of it. They told no one in fact except Miss Celandine, whose promise to receive and shelter Shushan was readily given.

Jack went to Muggurditch Thomassian, and asked him to lend him a sum of money. To this the merchant made no objection, for he felt certain the young Englishman would eventually have funds at his command. Jack gave him a written acknowledgment and promised him good interest, requesting him at the same time not to mention the matter to the Vartonians, who might be hurt at his not applying to them in the first instance. There was indeed little danger of his doing so, for the cousins, at the time, were not upon friendly terms. The Vartonians, like other Armenians, rich and poor, had contributed liberally to the needs of the unfortunate fugitives from Rhoumkali, even taking some of them into their house. They were indignant with their wealthy kinsman, who had given a handsome subscription to the cause, but seemed to be recouping himself by heavy charges upon the drugs and medicines supplied to the sufferers; and the younger members of the family expressed very freely their opinion of his conduct.

With part of Thomassian's money Jack bought Kourdish dresses for himself and for Kevork, and also a smaller one, fit for a boy of about fourteen. He had still the good horses upon which he and Gabriel had ridden to Urfa. After a sharp conflict with himself, he decided not to wait for the Consul's communication. Shushan could be still his betrothed; as such he and Kevork could bring her to Urfa, and place her under Miss Celandine's protection. The marriage could take place afterwards.

However, to his great delight, just as they were starting, the necessary papers arrived. Miss Celandine's influence had obtained them, and she also procured for the travellers a zaptieh to guard them on their journey. They took an affectionate farewell of the Vartonians, whom they told simply that they were returning to Biridjik, and of Gabriel, now an ardent and delighted pupil in the Missionary School.

Their journey to Biridjik was without adventure. On the way they agreed together that they would not say much to their friends about the massacres. But the precaution was a needless one, for already they knew enough.

As it was September and very hot, they travelled by night, arriving in Biridjik on the morning of the second day. The remaining hours were given up to talk, to rest, and to making arrangements for the future.

In spite of all the dangers that surrounded them, Kevork could not be unhappy as he sat with his mother's hand in his, his father looking on with interest, and his brother Hagop with adoring admiration, while he told of his wonderful eighteen months in the Missionary School at Aintab. And if the name of Elmas Stepanian slipped sometimes into his story, was there anything wrong in that? Did he not see her every Sunday in church, and did he not hear of her splendid answering at the examinations, and of the prizes she gained? Had not his teacher told him and the other youths about it, that they might be stirred to emulation by the grand achievements of the girls?

For Jack there were even sweeter joys that day. It is true that he was only permitted to see Shushan veiled, and in the company of her mother, or of some of the other women. Still, he could whisper a few words of cheer about the home they hoped to have by-and-by in free, happy England. And when she murmured doubtfully, " But my people, Yon Effendi ? " he said the whole household must follow them to England. There Kevork could find a career, the younger boys an education, and all of them peace and safety, and bread enough and to spare. It is true the difficulties in the way of these arrangements would have seemed to him, in his sober moments, almost insurmountable ; but in certain moods of mind we take small account of difficulties.

There was much to be done that day in arranging for the wedding, which all agreed should take place the next morning. According to custom, Jack ought to have provided the dress of the bride ; but this, under the circumstances, he could not do. Avedis however came to him privately, bringing a beautiful robe of blue satin with long sleeves, trimmed with gold embroidery. " You know," he said, " I was to have married Alà Krikorian. Sometimes I think it was well she died, for she has escaped the woes that are coming on our people. But I had the bridal robe all ready ; and I shall never marry any one else. Take it as my gift to you ; give it yourself to Shushan ; and God bless you both."

His own best garments Jack laid ready, with care, for the morning. Rising very early, he put on his ordinary clothes, and went forth to meet Der Garabed, who came by appointment to bless the bridegroom's apparel. This ceremony accomplished, Jack arrayed himself for the wedding, and, with Hohannes and the other men of the family, went to the church. He sat in his own place on the men's side, Shushan coming in afterwards with her mother and other female relatives, and sitting among the women. The service proceeded as usual, until, at the appointed time, Jack, with a beating heart, stepped out of his place, and came and stood before the altar. Shushan also was led to the spot, and stood there beside him. Neither dared to look up.

Der Garabed read from the Holy Book of the first bridal in Paradise ; and again, from its later pages, of how Christian wives and husbands ought to love and cherish one another. Then, as they turned and stood face to face, each for one instant looked into the other's eyes, and read there the secret of the love that is more strong than death. They had to clasp hands, and to bow their heads until each forehead touched the other. Old

Hohannes took a cross from the hand of the priest, and, his own trembling with many emotions, laid it on the two bowed heads. The priest recited a few prayers, and put the solemn questions that the ritual of every Christian Church prescribes. Then, raising their bowed heads they stood together, with the right, before God and man, to stand together until death should part them. The psalm was sung, and the benediction given ; and John Grayson led forth his Lily—all his at last. There was deep, solemn gladness in his heart ; he felt as if, in the expressive Scottish phrase, "his weird was won."

Peril might be behind them, before them, all around them, yet this one hour must be given to joy. It is true he had no mother to " crown him in the day of his espousals," no father to breathe the blessing his filial heart missed so sorely. Still he believed in blessing, Divine and human. His faith was strong, his hope was high. He thought it would be no hard task to bring his bride in safety to his English home—and hers. Once there, they could both work together for the deliverance of her people—"*our* people" was what John Grayson thought, with a throb of joy, of sympathy, and—is it strange to say it ?—of *pride*.

Chapter XI

AN ADVENTUROUS RIDE

"What if we still ride on, we two,
With life for ever old yet new,
Changed not in kind but in degree,
The instant made eternity."
—*R. Browning.*

ABOUT noon Kevork came to Jack with a pale, anxious face. "You see the state men's minds are in here?" he said.

"It is only too easy to see," Jack answered.

"Did you notice the scared faces in church?" Kevork went on. "There is nothing talked of here among our own people but death and massacre; and among the Turks, but how they are going to kill us and take all we have. And our own house is in the greatest danger of all. My uncle and the rest are afraid we will be held accountable for Shushan; and Heaven knows what the Turks will do to us when they find she is gone. In a word, they are all saying that if you go to Urfa and take her with you, the whole household must go too.   They think they will be safer there, lost in a crowd."

"But are they not afraid of coming so near Mehmed Ibrahim?"

"They think that very nearness will save them. He will never think of looking for them at his own door.   One and all, at least, are quite determined to go, except perhaps my grandfather, who is rather passive about it, and my father, who is doubtful.   Still they do not oppose the rest.   My grandfather says 'Heaven is as near in Urfa as in Biridjik.'"

"Very good," said Jack, "but then, can they go to-night?"

"To-night!" exclaimed Kevork.   "Heaven bless you!   It will take them a fortnight or three weeks to get ready; they must do it all quietly, you know, for fear of the Turks."

"Then, look here, Kevork," Jack said, with a determined air, "I am not going to leave Shushan in this place another day; the rest may follow as they like."

"You are right," Kevork answered.   "But as for me, I must stay.   Think of it! here are three-and-twenty souls, for the most part women and children, to be brought to Urfa; and not one of them has been twenty miles from home before— not even my Uncle Avedis, who is so shrewd and clever. And then we shall have to make all our preparations, and to sell off everything we can, but with the greatest secrecy, lest the Turks should find out and stop us. Yes, I must stay. You shall take the horses."

Jack nodded. "We must start at midnight," he said. "I am going now to arrange matters, and to tell the women."

He went, and was fortunate enough to find Shushan for the moment alone. He held in his hand a large bundle, which he laid on the ground beside her. "My Shushan," he said, taking her hand tenderly, "I know you trust me utterly. I am going to ask you for a proof of it."

She looked up at him, and her eyes said for her, "But prove me what it is I will not do."

"Dearest, put on this clothing I have brought, kiss your father and your mother, and be ready at midnight to ride with me to Urfa."

She looked at the garments, as he unfolded them, with an involuntary shudder. "They are Kourdish clothes," she said.

Jack smiled. "At least they are clean," he answered. "They have never been worn. And there is no law, that I know of, against sheep in wolves' clothing."

"Oh, but all want to go, father, and mother, and Hagop—all of us."

"They shall follow us, my Shushan."

"But to leave them in such peril! And, Yon Effendi, it is I who have brought it on them."

"Not altogether, my beloved. Now it is not one here and there who is persecuted; the danger threatens your whole race—*our* race," he said, with a sudden throb of the passionate, pitying love that was springing up in his heart for the people of his adoption. "Without you," he added, "their danger certainly will be less. And if God wills, we will all meet again, in Urfa."

"I will do what you tell me,—my husband," Shushan said, and the words, if low, were quite steady. The whole trust of her simple heart was his; and although tender, modest, refined, it was still a hot, impulsive Eastern heart.

At midnight a group assembled in the court-yard of the Meneshians house. There was no moon,—all the better for their purpose; but from the cloudless sky the great, beautiful stars shone down upon them. Avedis brought out a lantern, which showed two strange figures. In the midst stood a young Kourdish warrior, his head protected by a gay "kafieh" of yellow silk, bound about it with rolls of wool, and having the front thrown back to reveal the face, which was nearly as dark as a mulatto's. His zeboun was of bright scarlet, and it boasted, instead of a skirt, four separate tails, or aprons, which showed beneath them Turkish trousers of crude and staring blue, while a crimson belt contained the perilous revolver, its two available barrels loaded. It was not necessary now to conceal it, for it was part of the equipment.

A Kourdish boy, attired in similar fashion, and with face and hands yet more carefully blackened, clung to the breast of Mariam, as if they could never part.

" Come, my daughter," Boghos said at last ; " the moments are precious."

" 'Tis not as if the parting were a long one," Kevork said cheerfully. " A few weeks, at most, and we follow you to Urfa."

" As we stand now," old Hohannes said solemnly, "*every* parting may be as long as life, or death ; but we Christians are not afraid of death. Shushan, my Lily, in Christ's name I bless thee, and bid thee God-speed."

Shushan had been given into his arms by her mother, and now her father stood waiting for the last embrace. As he gave it with tear-dimmed eyes, Jack turned to Hohannes ; " You have been as a father to me," he said. " Bless me also, as a son."

In a broken voice, the old Armenian spoke the words of blessing. The Englishman bowed his young head in reverence, then shook hands with the others, and turned to lift into her saddle the shrinking girl in her boy's attire. Next, he sprang lightly upon his own horse, which Kevork was holding for him. "Good-bye, *brother*," he said, stooping down to wring his hand.

Slowly and silently they moved along, the good horses climbing the terraces that led out of the town. A bribe,—cleverly administered beforehand by Hohannes, who had a life-long practice in these matters,—opened to them the ancient gate of Biridjik, and they found themselves in the road outside.

"Softly, softly," Jack whispered, stroking the neck of his steed, who seemed quite to understand him. He wondered if, in this strange country, even the dumb creatures learned to accommodate themselves to the exigencies of a hunted life. Both their horses might almost have been shod with felt, for all the noise they made.

When the terraces and gardens were left behind, a running stream or two had to be crossed, and they found themselves beside the ancient reservoir which supplied the town with water. After passing this, they came to a place where three roads met, and where a Turkish guard was always stationed. This was a serious danger ; he might demand their passports, and they had none.

"What shall we do if he does?" Shushan whispered. Jack pointed to his purse. But, happily, the Turk gave them no trouble, being fast asleep in his little booth by the roadside.

When they got into the open country, their road lay over rocks, which rang to the feet of their horses. At first the sound almost scared them, used as they were to fear. But for the present, in all the wide landscape, there was no one to hear, and nothing to dread.

They rode out into the still night—no mist, no dew, the stars flashing down, the great planets bright enough to cast perceptible shadows. The brilliant, shimmering starlight lent the campaign a beauty not its own; there was a kind of glamour over everything. Jack's spirits rose with the sense of freedom and solitude. He and Shushan put their horses at full speed, and they seemed to be flying through the clear still air,—not cold, but cool enough after the hot day to be refreshing.

"Are you frightened, love? Are we going too fast for you?" he asked, hearing a little sigh, and slackening his pace accordingly.

"No; but I never rode like this before. When Cousin Thomassian brought me to Biridjik, it was "*Jevash! Jevash!*" (a Turkish word, which may be rendered in English, "Take it easy").

"Do you like it, my Lily?"

"I like it well," she answered, breathless but rejoicing. "Go on fast again; I like it well."

Did Jack like it? There was a light in his eye, a bounding rapture in his every vein, as they flew along, alone with each other in that desolate waste, which to them was as the Garden of Eden.

After a while they drew rein again, that they might talk. "They tell me"—Jack spoke dreamily, out of a depth of half-realized delight—"they tell me the Garden of Eden was *here*, in this land of yours."

"So our fathers say," Shushan answered. "And it is lovely enough, at least in spring, when the flowers are out. If only we were not afraid,—always."

"That was what struck me," Jack said, "when, after my long illness, I began to get strong, and to notice what went on about me. Always, over every one, there seemed to hang the shadow of a great fear."

"But I suppose, in your England also, there are sin and sorrow."

"A great deal of both, my Lily. But in England law is *against* wickedness and cruelty, and stops them if it can. Then there is the same law in England for all. There are not two kinds of people, one booted and spurred to ride, and the other bridled and saddled to be ridden. It took me a good while to understand that was the case here, and *I* was among the bridled and saddled."

"Because you were not born here. You know, Yon Effendi, we always *expect* to suffer, because we are Christians. Ever since I can remember, every one was afraid—afraid of the Turks in the street, afraid of the Kamaikan, afraid of the zaptiehs, afraid of the Kourds. Kevork and I were great companions, but I do not think we played much. Sometimes I played with the little ones, but I liked better to help my mother, or to hear the talk of the elders. Then came the dreadful time when Mehmed Ibrahim, our Kamaikan——"

"Don't talk of it! You shall never see his face again, my Shushan."

"I never have seen it, to my knowledge. I was only ten years old."

"When a little English girl would still be playing with her doll, as my cousins used to do. Poor child!"

"My childhood ended then. They sent me to Urfa, with some merchants from our town, who were going there. Oh, I was happy there! I had the school, and the dear foreign ladies, and my cousins the Vartonians, and, above all, Elmas Stepanian."

"Do you know, my Lily, that Kevork loves Elmas, just a little bit in the way I love you?"

"How could he help it?" Shushan said, and smiled quietly. "In the school," she went on, "I learned many things about the Bible, and about our dear Lord, that I did not know before, though I think I always loved Him. They helped me to understand why all the troubles came to us. Has He not said, 'In the world ye shall have tribulation'? But He has said also, 'I am with you always.' If one is true, so must the other be."

"Yes," said Jack thoughtfully, "I think I can believe it now."

"It all seemed so real in the happy years at school; and afterwards, when I first came back to Biridjik, I felt as if all day long He was close by me; and then all the fear went out of my heart. There was no room for it when He was there."

Jack was silent. He feared God, prayed to Him devoutly, and desired sincerely to do His Will; but this experience of His personal presence and nearness was beyond him as yet.

"But I could not help seeing how things went on about me," Shushan resumed. "And for a year and more we have been hearing of worse things yet. I did not talk of them, for what was the use of frightening everybody? We could do nothing; we were helpless. But they sank into my heart. Then the horror—about Mehmed Ibrahim—came again. I began to think God had forsaken us. Do you know the sad things about that in the Psalms? They seem just written for us. 'But now Thou art far off, and puttest us to confusion . . . so that they that hate us spoil our goods. Thou lettest us be eaten up like sheep, Thou sellest Thy people for nought, and takest no money for them. Thou makest us to be rebuked of our neighbours, to be laughed to scorn, and had in derision of them that are round about us. For Thy sake also we are killed all the day long, and are counted as sheep appointed to be slain.' "

"Oh, Shushan, stop! It is too sad."

"Only one word more. 'Up, Lord, why sleepest Thou? Awake, and be not absent from us for ever. Wherefore hidest Thou Thy face, and forgettest our misery and trouble?' That was what I feared—that He forgot—that He did not care." Shushan's head bent low. Jack stretched his hand out to touch hers; she raised her head, and turning her face to his in the dim light, said, ' He did not forget *me*, He sent me you. And it is not likely He has remembered Shushan Mene-shian, and forgotten all the rest."

In talk like this, passing gradually into lighter topics, they rode along, now fast, now slow. Shushan, little accustomed to riding (save to the vine-yard on a donkey), grew very tired, though she

would not have confessed it for worlds. They had
a mountain gorge to go through, where the narrow
path, only wide enough for one, winds along the
mountain side, a slope above, a deeper slope—
almost a precipice—beneath. One false step, and
the unlucky traveller would lie, a mangled corpse,
in the rocky gulf below. They had only starlight to guide them, and the mountain on the
other side increased the obscurity.

"Trust your horse, my Shushan," Jack said.
"Horse sense is better here than ours."

Shushan did so; and though she trembled, no
cry, no word of fear, passed her lips. Only she
murmured the favourite prayer of her people,
"Hesoos okné menk"—Jesus, help us.

Her prayer was heard: they emerged safely
from the perilous gorge. Then presently, in the
soft starlight, there fell upon their ears a perfect
burst of song—sweet, liquid notes, rising and
falling in thrills and gushes of delicious melody
that seemed to fill the air around them. "The
nightingale!" Shushan whispered; "Listen, oh,
listen!"

Hitherto, not a tree had relieved the monotony
of the waste and dreary path, which indeed was
rather a mule track than a road. Now they were
drawing near a couple of stunted thorn-bushes,
one of which gave a shelter to the sweet songster.

"There is a well here," Jack said. "Kevork tells me travellers always rest and sup—or breakfast as the case may be—beside it. Ah, there it is!"

He sprang from his horse, and helped Shushan down from hers. Then he spread the saddle cloths beneath her on the ground, and took from the small bag strapped beside him on the horse the viands it contained—bread, white delicious cheese in small squares, apples, pears, and peaches. He had with him his father's little flask and cup, one of the few things that had escaped the rapacity of the Syrians; and they needed no better beverage than the cold, pure water with which the well supplied them. Very happily they ate and drank together in the starlight.

Shushan refused the last peach, saying, "No more, I thank you, Yon Effendi."

"My Lily must not call me that again. English wives do not speak so to their husbands. '*Mr. John!*' how odd it would sound!"

"I think it has a very pleasant sound—*Mis-ter John.*"

"No, dearest, you must call me, as my father used—*Jack.*"

"Shack? Oh, that is so short, so little of a name for a great, tall Effendi like you!"

"But I love it best, Shushan. And I will love

it, oh, so much better! when I hear it from *your* lips."

"Now I will say it—Shack."

"Not 'Shack'—*Jack*, like *John*, which you say quite right."

"I will say that quite right too.   Don't you think we ought to ride on, Shack?"

"Not 'Shack'—those naughty lips of yours, Shushan, must pay me a fine when they miscall me so."

He exacted the fine promptly, saying, "I have the right, you know."

Nevertheless Shushan adhered to the name of "Shack," which she softened until it sounded like the French "Jacques."   Evidently she thought the harsher sound uncouth, if not disrespectful.

"But don't you think we ought to ride on?" she resumed.

"Presently.   In three or four hours we shall come to that queer little village with the black, egg-shaped mud huts—Charmelik, that is the name.   The people are Kourds, and will want to talk to us.   What shall we do?   You do not know Kourdish, any more than I."

"No; but I know Turkish. Some Kourdish tribes speak Turkish, and we can give them to understand we come from one of these.   I will talk for us both," said Shushan, whose courage was rising to meet the exigencies of her life. Jack, as yet, knew only the few words of Turkish he could not fail to pick up in a town partly inhabited by Turks, like Biridjik.

"They will think that odd," he said, "unless I were deaf and dumb."

"*Be* deaf and dumb then," she answered, after a thoughtful pause. "You are going to Urfa, to be cured by a wise Frank hakim there ; and I, your young brother, go with you, to be ears and tongue to you."

"A splendid notion!" Jack said. It was not the first time he had had occasion to admire the Armenian quickness of resource, and dexterity in eluding danger. These were nature's weapons of defence, developed by environment, and the survival of the fittest. Yet they had their own perils. Does the world recognise how hard—nay, how impossible—it is for oppressed and persecuted races to be absolutely truthful ?

Just as they rode on, the glorious sun shot up with tropical splendour and tropical swiftness. It was late September now ; the heat was still great, and the travellers were not sorry when at last they saw in the distance the black huts of Charmelik, the walls of the khan, and the minaret of the little mosque. Shushan, in spite of her fatigue, seemed to have changed places with Jack. She planned and exhorted; he listened to her meekly. For fighting, the Englishman comes to the front; for feigning, the Armenian. "Now, I pray of you, Yon Effendi—that is, Shack—remember, you are not to speak; and also, which is harder, you are not to *hear*—not if a pistol goes off close to your head. You may talk to me by signs, or on your fingers."

Jack gave his promise; and, as both their lives depended on it, he was likely to keep it. At first they thought the khan might be safer to stay in than the huts, but a caravan from Urfa had just stopped there, and both the open enclosure and the rooms round it (if rooms they may be called) were quite full. Moreover, the Kourds of the village came about them with welcomes and questions and offers of hospitality. So Jack gathered from their looks and gestures. He stood among them, gazing about him with as vacant an expression of face as he could manage to assume, only praying they might not be rough with Shushan, for such a set of wild-looking savages, as he thought, he had never seen before; although, of course, since coming to the country, he had seen many Kourds.

After a while Shushan touched him, and motioned to him to come with her. One of the Kourds led them to a hut; and, as it appeared by his looks and gestures, invited them to consider it their own mansion, with the same magnificent air with which a Spanish grandee might have said, " This is your own house, señor."

As soon as he had attended to their horses and brought in the saddle cloths, Jack surveyed the miserable hovel—some twelve feet in diameter, and with no furniture save a couple of dirty mats and cushions—and wished with all his heart for a decent English pig-stye!

" You *must* get a sleep, Shushan," he said aloud. " But how I am ever to make you comfortable here——"

" *Hush!* " Shushan breathed rather than spoke, with a warning hand laid upon his arm.

" Well ? " said Jack, speaking low, but surprised at her evident alarm.

She pointed to the one little unglazed hole in the mud wall that served as a window. " They sit under that, and listen," she said. " I know their ways."

After that, only low whispers were exchanged. A meal of pillav, with kabobs (little pieces of roast meat), was served to them by their hosts, who were presently—as Shushan ascertained with much relief—going in a body to some neighbour-ing vineyard, to cut grapes.

When they had finished eating, Jack spread

the two horse cloths for Shushan, and exhorted her to lie down and sleep. He thought he was far too anxious to do so himself. He sat up manfully near the door, with his back against the wall, for fear of a sudden surprise ; but nature in the end was too strong for him, and even in that unrestful position she managed to steep his senses in a profound slumber.

Chapter XII

THE USE OF A REVOLVER

"So let it be.   In God's own Might
We gird us for the coming fight."
—*Whittier.*

IT was Shushan who awoke her guardian, near the going down of the sun. "Shack," she whispered, "let us get the horses and begone. I· like not the looks of these people. Some of them have come back from the vineyard; and I saw them looking in at the window, and whispering."

Jack shook himself. "So I have slept," he said, surprised. "I did not mean it. What time is it?"

They ate of the provisions they had with them, went together to make ready the horses, bestowed some silver on their hosts, and rode away. As soon as they were really off, Jack asked Shushan if she thought the Kourds were content with their backsheesh.

"Oh yes, content enough," she said. "Still, I do not like their looks. Let us ride on, as fast as we can."

They had some hard riding over the bare,

burned-up ground, where not a blade of grass or a leaf of any green thing was to be seen; and then they came again to a mountain gorge. The sun had gone down now—a great relief, for it had been very hot. Shushan, who had scarcely slept at all, was suffering much from fatigue; and though she tried to answer cheerfully when Jack spoke to her, she was evidently depressed and anxious. He asked tenderly what was troubling her.

"Nothing," she said,—"nothing, at least, that I ought to mind. This morning one of those Kourds asked me if we had come down from the mountains to help in killing the Giaours, and to get some of their goods. I asked, why we should kill them when they have done us no harm. And they asked me again where I had come from that I did not know it was the will of Allah and the Sultan, and that the true Believers, who helped in the holy work, were to have their gold and silver and all they possessed. Then they began a story that made my blood run cold—I will not tell it thee. But, Shack, I fear the worst—especially for my people in Biridjik."

"Let us ride on," said Jack, after a sorrowful pause. "It will not do for us to stop and think. And certainly not here."

The darkness, or rather the soft half-darkness,

of the starry Eastern night had fallen over them quickly, like a veil. And now they were getting among the mountains, and the wretched track called a road was growing more and more indistinct. Presently they entered another narrow gorge, deeper and gloomier than the one before Charmelik. But for their dependence on their sure-footed horses, they never could have faced it, so narrow was the level track, so steep the precipice below, so dark and frowning the heights on either side above them.

But even the horses seemed to get puzzled. The track became fainter and more broken, until at last the travellers found themselves on sloping ground where it was hard to secure a foothold.

Not all Shushan's self-command could keep back a little frightened cry: "I shall fall! Hold me, Shack!"

Jack turned to help her, heard the slip of a horse's foot in the dry, loose clay, and for one awful moment thought both were lost. However, foothold was regained somehow; and Shushan's fervent "Park Derocha!" gave him strength to breathe again and to look about him. He saw distinctly before them another gorge, crossing almost at right angles the one beneath them, and cutting off their path, as it seemed to him. How were they to traverse it? How had it been done before, when he rode in hot haste with the zaptiehs and the Post, or back again, with Kevork?

And where was the path itself, from which they had wandered—he knew not how far? Great Jupiter shone above them, bright enough to outline. their forms in shadow on the bare brown earth; and, looking carefully, he had light to discern a narrow, crooked thread of white winding some thirty feet below their standing place. He pointed to it. "We must get back," he said.

Shushan drew her breath hard, and looked, not at the perilous slope, but at *him*. "Yes," she said. Jack would have proposed to dismount, trust to their feet, and let the horses follow, but he knew it was not best. He knew too that he must restrain his longing to take Shushan's bridle and lead her horse—*that* was not best either. How she held on he did not know, nor did she know herself.

They were getting down the steep incline with less difficulty than they expected, and had nearly regained the path, when Shushan cried out suddenly, "Shack, I hear shouts." In another moment horse and rider both were on the ground. Jack could not tell until the end of his life what happened next, or what he did, until he found himself sitting on the path with Shushan's head in his lap, seeing nothing but her face, white through its dark staining.   Her horse had narrowly escaped slipping down into the gorge, but had found his feet somehow, and now stood beside Jack's, gazing solemnly at the two dismounted riders.

Happily, Jack had his flask in his wide sash. He got at it, sprinkled Shushan's face with the water, and put some between her lips.   After a few moments—it seemed like an age—she looked up.   He began to lavish tender words and caresses upon her, asking anxiously if she was hurt, but she stopped him quickly.

"Oh, what does it matter?" she said.   "Listen, Shack!"

He had been deaf as well as blind to all except her state.   Now he listened.   The mountain echoes rang with wild, discordant shouts.

"The Kourds!   They are pursuing us," said Shushan, sitting up.   Terror had restored her senses more rapidly than all the arts of love could have done.

"Another set of them?" asked Jack, bewildered.

"No.   The Kourds of Charmelik," said Shushan in a frightened whisper.   "I feared it.   They heard us speak, and knew we were no Kourds." Even in that moment's agony she said "heard *us* speak," as Jack remembered afterwards,—lest he should blame himself.

"I will run round the corner, and look," he said. "Do you fear a moment alone, my Shushan?"

"No; but take care. Keep under cover of the hill."

Jack ran to a turn that gave him a view of the road from Charmelik. As far as he could see along the track no creature was visible. But high up on the hill he saw dark forms, descending, doubtless by some goat-track known to themselves alone. They could reach Shushan almost as soon as he could.

He tore back to her, possessed with the thought that he would set her on horseback, and make a race for it. But when he came near, he saw their horses had moved away, and were both out of sight.

The shouts sounded nearer and nearer; he saw the flash of a gun, and heard the report.

"Shack!" said Shushan. She was still sitting on the ground, having sprained her ankle in the fall. "Shack!"

He bent down to her. He had been looking to his revolver, and held it in his hand. "If the worst comes," she said, "you will kill me with that—promise."

Jack set his teeth for an instant: then he said firmly, "So help me God."

Another pistol shot—not near enough to harm them. But the Kourds were upon them now. Jack saw the face of the man who had given them his hut—an evil face. He took aim, fired, and the Kourd fell in a heap, and rolled down the sloping ground to his very feet.

But there were twenty following him, and most of them had guns, while Jack had no other shot—*for them*. He stood at bay between his wife and the robbers, keeping his hand on the revolver as if just about to fire.

The Kourds desire close quarters with a dead shot as little as other men. They wavered,—hesitated. Presently one fellow, braver than the rest, discharged his gun, the shot passing close to Jack's head, then sprang down the slope and flung himself upon him. They closed in mortal conflict, hand to hand, foot to foot, eye to eye. At last Jack turned suddenly, dragged his foe to the edge of the abyss, tore himself loose with one tremendous effort, and with another, flung him over. Down—down—down, still down, he rolled and fell, fell and rolled, till he lay a mangled heap amongst the boulders at the bottom of the gorge. Jack would assuredly have followed him, had he not fallen, or rather thrown himself, backwards at full length on the path. As he lay there two or three bullets whizzed over him.

They were the last salute of the departing foe. The Kourds by this time had had enough of it, and beat a retreat more rapid than their advance. When they found out their guests were not what they appeared to be, brethren from a distant tribe, they had supposed they might be Armenians carrying communications from the revolted Zeit-ounlis [1] to Urfa, and that therefore they would be worth intercepting. But now they came to the conclusion they were too well armed to be molested any further.

It was long before Jack and Shushan dared to breathe again. "Park Derocha!" said Shushan at last. "Thank God!" Jack responded. He had risen to his feet, and was looking anxiously around to see that all was safe.

"Shack," said Shushan presently, "my foot hurts dreadfully now—praised be the Lord!"

Jack had no linen, but he tore his sash, poured on it all the water remaining in his flask, and wrapped it round the ankle, which was beginning to swell. "I meant that word," Shushan added smiling, "for pain is not felt until danger is past, and danger is—oh, so much worse than pain! But, Shack, the horses!"

"True, we must get them; I daresay they have not gone far. Dare I leave you here while I go to look for them?"

[1] See the Appendix.

"You *must*. Our lives hang on it. God will take care of me."

Jack drew her gently into a sheltered place under the rock. Then he set off at a brisk run, not letting himself think there was danger for her, since he *had* to go, and yet intensely, cruelly anxious about her.

He had a much longer chase than he anticipated, for the horses had quite disappeared from view. Still he went on, keeping the path, and uttering now and then the calls they were sure to recognise.

On account of the intervening gorge, the path descended almost to the very bottom of the valley, through which there ran a little mountain stream with a narrow fringe of green, stunted herbage on each side. Instinct had led the horses to this desirable spot, where having quenched their thirst, they stood contented, cropping the few mouthfuls of short grass. Happily, in this position, the Kourds could not see them.

Jack lost not a moment in leading their reluctant steps from the haunts of pleasure to the very dry and very stony path of duty. Joyfully he brought them back to where Shushan was, and met her joyful welcome.

"Is the pain *very* bad now, my Shushan?" he asked.

"No," she answered, smiling. "It is only *a*

little very bad, as you say in English. Is not that right? Now you shall lift me on my horse again, and we will go."

In a few minutes more they were on their way. When they came near the little stream, they halted for a while, that Jack might bring water for Shushan to drink, and bathe her ankle with it. She was very weary, and suffering considerable pain, but she kept on bravely, making no complaint. "It would be very ungrateful," she thought, "when God has been so good to us."

"Shushan," said Jack, as they rode along, "do you know what they call this gorge we are coming out of? They call it 'Bloody Gorge,' from the robberies and murders there have been in it. Kevork told me when we rode back together, but I did not want to tell you until we had passed it."

"Yesterday the Kourds told me the same," said Shushan, "but *I* did not want to tell *you*."

At length the mountain gorges were left behind, and a Roman road was reached, leading to the plain, which now began to assume an appearance of cultivation. There were wheatfields, and many fine vineyards laden with grapes. But if the prospect was pleasing, the road was vile. The great cobble stones the Romans loved had fallen apart, and the mud and gravel between them had caked into a hard cement. Not the surest-footed of steeds could avoid constant slips and stumbles, which filled up the measure of poor Shushan's suffering. She could scarcely hold herself upon her horse.

A little comfort came when the sun shot up in splendour. About the same time they got upon a smoother piece of road, and presently Jack said: " My Shushan, art thou too weary to look up, and see old Edessa in the morning light ? "

Shushan looked up. " It is a sight to take weariness away," she said, faintly, but joyfully.

Before them rose a hill, crowned with a magnificent ruined castle, and the slopes beneath it covered with buildings, interspersed with fair green patches, telling of shady trees and pleasant gardens. But still the eye turned back to the noble ruin, with its two very tall pillars, the use whereof no man knows, rising upwards towards the sky. Fragments of a great wall remained, enclosing not the castle alone, but all the hill on which the large town is built, with its dense mass of flat roofs, varied by minarets and mosques. Everywhere white was the prevailing colour ; so that, in the fair morning light, the old city of King Agbar seemed to have donned a mantle of spotless snow.

A very high, very long roof of white attracted the eye. It belonged to the great Gregorian

Cathedral, a noble structure, of enormous size, capable, it is said, of holding eight thousand persons. Jack turned to point it out to Shushan, but a glance at her face made him say instead: " My Shushan, you are ready to faint. You shall rest a little here. I will lift you from your horse."

" No, Shack, no. We are just at home now. I will keep up till I see Miss Celandine's face."

Through the city gate they rode, unchallenged and unhindered. Then they passed a little market place, rode on through narrow streets, and round the Protestant Church and churchyard, till they reached the gates of the Mission premises. Eyes that loved must have been looking from the window above the front door, for Jack had scarcely time to knock with a trembling hand, and to lift Shushan from the saddle, when the door opened, and a tall, spare figure stood within. The face was the face of one who had thought much, done much, suffered much, and above all, loved much. Jack gave Shushan into the motherly arms that opened wide to receive her ; she laid her weary head upon that strong, kind shoulder, and fainted entirely away.

" Do not be afraid for her, Mr. Grayson," Miss Celandine said. " Peace and safety are good physicians."

Chapter XIII

WHAT PASTOR STEPANIAN THOUGHT

" But he was holy, calm, and high,
As one who saw an ecstasy
Beyond a foreknown agony."
—*E. B. Browning.*

JOHN GRAYSON left his young bride, for the present, in the care of Miss Celandine. " She is safe ; she is absolutely safe !" he kept saying to himself, that one thought swallowing up all the rest. He went constantly to see her, and was relieved to find that she very soon recovered from the effects of her sprain, which indeed was not serious. Meanwhile he stayed with the Vartonians, and watched anxiously for the coming of the Meneshians to Urfa. Until he saw them settled there, and in some measure safe, he did not think he ought to apply for a passport for himself and Shushan, or, as she would then be called, Lily Grayson.

It was October now. The gloom of a great terror seemed gathering over the town. So accustomed had Jack grown to fears and apprehensions that he did not notice it as anything unusual. But he could not fail to notice a most astonishing and unexpected outburst of rejoicing and festivity that came suddenly in the very midst of the gloom. As sometimes in a day of storm, when the great thunderclouds sweep across the sky, the sun looks out for a moment, flashing a shaft of light through the darkness,—so here, when all seemed blackest, a sudden rumour passed from heart to heart, from lip to lip, " *The Sultan has granted the Reforms.*" Not only did the Armenians of Urfa whisper it within closed doors— as they were wont to do with anything bearing, however remotely, upon politics ; men said it aloud to each other in the streets and in the shops ; and women talked of it as they baked their bread, or drew their water from the fountains. What did these Reforms mean ? Did they mean—men said they did—no more plundering Kourds, no more tyrannous zaptiehs, no more dungeons and tortures for innocent men, and, best of all, no more of that wordless, nameless terror that made the life of the Armenian woman one long misery ? If indeed they meant *this*, ought not the whole community to go mad with joy ?

The tidings came officially, by telegraph, and were read aloud in the Gregorian Cathedral. There followed, throughout the Armenian quarter, tearful rejoicings, and many Services and meetings for prayer and thanksgiving to Almighty God.

One day, while these were still going on, Jack was walking in one of the narrow streets, when he met a young girl and a boy about Gabriel's age. The girl was wrapped from head to foot in an *eshar*, and closely veiled, but the boy he knew well, having often seen him with the Vartonians and with Gabriel—young Vartan Stepanian, the Pastor's eldest son. So he knew the girl must be Oriort Elmas, Shushan's friend, and he saluted both very cordially in passing.

He had not gone on twenty paces when a cry from Vartan brought him back. A tall, powerful Turk had come suddenly through a door in the wall, and being close to Elmas, for the street was scarcely two yards wide, seized her veil to pull it off. Vartan sprang upon him and tried to drag him away, but was not strong enough.

"None of that!" cried Jack in good English. He had no weapon, but he clenched his hand, and putting forth all his strength, dealt the Turk a blow between the eyes that sent him staggering against the opposite wall.

"Allah!" cried the discomfited follower of Mahomet, looking at him with a dazed, astonished air. An Armenian to strike a blow like that! Surely Shaytan had got into him!

"Come—come quickly," Vartan said, hurrying his sister on, for fear of pursuit. "More Dajeeks may come," he explained to Jack, who mounted guard on the other side of Elmas. "Let us go to the church. It is the nearest place where we can be safe."

"The Cathedral?"

"No; that is a long way off. My father's church."

They walked quickly, and were soon there. When in Urfa before, Jack had always attended the cathedral services; he had not entered the beautiful Protestant church since he saw the dead lying there in her peaceful rest, on the morning of his first arrival. Vartan led him through it; then, by the little side door, into his father's study. All around the room there were bookshelves, filled to overflowing, and with books in several languages. The Pastor was seated in a chair, before a little deal table, reading. He was dressed *à la Frank*, and when, after a few words from Vartan in Armenian, he rose and greeted his visitor in excellent English, Jack thought himself back in his own land again. He almost thought himself back again in the study of the good old clergyman who had been the pastor and teacher of his childhood.

It broke the illusion a little when that stately gentleman touched his own forehçad, and stooped down to kiss the hand Jack stretched out to him, instead of taking it in a hearty grasp. But this was in especial thanks for the service rendered to his children, and a few earnest words just touched with Eastern grace were added.

The pastor said a word or two to Elmas and Vartan, who left the room. Then he invited Jack to take the one chair, and seated himself on the little divan under the window.

Delighted at hearing his native tongue so perfectly spoken, Jack said impulsively and in English,—

"Pastor, you are more than half an Englishman."

Pastor Stepanian shook his head rather sadly, but did not speak.

Then Jack remembered the nationality of the missionaries, his friends.

"I beg your pardon," he said, "I meant—you are more than half an American."

"Neither English nor American," said Hagop Stepanian proudly. "Every drop of my blood, every pulse in my heart, belongs to my own race. But I am very grateful to the Americans, our benefactors."

The blood rushed to the face of John Grayson. "I am afraid," he said, "you have no cause to be grateful to *us*."

The pastor waved his hand. "I say nothing against the English," he said.—"Pardon me a moment."

He rose, looked carefully round, and opened both doors of the study, ascertaining in this way that there was no one within earshot, either in the churchyard or the church. Then he closed the doors again, sat down, lowered his voice, and began: "Have you been long enough in this country, Mr. Grayson, to have seen a dead horse, with half a dozen hungry dogs snarling round it? Each wants a bit, yet each is so jealous of all the rest, that if one dares touch it the others fall on him, and drive him off. Can you read my parable?"

"Yes; the nations, England and the others, stand thus around Turkey. Would it *were* dead, Pastor!"

"Take care, my young friend, lest some such word escape you as you walk by the way, or ride among the vineyards, or sit with a friend over your coffee in his private room, where the very hangings may conceal a spy."

"Oh, I am cautious enough. I have been here nearly five years."

"Were you here fifty, you might still have failed to learn your lesson. A word, a whisper, a scrap of paper found upon you,—nay, the assertion of some one else that you have given him a scrap of paper—may consign you any moment to a horrible dungeon, where you will be tortured into saying anything your accusers wish. Nor is that the worst. Men have been flung into prison, and tortured almost to death, without being able to guess the crime laid to their charge. I knew of one who was used in this way, and at last they found they had mistaken him for another of the same name. He was brought half dead before the Kadi, who said to him coolly, " My son, regard it not. It was an error. Go in peace."

" The stupidity of these people would be ridiculous, if the horror were not too great," Jack said.

" Nay, Mr. Grayson, it is not stupidity. It is savagery, and savagery dominating civilization, but that savagery is armed with an ingenuity almost devilish for the bringing about of the designs in view. All *special* outrages upon the Christians are cleverly timed for some moment when the eyes of Christian Europe are turned elsewhere. Our people are first entrapped, made to give up their arms if they have any, cajoled with false promises of safety, if possible induced or forced to accuse each other, or themselves, of seditious plans they never even thought of."

" Then, Pastor, are all the rumours of plots and seditions here and there mere fabrications ? "

"There are plots, no doubt, *outside* Armenia. Bands of desperate exiles, in the great cities of Europe, have committees, hold meetings, make revolutionary plans. And I do not say their emissaries may not find a foothold and gain a hearing in some of our towns, those near the Russian frontier, for instance. But *I* know of none such. And I do know what happened here a short time ago. A young man, with an air of importance, and dressed *à la Frank*, appeared one day in the Cathedral. The bishop noticed him, sent for him, and asked his business in the town. He said he had come to ask help for the Zeitounlis, and to establish communications between them and the Urfans. The bishop answered him, 'In two hours you will be either outside the city gate, or in the guard-house. You have your choice. It is not that I do not desire the deliverance and the freedom of my people, but they will never gain it in this way. This is only pulling down our house upon our own heads.' So much, and no more, sedition and disloyalty has there been in this city, Mr. Grayson."

"But do you not think the worst for your country is over now? These Reforms——"

The Pastor shook his head. "Only another snare," he said. "At least, I forbode it. The Sultan gives us reforms on paper to lull us into security, and to deceive our European friends, while he sharpens the dagger for our throats."

" You think then that the reforms are worth—"

" The paper they are written on. If the Sultan meant them even—which he does not—who are to carry them out? The Pashas, Valis, Kamaikans? They are our deadliest enemies. They want our lands, our houses, our gold ; they want—the dreadful word *must* be said—our wives and our daughters. And the Zaptiehs, the Redifs, the Hamidiehs, the Kourds and the Turkish rabble of every town want to share the spoil."

" Do they not think too that in killing us they do God service ? " Jack said "us " quite naturally now.

" In literal truth. Have you never heard the prayer they recite daily in their mosques ? ' I seek refuge with Allah from Shaytan the accuser. In the name of Allah the compassionate, the merciful ! O Lord of all creatures ! O Allah ! destroy the Infidels and Polytheists, thine enemies, the enemies of the Religion ! O Allah ! make their children orphans, and defile their abodes ! Cause their feet to slip, give them and their families, their households and their women, their children and their relations by marriage, their brothers and their friends, their possessions and their race, their wealth and their lands, as booty to the Moslems,

O Lord of all creatures!" Rather a contrast this to 'Our Father which art in Heaven!'"

"Is it possible they think God will answer such a prayer?" said Jack.

"They *do* think it. You must remember their God is not the God and Father of our Lord Jesus Christ, nor the Father of mankind. He represents Will and Power apart from love and righteousness. 'The will of Allah' means everything to them, but it is not necessarily a holy or a loving Will."

"Still people are often better than their creed, you know."

"They are. Moreover, the Moslems' creed has in it some grand elements of truth. They acknowledge one God, and they believe in the duty and the efficacy of prayer. Oh yes,—and there are some good and generous Turks, who are as kind to us as they dare to be. I have known such. There was one, a Pasha, who tried to rule according to the avowed·intentions of the Sultan, *not* according to his secret instructions. He was deprived of his office, and banished to a distant part of the empire. There a friend of mine, a missionary, visited him not long ago. At first my friend was disappointed, for though the Turk received him with all cordiality, he could not be got to talk. But when he returned the missionary's visit, and in his lodgings felt tolerably safe, he told him that every step he took was dogged, every word he said reported by the Sultan's spies : even in his most private chamber he never knew what safety meant ; a spy might lurk behind the tapestry or outside the door. ' I count my life,' he said, 'by days and hours. Soon or late I am sure to be murdered.' If he is, I think He who said, ' Inasmuch as ye have done it unto the least of these,' will have something to say to him."

" Surely in this land," Jack observed, " ' he that departeth from evil maketh himself a prey.' But what do you think of the outlook here just now, Pastor ? "

" Do you want to hear the truth, Mr. Grayson ? "

" Certainly."

" Then I think, in the words of your own poet, it is ' dark, dark, dark, unutterably dark,' and the darkness is over all the land."

"Darker than it has been yet ? Is that possible?" Jack queried.

"Yes, what was meant before was oppression. What is meant now is, I fear, *extermination*."

" But," said Jack, raising his head suddenly, while a new light shone in his eyes, " there is God to be reckoned with. Does *He* mean it ? "

" ' His way is in the sea, His path is in the great waters, and His footsteps are not known. ' Did you notice the name of my boy, whom you helped so kindly just now?"

"Vartan,—in English, 'Easter.'"

"It is a name dear to every Armenian heart, the name of the hero saint of our race. And yet, Saint Vartan died in a lost battle. He fought against the Persians, who summoned the Armenians to submit to them, and to exchange the law of the Christ for the creed of the fire-worshipper. The Persians were strong and many, the Armenians were few and weak; but this was their answer, and Vartan's: 'We are not better than those before us, who laid down upon this testimony their goods and their bodies. Ask us no more, for the covenant of our faith is not with men, but in bonds indissoluble with God, for whom there is no separation or departure, neither now, nor ever, nor for ever—nor for ever and ever.' That is what we said fifteen hundred years ago, that is what we say to-day, when the darkest hour of the darkest night is falling over our land."

A pause followed, broken by Stepanian. "He died in a lost battle. The battle is lost, but the cause triumphs."

Jack had covered his face with his hands; but at these words he looked up again. "Then you see, beyond the darkness, a gleam of light?" he said.

"Mr. Grayson, I will tell you a parable. Last

spring my little son Armenag came with me one day to the vineyard. I showed him two vines. One of them was beautiful, covered with luxuriant leaves and tendrils ; the other, a dry, bare stick, with branch and leaf and tendril cut away by a ruthless hand. 'Which of these two will you have for your own, to bear grapes for you by-and-by?' I asked the boy. Of course he chose the beautiful, leafy vine. But the other day, in the ingathering, I brought him there again. Lo! the vine that kept its leaves and branches had only a few poor stunted grapes, while the tree that had been stripped and cut down, was bending beneath the weight of its great clusters of glorious fruit."

"And?" said Jack, his eyes eagerly fixed upon the Pastor, who went on—

"I see some clusters ripening even now. Is it nothing, think you, that men and women, and children even, have been witnessing fearlessly unto death for the Lord they love? In very truth, like the witnesses of old, they have been tortured, not accepting deliverance. Many have already joined the noble army of martyrs. And many more are coming—ay, even from this place. Never of late have I stood up to preach, and looked down on the faces beneath me, without the thought that these, my people, may soon be standing in the presence of Christ. And I too—I shall see Him soon."

"Are you a prophet?" John Grayson asked, looking with amazement at the calm, refined, intellectual face of this gentleman of the nineteenth century, who spoke of his own martyrdom as certainly, as quietly, and as fearlessly, as if he had said, "I am going to France, or to England."

"I am no prophet, Mr. Grayson; but I think I can read the signs of the times. And though it becomes no man to answer for himself, there are things in which we may trust God to answer for us;—and things which He does not ask of us. He does not ask the shepherd to save himself when the sheep are smitten."

"But death is not the *worst* thing that happens here," Jack said very low, "nor even torture—would to God it were!"

"Don't you think I know that?" said the Pastor hoarsely, as a shade of anguish crossed his face. "Don't you think I thank God every hour for my Dead—my Dead, who died by *His* Hand?"

Jack remembered what he had seen in the church that day, and held his peace. A great silence fell upon them; then Hagop Stepanian stretched out his hand to Jack, and looked straight into his eyes. "Mr. John Grayson," he said, "do you trust God?"

Jack's frank blue eyes fell beneath the gaze of those dark, searching eyes, that seemed to have looked down into unfathomed depths of anguish and come back from them into peace. " I trust in God," he said very low.

" I am sure of it. But here, where we stand now, we want more. To overcome in this warfare, a man must have laid, wholly and without reserve, his own soul and body, and the souls and bodies that are dearer than his own, in the hands of his faithful Creator and Redeemer."

" Do you mean we must be willing, not only to suffer, but to see them suffer ? " Jack asked in a broken voice. "That's against nature — impossible."

" Therefore God does not ask it of us. All He asks is that we should be willing for His will."

" *Not* His will—oh, *not* His will ! " Jack said almost with a cry. " The will of wicked men—of devils ! "

" Even so ;—but He is stronger than they, and will prevail. Mr. Grayson, will you take my counsel ? "

" Except it be to leave this place and save myself, which at present I cannot do."

" I know it : you have others, you have *another* to think of,—No ; you share our peril, and unless you share also our strong consolation you will be as those that go down into the pit, and your heart will die within you. Remember, you must trust God, and trust Him utterly. In all the generations

He has never yet broken faith with one man who trusted Him so. He will bring you up out of the depths again, and you shall behold His righteousness, and one day you shall see His face with joy, and know wherefore He let these things come upon us."

The conversation was interrupted by the entrance of Vartan and a younger boy, bringing coffee and sweetmeats. The Pastor drew the little one towards him, saying in Armenian, "Tell the English Effendi, Armenag, what our fathers in St. Vartan's day said to the Persians, when they bade them deny the Lord Jesus."

The child answered steadily, and as if he meant every word: "Ask us no more, for the covenant of our faith is not with man, but with God, for whom there is no separation or departure, neither now, nor ever, nor for ever, nor for ever and ever.'

"And what has God said to them, and to us?"

The boy's young voice rang clear and high as he repeated his well-remembered lesson. "'The mountains shall depart, and the hills be removed, but My kindness shall not depart from thee, neither shall the covenant of My peace be removed, saith the Lord that hath mercy on thee. O thou afflicted, tossed with tempest and not comforted, behold, I will lay thy stones with fair colours, and lay thy foundations with sapphires. And I will make thy windows of agates, and thy gates of carbuncles, and all thy borders of pleasant stones.'"

"I teach my children words like these," the Pastor said, reverting to English, "that they may know we are watchers for the morning. Which assuredly our eyes shall see, here or elsewhere," he added with a bright glance upwards.

Jack sat in silence for a space. Then, rising to take his leave, he grasped and wrung the Pastor's hand in true English fashion. "I will remember what you said about trusting God," he murmured.

"God, who is not only above you in heaven, but underneath you in the depths," the Pastor said. "There is no abyss you can sink into, where you cannot sink down on Him. And yet," he added with a smile, "I have good hopes of your safe return at last to your native land, along with your sweet bride Shushan, the daughter of our people. For you are an Englishman, and such are always protected here. And, when God gives you deliverance, think then of this Church of His, which is afflicted, tossed with tempests, and not comforted. May yours be the hand He uses to comfort her." Then, once more in Armenian, "Vartan, do you go with Mr. Grayson to his home; you can take him by the shortest way."

"Yes, father, but I want to tell you"—the boy lowered his voice—"Osman has just been here, to let us know privately we should not try to hold a meeting for thanksgiving to-night. The Zaptiehs will disperse it by force."

"I will see what ought to be done.—So much for the Reforms, Mr. Grayson. But do not speak of this. Osman is a young Turk who bears us good will, as I have told you some do ; and an incautious word might bring him into trouble. Once more, farewell ; God bless you."

Chapter XIV

A MODERN THERMOPYLÆ

JACK often went after this to the Protestant church to hear Pastor Stepanian preach. He had been much impressed by his words, and still more by his remarkable personality; and there was the added pleasure of worshipping with Shushan, who sat demurely by Miss Celandine on the women's side of the church. Oriort Elmas was there too—a noble-looking girl, a good deal taller than Shushan, and far less regularly beautiful, but with a face full of intelligence. He heard much of her courage and charity in ministering to the poor and sick, as well as of her loving care of her young brothers and sister. He met her once or twice at the Vartonians, with whom she was very intimate; and he thought Kevork a fortunate man; with the mental reservation that he was much more fortunate himself—a reflection which makes it easy to "rejoice with them that do rejoice."

Jack heard from Shushan, when he visited her, many lamentations over the departure of her beloved young teacher, Miss Fairchild. Many stories lingered in Urfa, and were told him by the Vartonians, of those loving ministrations to the poor, and especially to the Sassoun refugees, which had nearly cost the young missionary her life; and also of the gratitude and affection with which they were repaid. Once during her illness, when her life was almost despaired of, a poor man, a seller of antiquities, heard that she had asked for fish. This seemed impossible to procure, for it was summer, and the Euphrates, from which fish was brought in winter, was two days' journey off. But, in the midst of the city is the beautiful Pool of Abraham, where are kept the sacred fish, which every one feeds, and which the Moslems esteem so highly, it is death to touch one of them. The poor Armenian watched by the pool until the darkest and most silent hour of the night; then, at the peril of his life, he caught some of the fish, and brought them to the Mission House. David's Three Mighty Men, who brought the water from the well of Bethlehem, did no more.

Very touching also was the story of the service held in the Cathedral to pray for her recovery. The

Gregorian Bishop, and all the priests in the city took part in it, and the great building was thronged from end to end.   " God *must* give her back to us," the Armenians said.

On Sunday, the 27th of October, Jack attended Pastor Stepanian's church.   After the service he went to meet his friends, who had most of them gone to the Cathedral.   He saw, before he reached it, that something unusual was going on.   All the Armenians he met seemed to be in a curious state of excitement ; most of them were hurrying some-where in hot haste.   Whatever possessed them this time however, it was certainly not fear.   The scraps of conversation that reached his car savoured of hope, and of confident appeal to Law.   " Have him up," — "Go to Government House,"—" See what they will do," and words like these.

" Oh, Gabriel, is that you ? " he cried, seeing the boy come towards him.   " You will tell me, what is all this about?"   Gabriel, who had been at the Cathe-dral, explained : "There was a crowd of us standing about in the churchyard after service, when a Turk came in.   He looked from one to another, no one caring to say anything to him—though of course he had no business there—till at last he lighted upon poor Baghas, the money-changer.   He began to curse him by the Prophet, and to give him all sorts of foul language.   How had he, a dog of a

Giaour, dared to come to *his* house, and ask him for money? Baghas stood his ground, with a courage that astonished us all. He told the Turk plainly it was all his own fault. What business had he to buy gold coins of him, if he could not pay for them? Let him give him the money he owed him, and make an end, that was all he wanted. There came to be a crowd round the two of them ; yet was no man quick enough to stop the Turk when he flashed out his scimitar, and stabbed poor Baghas to the heart. 'Take that for payment, Giaour,' saith he. But he said no more ; for our people closed upon him with a cry of rage. I heard them saying, 'Now we shall see the good of the Reforms !' 'Now we shall have justice !' 'Djanum[1]! are our men to be killed like dogs ?' and more of that kind."

"Heaven send they have not harmed the Turk," Jack said ; "the bill for that would be too heavy."

"I don't think they have. They got him in the midst of them, and they are taking him to the Government House, to lodge a complaint against him there."

"I remember once, in England, seeing a sparrow fly at a cat, in defence of her young. It reminds me of that" said Jack. "Gabriel, I want to see

---

[1] Djanum = "my soul." A common exclamation.

this thing through, but I don't want *you* to come. There may be rough work."

"Oh, I should *like* to come.   I am not afraid."

"But, if you were hurt, Shushan would not like that ; we must think of her."

"Yes," said Gabriel slowly. "Yon Effendi, I will go home."

With a self-denial Jack scarcely appreciated at its full value, he turned away and ran quickly down a side street.   Jack went on his way, and he had no difficulty in finding it, for cries and shouts, and the trampling of many feet directed him to a market place, some distance off.   Here, at first, he could not see the wood for the trees.   All the place seemed full of Turks and Armenians mixed together, shouting, struggling, swaying, and push-ing, now this way, now that.   It seemed to be a free fight, but what they were all fighting about was not clear to an onlooker.   Still, not to be left out when good things were going, Jack took his share by snatching a knife from the hand of a Turk who was threatening an Armenian with it.

Presently half a dozen Turkish horse—Regulars, with a splendid-looking officer at their head, came dashing into the square, and sending both Turks and Christians running in all directions.   But one Turk did not run, for he lay dying on the ground. It was the murderer of Baghas.   The soldiers took up the wounded man and set him on a horse. And then the Turks began to return ; a number of them gathered round the group, with a few Christians also. Jack heard them cry out that the man was dying.

"How did you get here, Yon Effendi?" said the voice of Barkev Vartonian beside him.

"I met Gabriel, and came. What are they going to do?"

"Going to take the man to the Government House, I suppose. They will never get him there alive."

"Barkev, who killed him?"

"The zaptiehs, of course, when they could not get him from us. I *saw* one of them stab him with a bayonet."

"I thought one of our people might have done it, seeing they wanted to take him from us."

"How, save with sticks or stones? We have nothing else, as you know. But the Turks will try to put it on us, no doubt. Come along to the Government House, and let us see what happens."

As they reached the place, Barkev exclaimed, "Djanum! there is Dr. Melkon, of all men, in the hands of the zaptiehs. What can *he* have done?"

"Not arrested as a criminal, I hope, but called in as a doctor," said Jack, as they came up.

If so, the wounded Turk was beyond his skill.

They heard those around him saying he was dead. At the same time Melkon's voice reached their ears. He could do no good now, he pleaded, entreating the Turks to let him go about his business, which was urgent. He had a serious case to attend to—a Mussulman Effendi.

No; he must stay, and certify to the cause of death. Barkev and Jack followed the crowd, which streamed into the Government House—an open court, where they could see all that passed.

They saw the body laid on a divan, and they saw Melkon approach to examine it. The Turkish officer stood beside him, a drawn sword in his hand.

"This man has been killed by the blows of sticks or bludgeons," he said, in a loud voice. Melkon stooped over the body; the officer stooped also, and whispered something in his ear.

Almost instantly Melkon stood up, his face pale as that of the dead man who lay before them. For once the noisy, chattering Eastern crowd kept a profound silence. Melkon's low, firm voice reached every ear,—

"This man has died of wounds inflicted by the bayonet."

"No case against us," Barkev said.

But Melkon had sealed his own death warrant, and he knew it. For one moment he faced the crowd—

"I can die, but I cannot lie," he said.

His voice was drowned in a howl of execration, and a dozen furious hands laid hold on him at once.

"To the rescue!" cried Jack and Barkev together, dashing in amongst the throng.

"Keep quiet!" muttered a voice beside them, and a Turk they knew laid his hand on Barkev's shoulder. "Keep quiet and go home," he went on in a whisper; "my brothers have got the doctor, and will hide him in our house. He has attended us; we like him, and we will not let him be killed."

Somewhat comforted, the young men went home. As they passed through the streets, the Moslems greeted them with threats and insults.

"We will soon make an end of you, dogs of Giaours," they cried. Boys threw stones at them, and women screamed curses—foul and hideous Turkish curses—at the top of their shrill voices.

"I do not like the look of things at all," said Barkev, when they got into their own quarter.

"Nor I," Jack answered. "I think it would be no harm for some of us to keep watch to-night. I volunteer, for one." And he went apart to clean his precious revolver, and to load the two serviceable barrels. He had not dared to get it set in order; that would have been far too dangerous.

The night, so far as they knew, passed quietly away. Many Armenians had shops or booths, or other business to attend to outside their own Quarter, and this was the case with some members of the Vartonian family. On Monday morning the women prayed of them to stay at home, and, indeed, the greater number did so. But others thought it the part of wisdom, as well as of manly courage, to go about as usual. Barkev Vartonian was amongst these, and Jack went with him for company.

They had not gone far beyond the limits of their own Quarter when a boy ran against them, screaming with terror, and caught Jack by the zeboun.

"What is it? What is the matter, poor child?" he asked; then looking more closely cried out, "Hagop! Hagop Meneshian! How is this? Have you all come? Where are you?"

"We came in at the gate," Hagop gasped out. "Then the Dajeeks set on us with sticks and stones and knives. Oh, they are going to kill us! What shall we do?"

"Don't be afraid; we will protect you. Where are the rest?"

"Down there—in the Market Place—the corner, by the dead wall. Kevork and the others are defending the women and children as well as they can. I slipped through somehow, and ran on to tell you."

"Don't come back with us. Run along that narrow street, keep to the right, and once in our Quarter you will be safe. Ask any one for Baron Vartonian's house. You can send us any men you find to help."

Barkev and Jack hurried on to the rescue of their friends. They were met on their way by a hideous rabble of Turkish men and boys, the very scum of the city, who were dragging along at the end of a rope, with shouts and ribald laughter— *something*. Was that a human form, so horribly torn and mutilated? Was that a human face? Was it the face they saw, not four and twenty hours ago, white and set, yet calm in its brave resolve?

"It is Melkon," Jack whispered in horror; "they have killed him. Oh, God, what things are done here!"

"Come on! come on! Don't look," said Barkev. "We have my cousins to save from a like fate."

They found the Meneshians in a corner of the Market Place, still keeping the foe at bay. They had the advantage of being, most of them, on horses or on mules; but the density of the hostile crowd, and the number of women and children they had with them, had kept them from breaking through, while they made all the better mark for stones and mud.

However, their tormentors were getting tired of a kind of sport which yielded no profit. Rather a pity, when their brethren were looting the well-stocked Armenian shops in the Bazaar! So the crowd soon gave way sufficiently to enable Jack and Barkev to extricate their friends, and they led the terrified party towards the Armenian Quarter. Some were bleeding from the stones that had been thrown at them ; all had their clothing torn and disfigured with mud. The children were crying, and two or three of the women were ready to faint.

Meanwhile, there was a roar behind them like the roar of many waters, breaking on a rock-bound shore. The mob—the savage mob of an Eastern city—was "*up.*" "Death to the Giaours!" was the cry that rose and surged, surged and rose again. The luckless Armenians who had ventured into the Turkish town were fleeing before the storm,—fleeing for their lives, many of them streaming with blood.

Would that mob pour on, like sea waves in a storm, into the narrow streets of the Armenian Quarter ? Would they slay utterly young and old, men and maidens and little children ? No, the weak should not die, if the strong could protect them.

Barkev, Kevork, Jack, and other young men sent the rest on before them, and took their stand in a narrow street at the entrance of their Quarter. It bade fair to be a little modern Thermopylæ. Surely neither Greek nor Roman ever fought in a holier cause, or for dearer issues ; nor against greater odds, nor with more determined courage.

Gabriel, just back from school, came with the rest. Jack sent him for his revolver. " You know where to get it," he said. The others armed themselves, as they could, with sticks and stones. Not another firearm was seen, save this revolver.

The Turks had plenty of firearms. With the rabble were mingled regular soldiers, Zaptiehs, Redifs, Hamidiehs, Kourds, all fully armed, all thirsting for blood and plunder. The Armenians could scarcely have held their own had they not had good allies on the flat roofs of their houses. These had all parapets of loose stones, treasuries of effective weapons for the men, the women, and the boys, who flung them down on the heads of the Moslems.

Jack's two barrels were soon emptied, as two of the Turks knew to their cost. But he could not reload, so a friend behind him snatched the weapon out of his hand, and thrust into it a stout bludgeon. With this he played the man, his whole soul in the blows he dealt. He was fighting for dear life—for dearer lives than his own. Was it minutes, hours, years that he stood there, struggling in that desperate *mêlée*? Were the Moslems giving ground at last? What did it mean? There certainly was a space growing before the defenders; they had room now to breathe. Two or three Turks lay in the street dead or dying, others were well bruised with bludgeons or cut with stones. A panic began among them. And presently—for an Eastern crowd does nothing by halves—the street was cleared with a rush. It was a regular stampede.

The Christians drew breath, and looked one another in the face. "Safe at last!" Jack said.

"For the present," said Kevork, wiping his brow. But the next moment he cried in horror, "My father! he is dying!"

The Christians, of course, had suffered in the fray. Several lay dead, others were sorely wounded. One of these was Boghos, who, though no longer young, had chosen to take part in the defence. Jack and Kevork, in great distress, carried him into a house at hand; the owner, a carpenter named Selferian, cordially inviting them in, and his handsome, intelligent wife, Josephine Hanum by name, bringing linen and cold water, while the eldest boy ran for the nearest doctor. Fortunately, the wound, when examined by him, did not seem to be immediately dangerous, though it was certainly serious.

When the Armenians had time to compare notes, it appeared that all the principal entrances to their Quarter had been defended with the same desperate courage and with equal success. There was considerable loss of life, inevitable when their assailants had firearms and they had none, but at least for the present they were safe, with their wives and children.

That is to say, they were safe within the limits of their own Quarter; outside of it, even at its very entrance, every Armenian was mercilessly slain. At least, to be accurate, the men and the boys were slain. Armenian shops, of which there were many, including the best and richest in the town, were given over to plunder, and Armenian houses shared the same fate.

Still, at first, in the Armenian Quarter, the feeling was one of relief. When a naked sword that has been held at your throat is suddenly withdrawn, your first sensation is delightful, whatever the next may be. It took the Armenians some days at least to realize two awful facts: that their friends and relatives outside were hopelessly lost, and that they were themselves straitly shut up and besieged.

Had the Meneshian family been twelve hours

later in entering the town, not one of them, probably, would have been left alive. Their journey from Biridjik to Urfa had been a most perilous one, as every Moslem in the country seemed to be in arms against them. They could scarcely have accomplished it at all but for an expedient of Kevork's. Jack had provided a Kourdish dress for him, as well as for himself and for Shushan, supposing that he would return with them to Urfa. He wore this during the journey, and rode boldly in front of the party, whose guide and protector he was supposed to be. He had changed it, however, before entering the city, as he never dreamed of danger *there*, and imagined it would expose him to ridicule.

Great anxiety was felt about Miss Celandine, and the other inmates of the Mission premises. But this, as far as Jack was concerned, was soon allayed, though in a way that caused his friends a terrible alarm. Two zaptiehs came to the Vartonian house, enquiring for one Grayson Effendi. Every one thought nothing less than that he had been identified in the crowd at the gate as the man who used the revolver, and that this summons meant imprisonment, as bad or worse than death. Great was the relief when it proved to mean only a polite request to visit Miss Celandine. True to his system—and he does everything upon system—the Turk would not willingly injure a foreign subject. Miss Celandine therefore was not only left unmolested, but given a guard of zaptiehs to protect her premises from the mob. These zaptiehs did their work faithfully ; and it seems that some of them at least were won to regard their charges with respect and liking.

Jack went to the Mission House, as safe in reality as if he had been walking in a London street, though under the escort of men who, at a word from their captain, would have torn him limb from limb with the greatest pleasure in the world. He found the mission premises crowded with persons who had taken refuge there during the late disturbances. Many of them were wounded, and all were destitute. The courtyard was filled with them, as well as most of the rooms of the house. Miss Celandine—who, since the departure of her youthful fellow-worker, had stood completely alone—looked ten years older than when he saw her last. Thinner she could scarcely be, but her eyes had dark circles round them, and her face an abiding look of horror. She led him into the only private room she had left, and made anxious enquiries about the state of the Armenian Quarter, which, although it was at her very gates, it was practically impossible for her to enter.   Then she said, " Mr. Grayson, I am sending to the Pasha to ask for a passport."

" It is what any one would do in your place—what any one else would have done long ago," he answered.

" This is why I do it.   The danger seems over here.   The massacre is stopped.   Yet I cannot resume my work amongst the people ; that is not permitted to me.   Here I am useless ; I am only witnessing misery I cannot relieve.   But in England or America I could do a great deal.   I could tell the truth—the very truth—about what is done here.   If England and America knew *that*, I think it would change everything.   I am persuaded better things of my fellow-Christians than that they would sit still and tolerate the destruction—with every aggravation of refined, diabolical cruelty—of a nation of Christians, only because they *are* Christians."

Miss Celandine seldom spoke in this way ; but her heart was hot and sore within her, she had just been hearing a recital of horrors such as may not be mentioned here, and was in no mood to guard her words.   The hatred of Turks for Armenians is a growth of centuries, rooted in complex causes ; but the fact that they are Christians lifts the bridle from the jaws of the oppressor, making every act of cruelty to them a merit—their extermination a holy war. And since by embracing Islam they would come under the protection of the Prophet, it *is* because of their firm adherence to their faith that these unhappy ones are given over to the sword, *and worse.*

"You are right to go," Jack said simply. "And oh !" he added, his eyes kindling and his whole face changing, "you will take Shushan with you? That is what you mean—why you sent for me. God bless you, ten thousand times !"

The smile that lit up the worn face made it very sweet to look upon. "Yes, my dear boy," she said. "I do mean that. But I dare not take her with me, either as Shushan Meneshian, or under the name she has now a right to bear. It would cause too much remark and enquiry. No ; she had better pass as one of my servants, a certain number of whom I have the right to take. But this is what I sent for you to ask : Will you also apply for a passport, and come with us ? "

Jack was silent. Indeed, he could not speak, for the fierce hope, the passionate longing that arose within him was too strong for words. To leave all this misery, to stand with Shushan on the shores of England—*free* !

"The thought grew frightful, 'twas so wildly dear."

But soon reflection came. It could not be. All

at once he threw back his head with a sharp, sudden "No," very startling to the lady, whose nerves were already strung to their utmost tension. "In the first place, everything would come out. I should be known as the Englishman, John Grayson, who married an Armenian in Biridjik, and who afterwards killed Kourds, and fired on Mussulmans with a revolver."

"They would probably be afraid to meddle with you."

"They might. You know their ways much better than I do. But I suspect they would find a way of paying me back my revolver shots in kind—or worse—before I left the country. And even suppose I got safe out, and Shushan too, what would be the fate of the Meneshians? Would not sevenfold vengeance descend on them — which, even if *I* could bear to think of—what of Shushan? There is another thing, though I scarce like to say it," Jack added in a different tone, and with a kind of relapse into boyishness : "all the people here, the Meneshians, the Vartonians and the rest—in some queer way I cannot explain—seem to cling to me. They give me far more credit than I deserve for the repulse of the Turks the other day, and somehow they fancy I can protect them. I suppose it is because I am an Englishman, come of fathers and mothers who have not been afraid—because they had nothing to be afraid of—for generation upon generation. So I want to stay, at all events, till this affair is over."

" John Grayson, you are a brave lad," said Miss Celandine, stretching out her thin, worn hand to him.

Jack took it with all reverence. What deeds of kindness and pity, and heroic beneficence that weak woman's hand had done! Like the people he dwelt amongst, he bowed over it, touching it with his lips and his forehead. Then he said, smiling, " But also I am a man now. If it please you, Miss Celandine, may I see my wife ? "

" Certainly. I will go and fetch her."

In a few minutes Shushan entered. She had grown a little pale with the anxieties of the last days, but he thought she looked sweeter than ever. She had much to hear from him about her family, and about her father, of whom he was able to give her a hopeful report.

An hour passed in earnest talk ; but what each said to the other, neither told afterwards. When at last the moment of parting came, neither cared to think how long a parting it might be. Lip met lip, heart throbbed against heart. Shushan was the braver now. " You know, Shack," she said, "the cross of Christ was laid on us together. Nothing can keep us parted after that."

"The cross laid on us together," Jack repeated ; "indeed, it looks like it. But do not droop, my Lily. With God's help we will win through yet, and have a joyful ending to all our troubles."

But something in his own heart gave the lie to his hopeful words, as he took one last lingering gaze, and sadly turned to go.

"Yertaak paré," said Shushan softly.

"Menaak paré," he responded, and went.

Chapter XV

DARK HOURS

" Oh, Thou that dwellest in the heavens high,
Above yon stars and beyond yon sky,
Where the dazzling fields need no other light,
Nor the sun by day, nor the moon by night ;

Though shining millions around Thee stand,
For the sake of Him at Thy Right Hand,
Think on the souls He died for here,
Wandering in darkness, sorrow and fear !

The Powers of Darkness are all abroad,
They own no Saviour, they fear no God ;
And we are trembling in dumb dismay—
Oh, turn not Thou Thy Face away ! "

—Cameronian Midnight Hymn.

IF the Armenians were safe, for the present, in their own Quarter from actual murder, it was the most that could be said. They dared not stir an inch beyond its boundaries ; and within it, the Redifs who were quartered upon them, ostensibly as protectors, but really as spies, committed many horrible outrages.

They were continually pressed to surrender fire-arms, which they did not possess. To satisfy the authorities, any pieces that could be found by diligent search amongst the few who had dared to conceal them, were given up; and this, much to his regret, was the fate of Jack's revolver. Still the Turks persisted in the assertion that the Armenians had a large number of Martinis, supplied to them by foreigners, and that these must be produced before they could promise them security for their lives and their possessions. Vain were their protestations that these Martinis had no existence—that they had never even heard of them. In the end, the persecuted community actually *purchased* arms from the Turks themselves, which they then gave back to the Government. This might appear at first a mere trick of the officials, to secure a trifle of dishonest gain. It was much more; it was part of the subtle, skilful, elaborate plan by which a net was drawn around the doomed race, and they were made to appear, in the eyes of those who might have befriended them, as the doers, not the sufferers, of violence. In a European newspaper, English or German, the transaction might have read thus: " At Urfa, a town on the Euphrates (*sic*), a disturbance was caused by the Armenians, who attacked a party of zaptiehs as they were conveying a prisoner to the guard-house. They overpowered the zaptiehs, and killed the prisoner, against whom they had a grudge. Some rioting ensued; shops were plundered, and several persons, both Mussulmans and Armenians, were killed. But the Armenians having surrendered their fire-arms, and being restricted, for the present, to their own Quarter, order and tranquillity have now been completely restored, through the firmness of the Government." This was the sort of thing John Grayson might have been reading if he had stayed in England. He would probably have dismissed the subject with the careless comment, " People are always fighting and killing each other in those out-of-the-way places," and turned with quickened interest to the great cricket match on the next page.

But now he was himself in the midst of the agony, which made all the difference. He was shuddering and starving with the thousands packed together in those close, unhealthy streets. At first a danger threatened them, almost as terrible as the sword of the Turk. The water of the fountains they used came to them through the great ancient Aqueduct; and this supply the Turks could, and did, cut off. But there were, in their Quarter, some old, unused wells, which they cleaned out and made available, though the water obtained in this way was neither pure nor healthful. Their stores of rice, bulghour, and other kinds of food, which happily they had just laid in for the winter, were husbanded with all possible care.

Jack took an active share in everything that was done. His leisure time he employed in learning Turkish; for he saw how greatly his own and Shushan's dangers, on their journey, had been increased by his want of it. It was not a difficult task; many Turkish words and phrases, which were in common use, he already knew; the Turkish language moreover is very poor and scanty, containing, it is said, not more than seven hundred really indigenous words.

He continued to live with the Vartonians; and indeed the whole Meneshian family contrived to stow itself away in their large and hospitable house, with the exception of the wounded Boghos, now slowly recovering, and his wife, who remained for the present with the Selferians.

It was thought that Thomassian might have received some of the Meneshians, as they were his kinsmen also; but his mind at this time seemed to be wholly absorbed in grief for the destruction of his property. His large, well-stocked shop had been looted; and fresh stores coming to him from Aleppo had been intercepted and seized. Unhinged by these catastrophes, and by the apprehension of worse to come, he fell into a state of morbid depression. He used to rouse himself however to take part in the meetings for consultation which were held, with many precautions, by the Armenian " Notables " ; and he often gave very good and sensible advice. He was not fond of giving anything else.

" 'Tis making a hole in the water to ask *him* to do anything for you," said the younger Vartonians. " But he might comfort himself, under his losses, with the thought that the Turks are sure to poison themselves with some of his drugs, not knowing the use of them."

Communication with the Mission House had now become very difficult, though the Armenians knew that their friends were still in safety there. It was no longer practicable to hold service in the Protestant church ; so Jack's opportunities of seeing Shushan, and Kevork's of seeing Elmas, were no more. Miss Celandine however contrived occasionally, through her zaptiehs, to send news of Shushan to Jack, and to get tidings in return for her, of him and of her family. In this way she informed him also that she had not yet succeeded in obtaining her passport. The Pasha made fair promises ; but continually put off the granting of her request on the plea of the disturbed condition of the country.

The Gregorians still assembled, very constantly,

for the prayer they so much needed, in their great Cathedral; and it was before or after these services that they used to deliberate together on the state of affairs.

In one of these consultations they were lamenting, as they often did, the impossibility of sending news of their condition to those outside who might help them. Post and telegraph were closed to them; and, as they surmised, to Miss Celandine also. Two or three messengers, with letters concealed about them, had gone forth secretly, and at terrible risk, but they had never been heard of again. The presumption was that they had fallen into the hands of the Turks. What more could the Armenians do?

Then John Grayson rose up in his place, between Kevork and Avedis, and these were the words he said,—

"Friends, I will be your next messenger. Will you trust me?"

A murmur of astonishment ran round the assembly. The personal friends of Jack, and they were many, began to protest against his exposing himself to so great a danger; and indeed every one thought his life too valuable to be lightly risked.

"What would my sister say?" Kevork whispered.

And Jack answered, "She would say, ' Der-ah haadet allà ' (The Lord be with you). Then raising his voice, " It is the best way all round, if you will look at it. You need not endanger me or yourselves by writing anything ; for I know all, and can tell it. If I am caught, I have still a good chance of escape ; for I will tell the Turks I am an Englishman, and that they touch me at their peril."

" They will not believe you, and you have no proof to offer," said old Hohannes, with a face of much concern, for he loved Yon Effendi as a son.

" I *have* proof, father. I can speak and write English for their edification, and talk big about Consuls and International Law, and the power of England. Whereas, if I am *not* taken, the gain is great. An Englishman who has seen what I have, can say things the English—and the rest of the world—ought to hear, and there is none to tell them."

" Amaan ! That is true," several voices said.

" And do not forget, for *I* do not," Jack went on, " what I stand to win. Once free, I think I can help myself, and you too, far better than by staying here. If it were to abandon you, I would never go. Here or there, I mean to see this thing through with you. But it seems to me that I can do more, just now, there than here."

"How will you disguise yourself?" some one asked.

"I can wear the Kourdish dress that served me coming here."

"But you do not know the country," another objected.

"As far as Biridjik I know it well.   Trust me to find out the rest."

Finally, Jack's proposal was agreed to by all; except indeed by Hohannes, who kept silence, but did not change his mind.   The meeting broke up, as soon as the heads of it had arranged for Jack to come to them at a later hour, to receive messages and other instructions for his dangerous mission.

As they went out together, Kevork laid his hand on his shoulder: "Brother," he said, "do you not desire to see Shushan again before you go?   I think it might be managed for you, with back-sheesh to the zaptiehs."

Jack thought a moment; then he answered with a decided "No.   We have had our farewells," he added.   "It is best not to alarm her."   In his own heart he said, "I had rather keep the last words she spoke to me, 'The cross of Christ has been laid upon us together.   Nothing can part us after that!'"   But he took his father's note-book, the one precious relic that remained to him, wrote a few tender words in it, wrapped it up carefully and gave it to Kevork to give her, in case anything happened to him.

At the later consultation it was decided that Jack should not wear the Kourdish dress: it was thought he could not keep up the character sufficiently to disarm suspicion. A proposition that he should go dressed *à la Frank* was negatived also, since a person so attired would never be found travelling alone. At last a disguise was found for him,—the dress of an Armenian peasant of the very humblest class, a countryman. It was hoped that the appearance of utter poverty and of ignorance might secure his safety.

It was December now, and the nights were dark, as dark as they ever are in that southern land. There are many places in which the ancient wall of Urfa is much broken down, in some it is only three feet high, with stones and rubbish and broken masonry all about. Stealthily and noiselessly Jack crept towards one of these. There was no difficulty in getting over the wall, but then at the other side there was a natural rock to be descended—almost a precipice. This also however the agile youth accomplished, and stood in safety at the bottom. His next difficulty was to elude the Turkish patrol, which passed frequently during the night. Seeing it at a distance, he laid himself down quite flat amongst the stones, until the men had passed, and everything was perfectly quiet. Then he cautiously set out upon his journey, passing through fields and vineyards, and striking into the Roman road where he had ridden with Shushan three months before. Although the weather was now cold, he intended to travel by night, and rest during the day, in order to minimize the dangers of discovery.

Yet, three hours later, the die was cast, and his fate was sealed. A party of Turkish horsemen, who were conveying some prisoners into the town, saw at a distance in the morning light his dark figure thrown out by the white path behind him. He knew they had seen him, but there was no place near where it was possible to conceal himself, so his only chance was to pass on boldly in his assumed character.

The captain of the troop took little heed of him, just flinging him a curse in passing as one beneath his notice. Unhappily, amongst the band of wretched prisoners—all the more wretched for having had to keep up on foot with the riding of the Turks—Jack saw a face he knew, Der Garabed, the priest of Biridjik. No fear of consequences could keep the look of grief and pity out of his eyes. It was observed, as also was the captive's quick glance of recognition, changed though it was immediately into the dull, vacant stare his race have a wonderful power of assuming.

The Captain gave a rapid order, and Jack was surrounded and seized. Asked what his name was, he answered boldly, "John Grayson. I am an Englishman."

This was received with a shout of laughter. "By the Prophet, a likely story!" the Captain said. "English Effendis do not go about the country alone and in rags. More probably a Zeitounli prowling about to stir up rebellion."

"I can prove my words," Jack said. "I am an Englishman. I put on this dress to get down to the coast in safety, as the country is disturbed. I have never been in Zeitoun. I can prove what I am. Those who hurt the English have to pay for it. Those who help them get well paid themselves, in good medjidis."

The last word had rather a softening influence. "Of what religion are you?" the Captain asked.

"Of the religion of the English," Jack answered promptly. The Captain hesitated for a moment.

"Captain," shouted a Turk from his following, "the Giaour is lying. He is no English Effendi, but an Armenian of Urfa. I saw his face that day there was fighting. He had a revolver in his hand, and shot true Believers with it."

"Is that so? Then he goes to the Kadi," said

the Captain, his momentary hesitation at an end. "Bind him, men, in the Name of Allah, the Merciful. You are an impudent liar, like all your race," he said to Jack, turning away with a curse.

Jack hoped he might be able to speak to the priest; but this boon was denied him. He was placed at the other end of the file of captives. The man to whom he was bound seemed either afraid, or too thoroughly crushed and dejected to speak to him. His own state of mind was not enviable. His first feeling was that he had failed. He meant to do such great things; he had gone forth full of hope and courage, as one who should work a great deliverance in the earth. And now? —and now?—What would they all feel, all the friends who loved and trusted him so? They would be waiting, wondering, speculating about his fate. Their anxiety would change into suspense, their suspense would deepen at last into sad certainty. Yet, most likely, there would be none to tell of his fate. And Shushan? The thought of her sorrow swallowed up all other thoughts, all other regrets. And Shushan? For her dear sake he would not give up hope, he would struggle on even to the end. His English name and his English race might save him yet.

Not likely, after those fatal shots. Meanwhile, at the present moment, where was he? Whither was he going?   All the stories which, in the last five years, he had heard spoken with bated breath of the horrors of Turkish prisons rushed like a sea of bitter waters over his soul.   They brought with them a sensation absolutely new to him—utter, unreasoning, overpowering *fear*.   Terror and anguish took hold on him; large drops, like the touch of cold fingers, stood upon his forehead; he shivered from head to foot.   He had faced death before this, and it had seemed to him but a light thing. " After that, no more that they can do."   After that; but how much before—oh, God of mercy, how much before!

All at once Stepanian's voice seemed sounding in his ears.   "You must trust God utterly." Wherever they might bring him, whatever they might do with him, *God would be there.*   He could not get out of that Presence, nor could they.   A thrill shot through him of hope restored and strength renewed; a vision of conflict over, and victory won at last.   As a cry "unto One that hears," his prayer went up: " Oh, God of my fathers, I beseech Thee, suffer me not through any pains of death to fall from Thee.   Suffer me not to deny my faith, nor yet to accuse my brethren, in the Name of Christ, my Redeemer ! "

While he thought of God he was calm.   When he thought of his chances, of what might happen to him, of whether any one would believe his story, the dark fears came again. Even of Shushan it did not do to think too much just now—he could only commend her to God. Constitutionally, he was brave and fearless. But to think of a Turkish prison without shuddering requires much more than constitutional bravery,—either nerves of adamant, or faith to remove mountains. Perhaps not either, perhaps not both together could prevent the anguish of anticipation, whatever strength might be given for actual endurance.

Back again in Urfa, and at the Government House where he had seen Melkon witness his brave confession, Jack found that his story would not be listened to for a moment. Some of the captives were taken away, he knew not whither; others, along with himself, were led within the gloomy gates of the prison, and after passing through several dark passages, thrust into a room or cell. As well as he could discern by the light that streamed from a narrow window high up in the wall, this cell was already full—nay, crowded—men standing packed together as those who wait for a door to open and admit them to some grand spectacle. "I suppose," he thought, "they will take us out by-and-by for some sort of trial. But what stifling, foetid, horrible air! Enough to breed a pestilence!"

It was utterly impossible to sit down, difficult even to raise a hand or move a foot, so dense was the crush. Occasional thrills through the living mass told that some wretch was making a frantic effort to get a little air, and thus increasing the misery of his neighbours. Jack contrived to say to a companion in misfortune, whose ear touched his mouth, "How long will they keep us here?"

At first the only answer was a mournful "Amaan!" followed by piteous groans.

He repeated the question—"How long will they keep us in this horrible place?"

"As long as they can," gasped the man he had addressed;—"until death sets us free.—Why not? —It is the prison."

But another hissed into his ear, "No; it is hell—*hell.*"

"'If I make my bed in hell, behold Thou art there,'" John Grayson thought. With a brave effort to cling to his Faith and his God, he said aloud, "God is here. Let us cry to Him."

"God has forsaken us," said the last speaker; but from two or three others came the feebly murmured prayer, "Jesus, help us!" "Jesus, help us!"

Time passed on. Jack would have given all the wealth he could claim in England, were it here and in his hand, simply for one square yard of the filth-stained ground beneath his feet to rest upon.

It was long since every limb had ached with intolerable weariness ; now the dull ache was succeeded by shooting, agonizing pains. He was too sick for hunger, but the thirst was terrible, and the sense of suffocation came in spasms that made him want to tear a passage with teeth and nails through the living mass about him. Once the pressure, becoming heavier, made him try to look round. Near him a man had swooned. Was it a swoon, or was it death? He caught a glimpse of the livid face between two others ; for there was no room for the fainting, or even for the dead, to fall.

Time passed on. He felt his strength forsaking him. He tried to speak, but his voice sounded hollow and unlike itself. Was he dying? He thought this numbness and faintness might mean *that* ; but then perhaps the wish was father to the thought. He was young and strong, and such do not quickly die.

Time passed on. Shushan was in his thoughts continually, with the wish—with the prayer often— that she might never know. Thank God—there was something to thank God for even here—she did not know now ! Miss Celandine would take care of her,—and sometime, somewhere, when all this agony was over, they would meet again. Was *this* the cross of Christ?

Time passed on. The numbness in his limbs increased. He began to lose himself a little now and then. He was at Pastor Stepanian's church— in Biridjik—in England even; then he would come suddenly back again, with a thri of anguish, to the horrible present. Yet he was not dying, he was not fainting even; strange to say, he was only falling asleep. Even upon the cross, men have slept. At last no more light came in through the little grated window. It was night.

Time passed on. A sounder slumber than before came mercifully to steep his senses in oblivion. He was in England, in his old home. In the orchard was one particular tree he used to be very fond of climbing, in spite of his father's warning, "Take care, my boy, you will break your bones some day." He thought now that he had fallen from the highest branch, and was laid on his bed, a mass of fractures and bruises, calling on the surgeons, whose faces he saw distinctly, to give him chloroform—anything to stop the pain, and bring unconsciousness. Was he crying out at the pitch of his voice, and doing shame to his manhood?

He awoke in horror. Shriek after shriek, though not from *his* lips, rent the midnight air. To those who only know what the human voice can do by the cries of childish pain or fear, a strong man's shriek of agony is an unimaginable horror.

"Oh, what is it?" Jack cried aloud, his own voice a wail.

"Some one is being tortured in the next cell to this," a weary, indifferent voice made answer.

The shrieks went on, interspersed with short intervals of silence, and with deep, heavy groans. There were words too, heard more or less distinctly, cries for mercy, agonized prayers. Then in a higher key, "I know nothing—nothing. You are killing me." And again, Kill me, in the name of God. I implore of you to kill me!" Once more, as if flung out with all the remaining strength of dying lips, "No!—No!—No!—No!"

"It is only," said the man who had spoken last, "some one who refuses to accuse his friends."

"God help him!" Jack murmured feebly. For a little while the cries died away; then they began again, culminating in a shriek so appalling that Jack's senses failed him with the horror, and at last unconsciousness took him out of his misery.

A waft of cooler air revived him. When he came to himself, he lay amongst a number of fallen or falling bodies. Then some one was dragging him along, as it seemed, through some passage towards the light. "Where am I?" he asked, trying mechanically to shake off the hand that held him. Then he saw that he was between two zaptiehs, who were laughing at his feeble efforts to get free. He thought it very likely they were going to kill him, and he did not care.

Yet their intentions did not seem at the moment particularly cruel. One of them pointed to a place near the wall, and told him to sit down and rest; the other fetched him a cup of water, incomparably the most delicious draught he had ever tasted. Then they half led, half dragged him into an open court, where many other prisoners were waiting.

He looked on dreamily while several of these were led up to the Kadi, who sat in state on the divan at the end of the room, and after a brief examination, sometimes a few words only, were led away again by the zaptiehs. At last his own turn came. He could manage to stand alone now, though he still felt confused and bewildered.

He was asked his name, and he gave it in full. But here strength and memory seemed to fail him together. He knew there was *something* he wanted to say, but he could not remember what it was. He looked around him blankly, helplessly—and the next moment would have fallen to the ground, if one of the zaptiehs had not caught him and held him up.

The next thing he heard was the voice of the

Kadi addressing him again. "Listen," said the zaptieh ; "His Excellency condescends to enquire if you are a true Believer."

"I am," said Jack.

"Are you then of the creed of Islam ? "

He stood up straight, and looked the Kadi in the face. "No," he answered.

"Will you become a convert to the creed of Islam ? "

"No," he said again.

"Since we are inclined to mercy, we will give you a week to think the matter over. After that, if you refuse again, you must die."

"I had rather you would kill me at once," Jack said.

"It is not the will of Allah," the Kadi replied. "Guards, take the prisoner away."

He was led presently to another dungeon, where at least there was room to stretch his weary, aching limbs at full length on the ground ; and where, from utter exhaustion, he almost immediately fell asleep.

Chapter XVI

"THE DARK RIVER TURNS TO LIGHT"

> "The thousands that, uncheered by praise,
> Have made one offering of their days ;
> For Truth's, for Heaven's, for Freedom's sake,
> Resigned the bitter cup to take,
> And silently, in fearless faith,
> Bowing their noble souls to death."

JOHN GRAYSON awoke from his long sleep. Though still aching all over, he was much refreshed and strengthened. Nature was putting forth her recuperative powers in his young and vigorous frame. For a while he lay quite still. The light was dim, the ground beneath him foul and muddy ; and he could see nothing, not even a mat, in the way of furniture. But he soon became aware that he was not alone. There were several persons in the room, or cell, and they were conversing together in low tones, mingling their words with many a sigh, and many a murmured " Amaan !" or " Jesus, help us !" One spoke of his large family of little children—how hard to leave them destitute ! Another of his wife ; a third of his aged father, who was blind ; a fourth of his brothers and sisters ; and in him Jack recognised the voice of a friend of the Vartonians, who had been away at the vineyards when the storm burst upon his people.

He raised his head.   "Is that you, Kaspar Hohanian ? " he asked.

' Djanum ! " cried the young man, coming towards him and looking at him attentively. "Friends, this is Yon Effendi, the Englishman who married Oriort Shushan Meneshian."

Most of the twelve or fifteen prisoners who were shut up there together knew his story, and all gathered round him with sympathy and interest. In the awful strain of their position any momentary distraction was a relief. "How had he come there ? " they asked. It happened that they had all been imprisoned before he set out on his desperate errand : some, like Kaspar, had been found outside the Armenian Quarter ; others had been arrested by the Redifs, on various pretexts, within it. But Jack, before he told his story, asked if they could give him any food, for he was exhausted with hunger. All they had to offer was a piece of hard black bread, defiled by the mud and filth into which it had been purposely thrown by their jailors ; and a draught of water, by no means either clean or fresh. But even for these he was very thankful, and ate and drank with eagerness.

Kaspar Hohanian quoted to him a proverb of their race. "'Eat and drink, and talk afterwards,' says the Turk. 'Eat and drink, and talk at the same time,' says the Armenian."

"At all events, while I eat you can talk to me," Jack said, with his mouth full. "Your people thought you were dead, Baron Kaspar."

"The Turks killed all my companions—oh, and so cruelly!" he answered with a shudder. "But an acquaintance I had among them persuaded them, instead of killing me at once, to tie me to one of the tall, upright tombstones in their cemetery outside the gate. Their thought was to leave me there to die of hunger; my friend's, as he whispered, was to come back at night and release me. But, Amaan! the patrol came along before he did, took me, and brought me here. And now I have a week given me to choose between Islam and death. It is hard."

They were all, as it seemed, in like case, only the period of respite varied a little. Meanwhile, it relaxed the intolerable tension of their thoughts, and wiled away a few weary hours, to tell and to hear each other's histories. Jack accordingly gave his, expressing sorrow for the fate of Der Garabed, the priest of Biridjik, and asking if any one present knew anything about him.

No one did ; and while they were discussing the matter, the prison door was opened, and another captive led—or rather thrust—in, to join their mournful company. He was a man of middle age, good-looking, and well dressed in European fashion. But his head was bowed down and his fez pulled low over his face, his arms hung helplessly by his side, and his whole manner and bearing showed the most utter dejection.

Jack sprang up and came to him at once, with an exclamation of pity and sorrow. "Baron Muggurditch Thomassian!" he said.

"Don't speak to me!" said Thomassian, turning on him a look of unutterable anguish.

He went to the most distant corner of the prison, the rest making way for him. No one ventured to approach him with enquiries or condolences, though they all knew him by sight, and several were amongst his acquaintances.

He sat down—or rather, lay down—upon the ground, and turned his face towards the wall.

Low, furtive whispers passed among the others.

"So much to lose. What can all his money do now?"

"Better had he shown mercy and given to the poor."

But these were quickly hushed, lest he should overhear. They did not want to hurt the feelings of the unhappy man, whom indeed they would have gladly comforted, if they had known how. But, as this seemed impossible, they left him to himself; and their talk soon wandered back to their own situation, and the momentous choice that was set before them.

Some were steadfast and comparatively serene. Others wavered, and two or three seemed disposed to give way. All prayed much and often. Most of them could sing, and, led by a few of the braver spirits, they made the gloomy walls resound with Psalms and hymns, especially with that favourite of the Armenians,—

"Jesus, I my cross have taken."

Once John Grayson's voice broke down in singing it, for he heard Shushan saying to him, "The cross of Christ has been laid on us together." Only, if it could be, that he might bear the heaviest end, and that she need never know of all this!

Meanwhile, Thomassian never spoke, and scarcely ever moved from the place where he sat, or lay, his face turned away from the rest. He ate little, and they could not see that he slept. Once or twice they noticed that his tears were falling silently. But not even a groan or sigh told of the anguish of his soul.

The days seemed unending, but still they drew towards an end.   Ay, and far too quickly for those who looked forward with unutterable dread to what was to come after!   The only breaks in the monotony were the jailor's daily visits with bread and water.   Generally he came and went without a word ; but on the evening of their last day of grace he broke the silence.

"You Giaours had better be learning your 'La illaha ill Allah' to-night," he said, "for if you have not got it off by to-morrow morning, you die like the dogs you are."

Then he shut the door, and left them to themselves.

There was a long silence, only interrupted by a few sorrowful "Amaans!"

It was broken at last by the youngest in the room, a lad of some eighteen years.   "I would not be afraid," he said plaintively, "if I thought they would kill us at once.   Were it only a shot or a sword-thrust, that were easy to bear.   But to be killed slowly—cut in little pieces—or perhaps like some——"

"Hush, boy!" Kaspar Hohanian interrupted. "Whatever they do to us, it must be over some-time.   And then—there is heaven beyond."

"Ay," said an older man, "there is heaven for *us*, after a brief agony.   But, friends, we have not ourselves alone to think of; there are our wives and children."

"True," another chimed in; "if we die, they starve."

"If we die, they do worse than starve," the former speaker resumed. "To *what* fate do we leave our women, our girls? You know it *all*, brothers. Whereas, if we turn Moslems, they will be safe, and under protection."

"You are speaking well," observed a third. "And I cannot think, for my part, that the Lord Jesus will be angry with us when He knows all. Has He not given us our families to take care of? Does not His holy Apostle say in his Letter, 'If any provide not for his own, and specially for those of his own house, he hath denied the faith, and is worse than an infidel'? If we *must* deny the faith, and be infidels, it seems as well to do it one way as another."

"And I have my old father to think of; he will die of grief," a sad voice murmured.

"'He that loveth father or mother more than Me is not worthy of Me; and he that loveth son or daughter more than Me is not worthy of Me,'" said another voice, unheard till then amongst them. Thomassian rose up in his place, and looked around him on the group. His whole appearance was changed—transfigured; his look firm and fearless, his eyes shining as if with some inner light.

"My brothers," he said, "you think I have no right to speak to you, that it ill becomes *me* to take upon my lips the words of my Lord and Saviour. And you think that which is true."

"No, no," murmured two or three, unwilling, in that supreme hour, to give pain to a fellow-sufferer.

But Kaspar said more frankly, "To confess the truth, we none of us thought you were a religious man, Baron Thomassian."

"I was *not*. I lived for the things seen, not for the things unseen, which are eternal. Very early I said to myself, 'I am an Armenian, one of an oppressed, down-trodden race. I cannot rise, make a mark in the world, and win its splendid prizes. Yet I have brains. I have the power to will, to plan, to execute. What can I do?' There was but one answer—'I can get wealth, and wealth means safety, enjoyment, influence.' So I tried to get wealth, and I got it by honest industry. At least in the beginning, my hands were clean enough. I prospered; I surrounded myself with comforts, with luxuries. I took to wife a lady, whom—God help me!—I love as truly as any man among you loves his own. But—ah me! —I forgot God."

"So no doubt have we all, some more, some less," said Kaspar Hohanian.

"If there is any one here who feels *that*, let him look up and take comfort," Thomassian went on, "for not one among you has gone from Him so far as I. But, though I forgot Him, He has remembered me. I was led on from one thing to another; until, for the sake of gain, I did some things of which the thought can sting me even now. I was hard upon the poor, and upon my debtors. I did wrong in various ways, and even to some who trusted me. Mr. John Grayson, you are one of those I wronged."

Jack started at the unexpected utterance of his name.

"It is no time now to think of wrongs," he said.

"No, for him who has suffered—yes, for him who has done the wrong. After that time I saw you in Biridjik, I went indeed to Aleppo, but I did not take your letter with me, nor did I speak for you to the Consul. For he and I, just then, were at daggers drawn. I had used his name and influence, and the presence of his dragoman, to pass through the Custom House some prohibited drugs. He was angry, and with reason. I did not dare to face him. I wanted to be rid of your letter, for fear of complications; so I just dropped it into the post office at Tel Bascher, where I have little doubt it lies until this day."

"Then my friends have *not* been false to me," Jack said, much moved. " And, if my letter had come to them, they might have saved me—and Shushan," his heart added.

Thomassian came over close to him, and stretched out his hand. " Can you forgive me?" he asked.

Jack was silent for just a moment. Then he said slowly, " '*As* we forgive them that trespass against us.' Yes, Baron Thomassian, I *do* forgive you, in His name whom we hope so soon to see." " But, oh! how I wish you had spoken!" he could not help thinking, tho' he crushed back the words in time. " Don't think it would have made a difference," he said. " I *do* forgive you, with all my heart."

" It might have changed everything, or it might not," Thomassian said mournfully. " I have no power now to undo that wrong, or any of the others I have done. Friends, while I sat in silence yonder, my face turned from you all, the sins of my whole life came upon me. They swept over my head like black waters, they seemed to choke my very life out. The thought of death was terrible. I *could* not die, and go into God's presence thus. And yet, to give up my faith would only be to add another sin, and one for which there is no pardon."

"Oh, no!" Jack threw in. "That is too hard a saying."

"Surely," Thomassian said, "if you go away from the light, you must remain in darkness; if you go away from the Christ, you must remain unforgiven. That was what I came to in those days of anguish. I thought I *could* not let Christ go. I know now it was Christ that would not let me go. My brothers, all that time that I lay silent there, not joining in your prayers, your hymns, your counsel-taking, my whole heart has been one desperate cry to Him, 'Oh, Christ, forgive me! Even now, at this eleventh hour, take my spoiled life, and receive me into Thy kingdom!'"

There was a silence.

"Has He heard?" Kaspar asked at last.

Thomassian bowed his head low, and veiled his face with both hands. "I stand among you confounded and ashamed," he said.

"Because God was silent to you?" said the youth Dikran, in a pitying voice.

"Because God was *not* silent to me," Thomassian answered, removing his hands, and turning on them a face full of awe-struck gladness, "because to me—the last and least of you—to me, who had forgotten Him and sinned against Him so, even to me He has revealed Himself."

" How ? " asked two or three, drawing near him with looks of reverence.

" How, I cannot tell you. That may no man tell, or understand, myself least of all. ' I called upon Thy name, oh Lord, out of the low dungeon. Thou drewedst near in the day that I called upon Thee ; Thou saidst, Fear not.' After all, though no man may understand it, yet it is a very simple thing. I, the worst among you, have taken God at His word, and claimed His promise of forgiveness for the Lord Christ's sake. I had so much to be forgiven, there was no other way. And He has forgiven. He has done more ; He has given peace, such peace as I could never dream of. I am *glad* to die for Him now. I have no fear of man—not from the fear, but from the love of Him. Not because if I forsake Him He will forsake me, but because I know He never will forsake me, neither in life nor in death, nor in the life beyond."

There was silence when he ended. At last the oldest man amongst them stretched out his hand to him and said, " Baron Thomassian, you have taught us a lesson."

" You are better than the rest of us," another said impulsively.

" Better ? No ; worse, a thousand times. Not worthy to stand amongst you as one of Christ's martyrs.   But since He has this joy to give to me, the last and least, think what gifts He must have for *you*, His true and faithful servants!"

"Certainly He will not forsake us in the hour of death," Kaspar said.   "Baron Thomassian, I take this answer of God to your prayer as a token of good for us all."

"My mind is made up," said a quiet, elderly man, who had not spoken hitherto.   "Let them do their worst.   I stand by the Lord Christ; and I trust the Lord Christ to stand by me."

Then Dikran, the youngest of them all, spoke up too.   "I think it is scarce so hard for me as for the rest of you.   For I am an orphan, and my only brother was killed in the fighting two months ago.   All through, it was not death, it was agony I feared.   But now, I know Christ will help me through that."

"And He will care for those we leave after us," another said in a low voice.

"Yon Effendi, *you* have not spoken yet," said Kaspar.

John Grayson started, as if from a dream. "There is only one thing to say," he answered firmly, "I stand by Christ."

"So likewise said they all." In prayer, and mutual counsel-taking and encouragement the long night wore on.   Amongst them all, there was only one who slept. Worn out with his long and bitter conflict, and at rest in the ineffable peace in which it ended, Thomassian fell into a dreamless sleep, with his head pillowed on John Grayson's knee. Jack himself feared to sleep, on account of the waking that must follow. He prayed, thought of his past life, of his father and all his friends ; above all, of Shushan. Often his mind would wander for a little amongst unconsidered, half-forgotten trifles, but it always turned back again to the things which made its home.

The morning light stole at last through their narrow grated window. Thomassian stirred, and sat up. He looked round upon them all with a smile ; but his eyes grew grave and full of thought as they rested on the face of John Grayson, who, just then, was absorbed in what he thought might be his last prayer for Shushan.

"Yon Effendi," he said, "are you ready to die ? "

Jack looked at him steadily for a moment, then bowed his head in silence.

"But you would rather live, if it were the will of God ? Is it not so ? "

"I do not seem to care *now*, not greatly," Jack said. "It seems easy to die *now*, with you all. But "— his voice sank low—"but there is Shushan."

"And if I can, in some slight measure, atone for

the harm I have done you, you will be glad, for her sake? But do not build on it—it is but a chance. Rather, since there is no chance really, it will be as God wills."

"Hush!" some one suddenly exclaimed.

The key was grating in the door. In another minute it was thrown open, and the jailor entered. He did not waste words. "Come," he said.

The band of confessors rose to their feet, and looked one another in the face.

"One moment, I pray of you," Kaspar said in Turkish to the jailor. Then in Armenian, "Let us bid each other farewell."

"Not so," Thomassian answered, smiling. "It is not worth while, we shall meet so soon with joy in the presence of our Lord."

As they went forth, John Grayson thought once more of the last words he had heard his father say, "The dark river turns to light."

It was the morning of Christmas Day, 1895.

Chapter XVII

A GREAT CRIME

" The clinging children at their mother's knee
  Slain ; and the sire and kindred one by one
  Flayed or hewn piecemeal ; and things nameless done
  Not to be told : while imperturbably
  The nations gaze, where Rhine unto the sea,
  Where Seine and Danube, Thames and Tiber run,
  And where great armies glitter in the sun,
  And great kings rule, and man is boasted free ! "
        —" *The Purple East,*" *by William Watson.*

MEANWHILE, over the crowd of anxious hearts the Mission House sheltered, the sad days went slowly by. Shushan's fears for her husband could find no relief, and they were intensified by apprehensions about her father, of whose state disquieting rumours reached her. Her entreaties prevailed on Miss Celandine to send a couple of her zaptiehs to ascertain the truth. The zaptiehs brought back word that Boghos Meneshian was dying, and prayed that his daughter might be allowed to come to him, in order that he might give her his blessing. Miss Celandine sent her accordingly, in the charge of a trusted Armenian servant, and with a guard of four zaptiehs. This was early on the morning of Saturday, the 28th of December.

She was left by her escort at the house of the Selferians, where her father had been staying, and was still supposed to be. The zaptiehs promised to return for her in an hour. The Armenian said he would be close at hand; he was going to see a friend in a neighbouring house.

"Oh, my dear Oriort Shushan," said Hanum Selferian, hurrying to meet her, "in the name of God, what brings you here?"

Shushan looked at her in amazement. "I have come to see my father," she said. "How is he?"

"Well enough, I suppose. He went to the Vartonians, cured, with your mother, Mariam Hanum, about a week ago."

"Thank God!" said Shushan, drawing a long breath of relief. "They told me he was dying."

"*Who* told you such a story, my dear? He is dying as much as we all are, no more."

Shushan felt surprised and uneasy, though she did not yet know, perhaps she was destined never to know, that she was the victim of a plot. "It may be," she said, a shadow crossing her face, "that they told me wrong about the house. I ought to go to my cousins."

"What? through the streets? You cannot—

not even if my husband went with you. Besides, if the zaptiehs should come back, and find you gone? No, Oriort Shushan; this is what we will do—my husband will go to the Vartonians, and, if possible, bring your father to see you here."

"I like not to take him from his work, Josephine Hanum."

"What signifies his work? There is little enough to do here now, and more than time enough to do it in."

Hagop Selferian, who was at work, stood up from his board, wiped his brow, and threw on his jacket. "Yes, I will go," he said.

Shushan remained with the women and children, and shared the pillav that formed their early meal, afterwards helping Josephine Hanum in her pleasant household tasks.

But, as time passed on, she grew increasingly anxious. "I wonder the zaptiehs do not come back," she said. It was now between ten and eleven in the forenoon.

Josephine Hanum went to the window that looked out upon the street. "There is no sign of them," she said. "But here comes my husband."

He crossed the court and came in, looking pale and frightened. "My father?" Shushan breathed, only one cause of distress occurring to her mind.

"He is well.   But there is an army on the slope of the hill.   In the town, the minarets are black with men, and the roofs of the Turkish houses with women and children.   Jesus help us, what is going to happen?"

"I would give my right hand to have you back in the Mission House, Oriort Shushan," said Josephine Hanum, looking at her guest in a sort of despair.   "Hagop, dost think thou couldst bring her there?"

Selferian shook his head.   "It is not *my* life I think of," he said.   "Wife, I met in the street that Syrian who used to work with me, Mar Tomas. He had a black turban on, and was hurrying to his church.   He is a Roman Catholic, you know.   It seems there is an order that all Christians who are not Armenians are to go to their churches, and stay there all the day.   And they are not to let a single Armenian cross the threshold, at their peril."

Here Krikor, the eldest boy, came running in. He had been up on the roof.   "Father, mother, come up," he said.   "Come and look.   Such a wonderful sight you never saw!"

"A sight that bodes no good to us.   What is it, boy?"

"Oh, so much, father!   I could never tell you. Come and look."

All four mounted the stairs that led to the flat

roof. The younger children followed them, eager to see.

The slope of the hill above them glittered with Turkish and Kourdish soldiers, the gay dresses of the latter lending animation to the scene, and the swords and bayonets of all flashing in the sunlight. Every point at which the Armenian Quarter could be entered bristled with soldiers drawn up in battle array, while behind them surged and swayed a savage mob, men and boys, and even young children amongst them. All were armed, many with guns, the rest with daggers, knives or bludgeons. In the Turkish Quarter the housetops swarmed with women; and above the confused noises of the great city, above the hoarse murmurs of the soldiers and the mob, was heard their peculiar throat-sound, called the Zilghit: "Tchk, Tchk, Tchk, Tchk," which means, "Go, men, and fight for Mahomet. We are with you."

White to the lips, Selferian turned to the women. "This means death," he said.

As he spoke, a glittering crescent shone out on the fort above the hill, catching the sunshine on its glassy disc. At the same moment, a green flag appeared on a minaret at the opposite side of the Armenian Quarter. From another minaret a Muezzin sang out over the town the Moslem call to prayer,—

"La ilaha ill Allah, Mohammed resoul Oullah."

Then came the shrill blast of a trumpet, and Shushan, who was looking at the troop of soldiers nearest them, saw them deliberately open their ranks, and allow the mob behind to pass with them into the Armenian Quarter.

All the family rushed down again from the roof. Selferian barred the door, and his wife drew the shutters across the windows. The children began to cry with terror; though, except Krikor, they scarcely knew what they feared. Selferian's aged mother was there also, weeping and wringing her hands.

Soon the sound of shots, the noise of hurrying feet outside, and the shrieks and cries that filled the air, told that the killing had begun.

How is it with men and women, and little children, in these dire extremities? Thank God that we do not know,—that we are never likely to know!

"Oh God, do not let them kill us!" children sobbed in their terror. "Oh God only let them kill us at once!" men and women prayed, their lips white with a deadlier fear.

It was deliberate, organized, wholesale murder. First came the soldiers—Zaptiehs, Redifs, Hamidiehs,—then the Turks of all classes, especially the lowest, well furnished with guns and knives. Their little boys ran before them as scouts to unearth their prey. " Here, father, here's another Giaour," they would cry, espying some unhappy Armenian in an unused well or behind a door. Then the Moslem, perhaps, would put his knife or his dagger into the hands of his little son, and hold fast the Giaour till the child had dealt the death blow, winning thus, for all his future life, the honourable title of *Ghazi*. After the murderers came the plunderers, a miscellaneous rabble, who took away what they could, and destroyed the rest. They would heap the provisions together in the midst of the living-rooms, mix them with wood and coal and other combustibles, then pour kerosene on the mass, and set it on fire.

The Vartonians, the Meneshians, and a few others, were gathered in the courtyard of the large Vartonian house. The two families were all there, except Baron Vartonian, who was still in Aleppo, old Hohannes Meneshian, who happened to be visiting some friends, Kevork, who had gone in search of him—and Shushan. They clung together, the women and children weeping, the men for the most part silent in their terror. Above the sorrowful crowd rose a voice that said, " Let us die praying." Immediately all knelt down, and their hearts went up to heaven in that last prayer, which was *not* the cry of their despair, but the voice of a hope that, even then, could pierce beyond the grave.

Thus the murderers found them, when they burst in the gate. Even in their madness the sight arrested them—for one moment. So the Giaours prayed! Then let them pray to Allah, and acknowledge His prophet, and they might be allowed to live. Cries were heard, " Say ' La ilaha ill Allah.' No, you need not speak. Only lift up one finger—we will take it for ' Yes.' "

Brave answers rang through that place of death. " I will not lift up one finger." " I will not become a Moslem." " I believe in God the Father Almighty, Maker of heaven and earth, and in Jesus Christ——" Ere the confessor could complete the sentence, he stood in the presence of Him in whom he believed.

Boghos and Mariam Meneshian died in each other's arms, slain almost by one stroke. Nor did Mariam greatly care to live, for she had seen Hagop, her youngest born, slain first, clinging in vain to his father. Gabriel remained ; and something in the boy's look and attitude seemed to touch the Moslems. They made a special effort to save him. " Only acknowledge the prophet ; only lift up your finger," they said.

The boy stood erect before them, and looked at them fearlessly, face to face. " Am I better than my father, whom you have killed? Am I better than my mother, whom you have killed, and who taught me the way of holiness? No; I will *not* become a Moslem, and deny my Lord and Saviour Christ." And he tore his clothing open to receive the death blow. They were angry enough now, far too angry to kill him at once. Blows and cuts rained on him, till at last he fell at their feet, bleeding from one and twenty cruel wounds.

It is enough. We can look no farther. "They had heaped high the piles of dead" reads well in song and story ; and it is not too horrible to think of, when brave men fall in equal fight. But those slain, lying in their blood, with their faces raised to the wintry sky,—it is best for us not to see them. Not now. It may be we shall see them one day, when those who were slain for the Word of God and the Testimony of Jesus Christ have part in the First Resurrection.

In the large courtyard of another house near by, there were many men together. The women of their families were gathered, for the most part, in a great room looking out on the court. The men were trying to conceal themselves, some in a disused well, some on the roof, some within the house. One man, however, made no effort to escape. He stood calmly at the top of the flight of steps which led to the room where the women were. It was Stepanian, the pastor. By his advice, the gate of the courtyard was left open, that the Turks might see they had no thought of resistance.

The howling, shouting mob came near, and nearer still. They poured in through the open gate; and, being men of the town, at once they recognised the Pastor. "Here is Stepanian; let us make an end of him," was the cry.

"Fellow townsmen, you ought to spare us," he said, "for we have done you no wrong. We are unarmed and defenceless, our little ones depend upon us, and will be left to starve."

"Down with him!" cried the mob. "It is the will of Allah!" "Preach us a sermon first," added a mocking voice in the crowd.

"Do not touch me here; I will come out to you," said the Pastor calmly, and began to descend the steps.

But ere he reached the last, a shot went through his breast, and he fell. No sound was heard, and no blood was seen.

Elmas, standing at the window, had witnessed all. Strong in her great love, that frail girl went out amongst the murderous crowd, knelt down beside her father, and put her hand upon his forehead.

He opened his eyes, looked up at her, and smiled.

"Father," she prayed, "father, speak to me! Only once; only one word more!"

That word was given to him, and to her. "Fear not, the Lord is with you. I have no fear, for I am going to my dear Saviour."

Again he closed his eyes, and in another moment, without struggle or suffering, he saw Him face to face.

She "sat there in her grief, and all the world was dark—blank" (the words are her own). She seemed to have no consciousness of the terrors all around her. The first sound that touched her broken heart was the wailing of her little brother, a babe of three, who wanted "father." He had followed her down the steps. She took him in her arms, and held him up that he might see. His sobs grew still at once. "Father is asleep," he said. So He giveth His beloved sleep.

Could they but have all lain down by his side and slept! But their rest was yet to be won. More Moslems crowded into the yard, slaying all the men they could discover. Then they seized the women, the girls, and the children, tore off their clothing and their jewels, and drove them in their midst as a flock of frightened sheep and lambs are driven to the slaughter.

The last thing Elmas ever saw of that beloved form on the ground, was that some Moslem had brought a mule, upon which he seemed about to place it.

She was dragged from her dead father to the unutterable horror that followed. Oh, that endless walk, with bare, bleeding feet, through the blood-stained streets! Oh, the clinging hands, the terrified faces, the piteous sobs and wailing of the children! Thus the crowd of women and girls, almost without clothing, were paraded through the town between files of brutal soldiers—and every now and then, some of them seized and dragged away, in spite of their shrieks and cries. Vartan pushed his way to his sister, and whispered, " Do not fear, Elmas. I have the knife my father gave me hid in my zeboun. It will do to kill you."

That was all Elmas remembered afterwards with any clearness—that, and the clinging of her baby brother's arms about her neck.

At last they came to streets that had no stain of blood, over which no storm of agony had passed. They were in the Moslem Quarter. On and on they went, until they reached the destined place—one of the great mosques of the city, the Kusseljohme Mosque. The iron gates swung open to receive them, and closed again on that mass of helpless misery, shutting out all mercy, save the mercy of God.

Chapter XVIII

EVIL TIDINGS

> "It is not in the shipwreck or the strife
>   We feel benumbed, and wish to be no more;
>   But in the after-silence on the shore,
> When all is lost, except a little life."
>
> *—Byron.*

JOHN GRAYSON sat alone in his prison room. It was a very different prison from the two he had known before—a room of convenient size, fairly clean, with a divan along one side under the grated windows, a mattrass to sleep on, a rug, and several cushions. A comfortable meal — almost untouched however — lay near him on a stool Moreover, he had been permitted a bath, and allowed to purchase clothing, anything he wished. He had chosen to have an ordinary jacket and zeboun, and a crimson fez.

He sat on the divan in an attitude of deepest dejection, his face covered with his hands. Continually the scenes of four days ago were passing through his mind, and before his eyes.

He saw them all again ; he thought he should

see them always, till his life's end. The band of confessors were led out of prison; they stood before the Turkish Kadi. A single question was put to them : Would they become Moslems, or would they not? Thomassian, in every way the foremost man amongst them, answered for the rest: "We follow Christ; we are ready to die for Him." With one voice all signified their assent.

The executioner began with Dikran, the youngest. John Grayson veiled his face, but not till he had seen too much. Could he ever cease to see it? A deadly faintness swept over him, from which he was roused by Thomassian's brave words of comfort and encouragement, spoken to the victim : "Dear boy, be strong; it will soon be over! you will soon be with Christ." Then came the poor lad's own murmured words of confession and of prayer, ending at last with one strong, joyful "Praise to Jesus Christ!"

John Grayson looked up again. It was time; he was wanted now. His turn had come. At that supreme moment, faintness and sickness, and every trace of fear, passed from him. One thought possessed him wholly—*God was there*.

Yet, he could have shaken like a leaf at Thomassian's sudden call to the executioners, "Hold, I have something to say!" Martyrdom could be borne, but the moments of suspense that followed seemed the most unbearable he had ever lived through. He heard Thomassian protesting, "It will be on your peril if you touch this man. He is an Englishman; I know it. He can prove it if you give him time; which, for your own sakes, you ought to do."

Jack might have said this himself till he was hoarse, and the Turks in their present state of frantic excitement would not have listened to, still less have believed, him. It was different when a man of mark, a "notable" like Thomassian, averred it solemnly and at the point of death. Their orders not to kill foreigners were precise and stringent, and hitherto had been wonderfully well obeyed. There might be trouble if they were transgressed. Jack was informed that it was not the will of Allah he should die that day; and, to his sorrow, was led away, without seeing what became of his fellow captives.

He was transferred that evening to a comfortable room, and told he might order any conveniences he desired and could afford. He begged to be told the fate of his friends, and was informed that several of them had died "with unparalleled obstinacy"; the rest were reserved for another time.

"Was Baron Thomassian amongst the dead?"

"No," said his informant, with an evil smile. He was much the worst, and should stay till the last.

As for himself, what were they going to do with him?

Let the Effendi give himself no uneasiness on that score. His Highness the Pasha had been informed of the circumstances, and would take care of him. Probably he would send him, under a safe escort, out of the country. But nothing could be done until order was restored, and the town quiet. "Let the Effendi be patient, and put his trust in Allah. The Effendi knew things had to go—*Jevash—Jevash.*"

Jack was very miserable. How could he take pleasure in the comfort of his surroundings, when he knew what his friends had suffered and were suffering? Only for Shushan, he would not have cared at all to live. He asked if Miss Celandine was gone yet.—No, not yet. There was some delay about her passport, his informant thought. But no doubt all would be ready soon, and she would go. Would the Effendi like to take exercise in the prison court? If so, he was quite at liberty. No one wished the Effendi to be incommoded; it was entirely for his own safety he was placed under restraint, until the rebellion amongst the Armenians should be put down.

Two long, slow days, Thursday and Friday, wore on. On Saturday morning he was aware of some unusual excitement in the court of the prison. The prisoners there, who were all Moslems, hung together in groups, talking eagerly, and more than once a word reached his ears about "killing the Giaours." Moreover, he heard shouts and cries from outside, increasing gradually until the uproar became terrible. The extraordinary sound of the "Zilghit" reached his ears, but he could not understand it.

The guards who brought him his food shared in the general excitement and exhilaration. After returning their "salaams," he said casually, "It is a fine day," to which one of them answered, "It will be a bad one for the Giaours"; and the other added, "It will be wet in the Armenian Quarter,— but the rain will be red."

He entreated them to tell him more ; but they would not. Evidently they had their orders. Did the Effendi want anything more? No. Then peace be with him.

They departed, securing the door behind them, as he thought, with unusual care.

Peace was *not* with him. Instead of it, a fierce tumult raged in his heart. On that strange Christmas morning, when he thought himself about to die for the Name of Christ, there had been a calm over him which was wonderful, "mysterious even to himself." The conflict was not his, but God's. God had called him to it, and would bring him through. He was very near him, and would be with him, even to the end.

But the chariots and horses of fire, which the prophet of old saw about him, did not stay. When the hostile hosts departed, the resplendent vision vanished too. Martyrdom at a distance, martyr strength seems at a distance also; sometimes it even seems unimaginable. Patient, powerless waiting is often harder than heroic doing or suffering. Perhaps the hardest thing of all is to be brave and strong *for others*, when they have the peril and the suffering, and we the bitter comfort of compulsory safety.

But the longest day must end at last. Evening brought to John Grayson the doubtful pleasure of a companion in misfortune. This was a handsome young Turk, who seemed much amazed, and still more annoyed, at the predicament in which he found himself. Paying little heed to his companion, he walked up and down, cursing certain persons, apparently his own kinsfolk, in the name of Allah and the Prophet, with true Eastern volubility.

In one of these perambulations he accidentally kicked over Jack's tray of food, and stopped to ask his pardon very politely, of course in Turkish. "I think," he said, looking at him attentively, "I think you are a Christian?"

"Yes," said Jack. "In fact, I am an Englishman; though I have been in this country for some years."

"Oh! Then I suppose you are the Mr. Grayson I have heard my friends speak of?"

Jack bowed, then added immediately, "I am unutterably anxious about dear friends of mine who are in the Armenian Quarter. Can you tell me how it has been with them to-day?"

The young man turned his face away and did not speak.

"For God's 'sake, say *something*," Jack cried; "say *anything*, only tell me all!"

"It was the will of Allah," said the Turk.

"Have you killed them?" Jack gasped out.

"Yes, a great many. Chiefly men and boys. But I did not see the end. That uncle of mine—Allah give him his deserts!—had me taken up and clapped in here."

"What? For killing our people?"

The Turk stared. "That were merit," he said. "No; what I did was to resist a soldier, a Hamidieh. In fact, I struck him. But what would you have? A man must have friends." He sat down, and taking out his tobacco pouch began leisurely to make cigarettes, apparently with the purpose of restoring his calmness, imperilled by the thought of his wrongs. "The matter was this," he resumed: "I passed by a long row of Giaours, fine young men, lying on the ground with their throats cut. In one of them I recognised a friend, and looking closer, saw he was not dead, for the work had been very ill done. Just then this Hamidieh came by, and wanted to finish him. Like a fool instead of giving him a couple of medjids, I gave him the butt end of my gun. I took my friend to my house, and thought no more of it; but, by the beard of the Prophet, what did that rascal do but go and complain to his captain, who knows my uncle, and must needs go to him? Then my uncle informs against me, and has me put in here, to keep me out of mischief, as he says. Curse his mother, and his grandmother, and his wife and his daughters, and all his relations, male and female, unto the fourth and fifth generations!"

Apparently, the Turk forgot that amongst these relations he was cursing himself.

Jack listened in horror. "Only tell me who are slain," he said. "How many?"

"How should I tell that? I could only see what I saw with my own eyes."

"Do you know aught of the Meneshians?—or of the Vartonians?"

"Yes; I fear that all of both families are killed, with perhaps one exception," he added slowly, stroking his beard. "I saw the mob burst into their courtyard."

"Oh God, it is horrible!" Jack said with a groan, and covering his face. After a while he spoke again. "The Stepanians?"

"Of them I know more. With my own hand I shot the Pastor."

Jack sprang on him, his eyes blazing, his hand at his throat. He had nearly been a martyr, but he was an Englishman, and a very human Englishman too.

"Let be," the Turk gasped, cool though choking. "A moment, if you please."

Jack loosened his hold. "You can strangle me, of course, if such be the will of Allah," the Turk continued. "But you may as well hear me first. For, if you get free, you can tell your people the words of Osman."

"*Osman!* Are you then the Turk I have heard the Pastor speak of so kindly? That you should sit there before me, and tell me you have killed him!—*killed him!* How could you?"

"Can't you understand?" the Turk returned with an expressive look. "There were his daughter and all his children looking on. His last thought was for them. 'Do not touch me *here*,' he said.

Was I going to let them see him cut to pieces? At least, I could save him—and them—from *that*. He had not a moment's pain."

Jack stretched out his hand to him impulsively, but drew it back again. "I cannot touch your hand," he said; "but I can say from my heart, God bless you!"

The Turk went on: "I could save the dead from insult, and I did. I wanted to save the children too, and might have managed it, but for my fool of an uncle."

"Is Miss Celandine—are the people with her in the Mission House all safe?" Jack enquired. He had little doubt of it, yet he could not help the beating of his heart.

"Oh, yes; they have a special guard of zaptiehs. Only an hour before the killing began the Pasha sent to Miss Celandine, to say that now she might leave the city; everything was safe and quiet. But she has not gone. Perhaps she thought she could help the other Giaours by staying. That however she cannot do. Even her own people are not safe beyond the Mission premises. A young lady in her charge had gone into the town with a guard of zaptiehs, to see her dying father at the house of one Selferian. She never returned. Mehmed Ibrahim, who has long wanted her for his harem, took care of that. In fact, I believe the summons to her father was a pretence, and the whole thing a plot of his. I saw them leading her away—*Allah*!"

With a cry of agony John Grayson fell senseless on the floor.

The Turk sat gazing at him, without stirring hand or foot. To use any means for his restoration was the last thing he would have thought of. Allah had stricken him, and Allah would restore his senses—when He pleased. A logical Western might ask, why he did not reason thus in the case of his Armenian friend, or of the Pastor and his family; but a man's heart may be sometimes better than his logic.

Jack at last recovered consciousness and struggled to his feet.

Osman did not know the story of his marriage, but he drew his own conclusions from what he saw "How hard you Franks take things!" he remarked by way of consolation. "Now there are in the world a great many girls, any of whom a man can marry, if he pleases."

"Don't," Jack said hoarsely.

"My dear fellow," the Turk went on kindly, "I am very sorry for you. See the advantage it would be to you now, if you were only a true Believer. We lose a wife, and we are very sorry—oh, yes! But then, you see, we have so many, it is only just like losing a cow. There are others quite as good."

Jack, fortunately, did not hear a word of this. He stood as one bewildered ; then made a sudden rush to the door, which he pulled and shook with all his might.

"What are you doing?" asked the Turk serenely.

"I must get out!" cried Jack. "I must get out and save her."

"You cannot save her. She could not be more out of your reach if she were up there in yonder sky. Take my advice, and be quiet. It is the will of Allah."

"I must get out!" Jack shouted, once more shaking at the door.

"You had much better stay where you are. If you were out, you would do something rash, and bring trouble on yourself."

"On *myself*?" Jack repeated in a voice of despair. "For myself, there is no trouble any more."

"I could tell you how you might get out, if it were really good for you," Osman mused; "but the truth is, I do not want more of you to be killed. I am sick of all this misery and bloodshed."

"Osman Effendi, I think you have a kind and pitying heart ; therefore I pray you to help me now, and so may God help you if you ever come to a bitter hour like this. I must get out, or I shall go mad."

" I wish I could do you a better service—but if you will try it, wait until the morning light. Then the killing will begin again. They are going to let the Moslem prisoners out that they may take part in it, and thus deserve their pardon from God and the Sultan. Tell the jailor, when he comes to us, that you want to walk in the courtyard. That he will allow. Once there, you may be able to slip out unnoticed among the rest. Take my scarlet fez instead of your crimson one, and see, here is a green kerchief to tie over it."

" The fez I take, and thank you ; the kerchief —no."

" As you please. I wish you well, Grayson Effendi, and if I can help you in anything, I will. Should you want a refuge, come to my mother's house. You know where it is. In fact, that is the best thing you could do," he added. " My people will make it known you are an Englishman, and then no one will even wish to hurt you. There will be a mark set upon you, as it were."

" Ay," cried Jack wildly—" the mark of Cain— ' lest any finding him should kill him.' To save my own miserable life, and see all I love perish around me ! Is *that* what it means, the mark of

Cain? He saved himself, others he did not save."

" I do not understand you."

" How should you ? I don't understand myself. I think I am going mad. Only I know it was not *that* mark which was put upon her forehead and mine; it was the cross of Christ, and that means just the contrary—' He saved others, Himself He did not save.' "

The young Turk took the cigarette from his lips and stared at him, wondering. Into his hard, black eyes there came for an instant a perplexed, wistful look, like that of a dumb creature who longs and tries to understand, but cannot pass the limitations of his being. At length he said in a softened voice, " When I get out of this cursed place, with the help of Allah and a handful of good medjids, I will try to do what I can to help your people. But now it is the hour of prayer. I will pray, and then try to sleep. Grayson Effendi, you ought to pray too. It may be Allah the Merciful will hear you, though you do not acknowledge His Prophet. He may remember you are a Frank, and make allowance."

For John Grayson there was no prayer that night. His anguish was beyond words; and as for tears, their very fount seemed dried up within him. Even the simplest cry to God for help seemed to freeze upon his lips. Where was the use of it? He had prayed with all his soul, and God had *not* heard.

How that long night passed, how he watched and waited for the morning, none would ever know. The morning light came at last, though it brought no joy with it. He continued however to hold off the anguish of his soul, as it were at arm's length, while he made himself carefully up to look as like a Moslem as possible, though avoiding the green *kafieh* for conscience sake. Assuming a tone of indifference, he made his request of the jailor, who, with his mind running on killing Giaours, muttered a careless assent.

For a good while he lingered about the court, joining one group or another so as to avoid suspicion. At last the prison gate was opened, and, lost amidst a crowd of Moslem criminals, who were rushing out with tumultuous joy to earn at the same time Paradise and pardon by killing Giaours, John Grayson made his way into the street.

Chapter XIX

A GREAT CRIME CONSUMMATED

"God's Spirit sweet,
  Still Thou the heat
Of our passionate hearts when they rave and beat.
  Quiet their swell,
  And gently tell
That His right Hand doeth all things well.

"Tell us that He,
  Who erst with the Three,
Walked (also) with these in their agony;
  And drew them higher
  And rapt them nigher
To Heaven, whose chariot and horses are fire."
                              —*C. F. Alexander*.

DREAD were the watches of that December night, amidst the unutterable agonies of half a city. In the Armenian Quarter the only sleepers were those—thrice happy!—who would never awake again—

"Until the Heavens be no more."

They were very many, like the slain in some great battle that decides a nation's destiny. They lay in heaps, in the open street, in the court-yards, in the houses. Tearless, wild-eyed women, strong in the strength of love, came and sought their own amongst them. Sometimes a wife who found her husband, a mother who embraced her son, wept and wailed and made sore lamentation, but for the most part they were still enough. Sometimes they thanked God that they had found them—*there*.

It went worse with those who sat in their desolate homes, and watched the slow ebbing, often in cruel anguish, of the lives they loved. The number of the wounded and the dying was enormous. For one thing, the murderers were unskilful, for another they were often deliberately—*diabolically*—cruel. Moreover, it was better economy to hack a Giaour to pieces with swords or knives than to shoot him, since every bullet cost two piastres !

It went worse still with the women, the girls, the little children even, who were dragged to the mosques and shut up there, in hunger, cold, and misery, until the murderers of their fathers, their husbands and brothers had leisure to come and take them, and work their will upon them. Oh God of mercy and pity, that these things should be in this world of Thine !

Had He quite forsaken Urfa ? Not always, standing outside the Furnace, can we see therein the Form of One like unto the Son of God. *In the Furnace*, men know better.

That night, in the vast Gregorian Cathedral, a great congregation met. Many, no doubt, came there as to a place of refuge, hoping that even Moslems would respect that sacred spot. But many more came to worship, perhaps for the last time, in the courts of God upon earth. A band of heroic Gregorian priests—men who were ready to be offered, and who knew that the time of their departure was at hand—made of this last service a solemn and sacred feast. They showed forth the Death of their Lord, giving the Bread and the Wine, which He ordained for all time as its hallowed memorials, to the kneeling, awe-struck multitude. Men, and women, and little children, thinking thus upon His Death for them, were strengthened to meet death for Him in faith and patience. On one of the pillars of that church, now in ruins, some hand, now cold in death, has traced the record that eighteen hundred persons partook of that solemn Sacrament. Never again should they eat of that Bread or drink of that Cup—

> "Until the Trump of God be heard,
> Until the ancient graves be stirred,
> And with the great commanding word
> The Lord shall come."

For those still left in the doomed city, that seemed indeed the last Trumpet which sounded in the early dawn of Sunday, the 29th of December. It sent a thrill of horror through every Armenian heart. They knew it was the signal for resuming the massacre, and completing the work of death and ruin left unfinished the previous day.

An orgie of blood and crime, worse than all that had gone before, began then. Many Moslems of the lowest class, who had hitherto been kept in check by the fear that the Christians might defend themselves, now joined the murderers. Moreover, all passions are blunted by indulgence, and require stronger and yet stronger stimulants. The passion of cruelty is no exception. Where it really exists, where men kill and torture—not for rage or hate, or greed, or fear—but for the joy they have in doing it, it is as a demon possessing the soul. It lives, it grows, it thirsts, it craves sacrifices ever greater and more ingenious. It develops a horrible, a Satanic subtlety. It inspires deeds at the mere recital of which humanity shudders. We may not tell, we may not even think of them. Involuntarily we close our eyes, we stop our ears. But ought we not sometimes to remember that our brothers and our sisters have *endured* them all ?

Hanum Selferian was sitting in what had been only yesterday the best room of her comfortable home. Now not a single article of furniture remained unbroken or unspoiled. Curtains were torn down, presses were smashed open, and their contents either taken away, broken into fragments, or strewn about. In the midst of the floor lay all the food in the house—bulghour, rice, meal, coffee, vegetables, bread—tossed together in a confused heap, over which charcoal had been thrown and kerosene poured. But no eyes for this, or for aught else, had the broken-hearted wife. On a bed in the corner lay her husband, dying. He was horribly mutilated ; but the hand of devoted love had bound up the fearful wounds, and done the little that was possible to assuage their anguish. All the long night she had watched beside him, her children clinging round her weeping and praying, the elder ones trying to help her when they could. No joy came in the morning, but a new and terrible fear. What if the Turks should return ? Flight and concealment were out of the question *now*.

The gate of their courtyard was broken the day before ; and now some one pushed open the door of the room where they were. Hanum Selferian started to her feet. A man stood before her, his eyes wild and bloodshot, his face stamped with an expression of unutterable horror. One short hour had passed since John Grayson went forth from the gate of the prison. In that time he had seen things which he never afterwards told to any one, and which he would have given a king's ransom for the power of forgetting. Now, like one walking in a dream—seeing nothing, hearing nothing—he strode up to her and asked, "Where is my wife?"

Hanum Selferian had seen him often, and knew all about him. But how could she recognise, in this broken, horror-stricken man, the bright, fearless English youth? He looked full fifty years of age. Besides, her own sorrow filled her heart, and dulled her senses. "Speak low," she said;—"my husband"—

"I am sorry," Jack answered mechanically. "But where is my wife, Shushan Meneshian?"

"Shushan?" She looked up now, her thoughts diverted for a moment. "You are not the Englishman?"

"Would I were *not!* No one will kill me. There is a mark set upon me, that none may hurt me. It is the mark of Cain.—Where is my wife? I was told she came here."

"Yes; to see her father, Boghos, who was not here at all. It was all a trick," said the poor woman. "Amaan! do not ask me more."

"Don't cry, dear Effendi," broke in the youngest of the little girls, taking his hand caressingly, and touching it with her forehead. "Mother hid me in the storeroom while the Turks were here, but I looked through the crack of the door and saw— I saw dreadful things. They hurt poor father, oh, so terribly! but they did not hurt Oriort Shushan at all—not the very least. They only took her away with them. I am sure they will be very kind to her, she is so dear and beautiful."

"*Hush!*" said the next sister, just a little older.

Krikor, the eldest boy, came running in. "Mother! mother! let us all go to the church. The neighbours—those of them who are *here*— say it is the best thing to do. The Turks will not touch us there."

One loving glance she gave to her dying husband, then she looked at Jack. "Perhaps," she said, "the kind English Effendi would take you children there. And your grandmother— Parooz, where is she?"

"Not one of us will stir a step without you, mother; there is no use in asking us. We live or die all together," the boy said firmly, disregarding the looks and gestures with which his mother tried to stop him.

Then a feeble voice was heard, speaking from the bed. "In God's name, let us all go. I think I could walk—with help."

In John Grayson's broken heart the instinct of helpfulness survived. It was as if he were dead within, and his shell, his outer self, went on mechanically, acting out the impulses impressed, and the habits formed, during his life-time. "I will help you," he said, going over to the wounded man and preparing to raise him from the bed. Almost dying as he was, he was still able to stand, and even to walk a little.

Parooz, the eldest girl, fetched the white-haired grandmother, who had gone apart to weep, and was found in an upper room sleeping for sorrow. The children gathered round them. Jack put his strong arm about the dying man, his wife supported him on the other side, and they all went out together.

The state of the streets was indescribable. People were rushing through them wildly, shrieking, screaming, crying for help ; and the dead and dying lay about under their very feet. Happily, the Cathedral was near at hand ; but, for one of the little party, peace and safety were nearer still. As they came in sight of it, Selferian's strength failed. "Let me rest a moment," he prayed. They put down some of their upper garments, and laid him gently on them ; and there he rested —from all his weariness and all his pain.

There was no time to mourn the dead. The

old grandmother went on first, taking with her the reluctant Krikor. Then Jack said to the new-made widow, " For your children's sake," and pointed to the Cathedral.

The sights of horror they had seen, even in their short walk, quickened their footsteps. They found the churchyard and the buildings around it, the dwellings of the priests and the school-houses, already full of people. Making their way through the throng, they got at last into the Cathedral ; and, after some further delay, went up into the gallery, some people the Selferians knew being there already.

Jack kept with them ; his behaviour outwardly was quite rational, but he had entirely lost control over his thoughts. Once he imagined he was back again in England, wildly imploring the Queen, the Government, the whole nation, to send men and guns and bayonets to Armenia—not to save the people, but to kill them—to kill them mercifully, all at once, and make an end of this agony. Shushan and Shushan's race seemed in his mind to have blended together into one. " 'And in these days,'" he thought, "'shall men seek death, and shall not find it ; and shall desire to die, and death shall flee from them.'"

All this time there were people pouring in, filling the vast spaces of the church till scarce standing room remained. At last the great iron door swung to, and was shut.

Not one moment too soon. The mob was already thundering at it. The yells and howls of the frenzied crowd outside mingled with the cries and groans of the terrified crowd within. At the same time shots came in through the windows, wounding some and killing others.

At last the storm prevailed, the iron door smashed in, and then the work of murder began in earnest. But the very density of the crowd of victims checked its progress. It was hard to cut through that mass of living flesh. One incident Jack saw which stamped itself upon his mind; though at the time he felt neither that nor anything else. Some Turk, mounted on a bench or stone, saw a face in the crowd he knew—that of a young Armenian singer, whose sweet voice was already winning him gold and glory, and who was a special favourite with the Moslems. He and others called to him by name. The youth sprang upon a pedestal, and in a minor key, with a voice of exquisite pathos and melody, began a plaintive Armenian song.

Then a strange thing was seen and heard—there were tears on Moslem faces, and sobs that broke from Moslem breasts. This would not do! Guns were pointed at the too successful singer. " Stop !"

cried the voice of one having authority. "Dear youth, be a Moslem.   We will save you alive, and give you wealth and honour, as much as you will."

"*Never!*" The dauntless word rang through the church, sweeter than melody of harp or lute sweeter than voice of song. It was the young singer's last utterance—the end came then, for him.

The work of death went on, the murderers hewing a way for themselves through the crowded aisles. Meanwhile, in the vast gallery, which ran quite round the building, the terrified multitude, mostly women and children, shrieked and wept and prayed, calling aloud on the name of Jesus. A few men tried to climb out through the windows; but this was impossible, and would have been useless, for the mob were waiting outside with firearms to pick off the fugitives. Jack stood where he was; for his own life he did not care the turning of a straw, and his instinct of protection kept him beside the Selferians. He saw all the work of murder going on in the church below. And now the Moslems had reached the altar. Some of them sprang upon it, while others tore the pictures, smashed the woodwork, and broke open anything they thought might contain treasure.

There was on the reading-desk a large, beautiful, and very ancient Bible, bound and clasped with silver. With a yell of triumph, a Moslem seized it, tore out the leaves, and flung down the desecrated volume. "Now, Prophet Jesus," he shouted, "save Thine own if Thou canst! Show Thyself stronger than Mahomet!"

For one brief moment a wild ecstatic hope sprang up in the heart of John Grayson. He looked up, and half expected the solid roof to open, revealing God's heaven above them, and in it the "sign of the Son of Man." His Christian lips re-echoed the Moslem cry, "Save Thine own! Show Thyself stronger than Mahomet!"

"There was no voice, neither any that answered." The silence of the ages—that strange, mysterious, awful silence—was not broken; it lasted, as it lasts still.

In the over-wrought brain of John Grayson some chord snapped then. "There is no Christ," he said. "He cannot hear us; He is dead long ago. There is no God; He is nothing but a dream—a dream of happy men, who sit at ease in quiet homes."

He did not know that he spoke aloud, but a woman near him heard the words. "How can you say there is no God?" she remonstrated. "It is not true;—but *God has gone mad!*"

The next moment a shot from below struck the

speaker, and she fell into Jack's very arms. The Turks were firing up into the crowd in the gallery.

But that process was by far too slow. Now they were dragging mattrasses, rugs, clothing, light wood work from the adjoining priests' houses, and piling them on and amongst the heaps of dead and dying in the church. Then they carried in great vessels of kerosene, and poured their contents over the whole mass. To this horrible sacrifice they set fire in several places. The flames arose ; the crowd in the gallery saw the awful fate prepared for them, and one wild, wailing shriek of terror drowned every other noise.

Turks, meanwhile, were rushing up the gallery stairs, seizing the younger women and girls, and carrying them out. A Turk forced his way between Jack and Hanum Selferian, "Do you know me?" he asked her. "I killed your husband yesterday because I want to marry you. Come with me, and I will save you and your children."

He seized her zeboun, but with an effort she freed herself from his grasp. Jack helping her, and the children keeping close to her, they pushed on to the front of the gallery, and looked down. A sea of fire was beneath them ; its hot breath scorched their faces. The Turk was following them. Then the Armenian mother lifted her youngest child, a boy of eight, in her arms, and looked at the three little girls clinging to her side. "Children," she said, "will you go with that man and be Moslems, or will you die for Christ with me?"

"Mother, we will die with you," said the little voices, speaking all at once.

She could do for them one thing yet. They should not suffer. In another moment they should be with Christ. Twenty feet down, right into the heart of the hottest fire, she flung her youngest child. Then followed the little girls; and then, just as the Turk's hand touched her shoulder, her own rest was won.

That was the last thing Jack saw in the burning church.

Oh, Christ, who that day didst keep silence in Thy Heaven, help us to remember that other day, when around Thy Cross the mocking voices sounded, "If Thou be the Christ, save Thyself,"—and Thou wert silent too. Help us to hold fast by that faith in Thee that lies between us and madness. Make us understand that these Thy people are indeed "members incorporate in Thy mystical Body." Not *with* them alone through sympathy, but *in* them through vital organic union Thou sufferest still. In them Thou art "in Thine agony until the end of the world"; until the last member is complete, the last sheaf of the great Harvest gathered in. Thou lovest them too much for the mockery of Thy foes, or even for the passionate prayer of Thy friends, to move Thee to come down from the Cross until the work of the Cross is finished, and the earnest expectation of Thy suffering creatures changed into the joy unspeakable of the manifestation of the sons of God.

Chapter XX

BY ABRAHAM'S POOL, AND ELSEWHERE

"But thou hadst gone—gone from the dreary land,
Gone from the storms let loose on every hill;
Lured by the sweet persuasion of a Hand,
Which leads thee somewhere in the distance still."
—Bayard Taylor.

A GROUP of Moslems were loitering idly beside the beautiful Pool of Abraham, watching the sacred fish and feeding them with crumbs and corn. They were talking over the events of the last few days. Some of them—who would not have hurt one of those little fishes for any consideration—were boasting how many Christian dogs they had killed, or detailing yet more horrible deeds of devotion and of prowess. "But now," observed one of them, "we are not to kill any more. The '*Paydoss*' has gone forth."

"Truth to say," another answered, "there are but few left to kill. And those are mostly old women and little children."

"It were well," a third remarked, "to take some order about the burying, and that quickly, or we shall have a pestilence among us, and true Believers have no charm against that any more than Christians.   Allah, who comes here? "

A weird, ghastly figure strode in amongst them, coming down to the very margin of the pool. His clothing was scorched and torn, his hair grey—almost white—and his hollow cheeks and wasted face gave the more awful expressiveness to large eyes full of horror.   He looked down into the bright, pure waters of the Pool.   " Much water there," he said ; " but it will not put out the fire. There is nothing will put that out, for ever and for ever."

One tried to lay hands on him, another drew a dagger.   But his pale lips only curled with a scornful smile.   " You cannot kill me," he said ; " I am an Englishman.   There is a mark set upon me that no man may hurt me.   It means, ' He saved himself : others he did not save.' "

" Put that up," said one of the Turks to his comrade with the dagger.   " Do you not see the man is mad ? "

Moslems think it wrong to kill a madman ; they even honour him, as one inspired by Allah.   Nor does their law allow them to receive a madman as a convert to Islam.

" Englishman ? " another queried.   " Nonsense about Englishmen !   There are no Englishmen here."

"That, no doubt, is part of his madness. He is a Giaour, whom it is the will of Allah to save alive."

A young man, dressed *à la Frank*, joined the group. "Whom have you got here?" he asked.

"Some Giaour, driven mad by the loss of his friends," answered one of the others.

The Giaour turned, and looked the new comer steadily in the face.

The Turk looked at him, with a perplexed, bewildered air.

"Osman Effendi, how many Giaours have *you* killed?" the Christian asked.

"*One*," Osman answered. "But he was a prince amongst them. It was enough. Madman, I seem to know your eyes. Who are you?" He gave him another long, scrutinizing look. Then he said with a start, "Can it be? Is it possible? Are you Grayson Effendi? How have you come here? I sought for you ; and heard you had gone to the church. Then I gave you up for lost."

"I *am* lost," Jack said.

"Nay, friend, you are saved, thanks to Allah the Compassionate. But how, in His Name, did you get out?"

"I have not the least idea," Jack said. "The last thing I saw was those children, falling down into the fire. The first thing I remember after that, I was walking among dead bodies in the churchyard. There were plenty of Turks about, but they did not kill me. No one will kill me."

" I fear you are right enough," said Osman aside to the others. "It is a pity." Then to Jack, "Come home with me, Grayson Effendi. I will take care of you, and give you meat and drink. Then you shall lie down and sleep——"

" No ; I shall never sleep again. I dare not. I should see the burning church, and the woman who threw her children into the fire."

" Poor fellow! He is certainly mad," said another Turk.

Jack turned and faced him. " I am not mad," he said. " I remember all my past life. I am an Englishman. My name is John Grayson. You have taken my wife away."

" *That* at least is madness," some one observed.

" Not altogether," whispered Osman. " There was a betrothal, or something, to a beautiful Armenian girl. Franks take these things hard." Then aloud, " But come with me, Grayson Effendi, you will be quite safe."

Jack yielded so far as to walk away with him from the group. But when they had gone a little distance he stopped, and said, very quietly, " Osman Effendi, I thank you. But I cannot enter the house of a Turk. I must go back to the ruined dwellings of my friends. I would say 'God bless you!' if, in the face of what I have seen, I could still believe in God. I cannot. Farewell."

He took the nearest turning which led to the Armenian Quarter, and soon found himself in the midst of horrors which the effects of no siege, no battle known to history, could have equalled. The dead—and the dying too, who lay undistinguished amongst them—were being dragged to the great trenches outside the town, which the Moslems had dug to receive them. There were many houses, like that of the Vartonians, in which no human creature, not even the babe in arms, was left alive.

On and on he wandered, from one horror to another. What he saw, in its details, is best left untold. He was *not* mad; the consciousness of the past was coming back upon him, every moment more clearly and fully. As the human heart will ever do, in the most overpowering, most universal agony, he still reverted to his own. "Shushan! Shushan!" was his cry, amidst the reeking ruins of the devastated city. Always, everywhere, it is not the "all" we care for, but the "one." We are made so.

He bore his burden alone, in the blank unbelief of utter despair. "Cold, strong, passionless, like a dead man's clasp," there closed about his heart the horror of " the everlasting No," choking it to death. No hope, no love, no God, no Christ.

How long he wandered in that ghastly scene of death he could not tell. Some desultory plundering was still going on ; parties of Turks, chiefly of the lowest class, sometimes met him, but no one thought of killing him. The killing was over, and even if it had been otherwise, his supposed madness would have secured his safety. Sometimes he saw an Armenian in the distance, gliding ghost-like in the shadow of a wall ; but if he hailed the phantom, it would vanish instantly into some hiding-place near at hand. He barely noticed the change of day into night or of night into day again. As the claims of his physical nature asserted themselves he took food, almost without thinking ; plenty of it lay about, uncared for, in the desolated homes. The one thing he did not dare to do was to sleep. He feared the dreams that would be sure to come—he feared still more the awakening.

After what seemed to himself a long time, he thought he heard a faint cry from the interior of a house in the courtyard of which he was standing. He went in, and was guided by the sound to a store closet, where food had been laid up. There, on the ground, her head upon a sack of bulghour, lay a woman quite dead, beside her a little baby, probably dying also.

Better let it die so, reason would have said, and perhaps kindness too. Nature is stronger than either. Jack stooped down, took up in his arms the little wailing babe, and tried to soothe its cries. Evidently it was starving. What should he do? He could not give it rice or bulghour, and hard, dry bread, even dipped in fruit syrup, would not be more suitable. How could he feed a baby?   Then all at once he thought of the Mission House. Miss Celandine would know what to do. He had often thought of her before; but either he supposed her out of reach, as for some time past she had almost been, or else unconsciously he shrank from going where he used to find Shushan. Moreover, for aught he knew, she might by this time have left the place. He thought Osman told him she had got her passport at last.

However, he soon found himself treading the familiar way by which he had gone so often to visit Shushan. How clearly he saw her now, in all her winning loveliness, her sweet eyes full of joy, coming to meet him with her little hand stretched out, English fashion, and on her lips the one word, "*Shack!*" He had not seen her so clearly since Osman's tale turned his heart to stone.

As he went he held the little babe close to his breast to keep it warm, and half feared it would die by the way. He found the great gate of the Mission House, and saw forms, like shadows, creeping in and out—wretched objects, most of them with bandaged limbs or heads. The spacious court-yard seemed turned into a hospital ; men, women and little children sat or stood about, waiting to be treated. He asked some one where he might find ·Miss Celandine, and was directed to the Church.

What a transformation that· beautiful church had undergone since he saw it last ! If the yard was the hospital for out-patients, the church was the ward where those lay who could not be removed. It was crammed from end to end with men and boys—the wounded and the dying. Their mats were placed on the floor, so close together that it was hard to move among them.

Still, the first thought of relief and softness came to Jack as he stood there and looked around him. There at least love reigned, not hate. Once more he was amongst beings who were human, and who pitied and helped one another.

He did not see Miss Celandine there, but an Armenian woman, with a sweet, serene face, came towards him and enquired what he wanted, He showed her the babe. "Can you save it ?" he asked.

"We will try," she answered, taking it gently from him. "Poor little one! I fear it is too late. Does it belong to you? Is it perhaps your little grandchild?" she asked, looking up at him.

It occurred to Jack that the question was a strange one; but—was anything strange now? He answered, "No; I found it just now, beside its dead mother. I know not who they are."

"Where is Miss Celandine, Anna Hanum?" asked a servant, coming up. "There is a boy here in great distress, who wants to speak with her."

"She will be here just now," said the woman who was speaking to Jack. "Where is the boy?"

He came running in after the messenger, pale and crying, as one in sore trouble. He seemed to know Anna Hanum, and began to pour out to her his tale of sorrow. Its burden was, "I have denied my Lord. I have denied the Lord Jesus Christ! Will He ever forgive me?"

"How was it, my poor child?" the woman asked pityingly.

"They killed my father and my mother," he said. "Then they held a knife to my throat, and asked me to be a Moslem and save my life. In my terror I said—I know not what. But it must have been 'yes,' for they spared me, took me to a Turkish house, and gave me food. They kept me shut up until now, when I ran away and came here. Will Christ ever forgive me? Oh, do you think He will ever forgive me?"

Ere she could answer, there came a faint weak voice from one of the sufferers lying at their feet. "Christ will forgive you. Only, you have lost a grand opportunity."

Something in the voice sent a thrill of strange, sweet memories through the heart of John Grayson. He turned towards the spot from whence it came. "Who said that?" he asked. A man, horribly mutilated, pointed out to him a boy who was lying beside him, with a light rug thrown over him. Threading his way with difficulty through the mats on which the patients lay, Jack came to his side and knelt down. He saw a young face, white, wasted and drawn with pain, yet full of a strange, unutterable peace. And he knew it was the face he loved best in the house of Meneshian— after the *one* through whom his heart had got its death blow. "*Gabriel!*" he said.

"Who is it?" asked the boy. "Is it—no, it is not, it cannot be! And yet you have the eyes of Yon Effendi."

"You used to call me that in the old days. Oh, Gabriel! I thought they had killed you all."

"Yes, *all*," Gabriel said; and into his eyes there came, instead of tears, a light from beyond the sun, beyond the stars. "We have all come home now, except me. I am just a little late for the first gathering-up there, but I forget my pain in thinking of their happy meeting all together, and of the joy they have in seeing the Face of Christ. Besides, He is here with me too; and I think He will let me go to them soon."

Then a wave of bitter pain surged over the soul of John Grayson. He supposed Gabriel did not count as any longer one of them her who, in the earthly home, had been the dearest of them all. Could he think the heavenly home would be complete without her? "*What* you must have suffered, Yon Effendi!" Gabriel went on, looking at his changed face and grey hair. "But I never thought to see you again! We all made sure the Turks had taken and killed you."

"Would they had!" Jack said. "Gabriel, how did *you* escape when all the rest were killed?"

"When they killed us all, and our cousins the Vartonians too, they cut and wounded me, and left me for dead. I suppose I was a long time unconscious. When I came to myself, I was lying among the bodies, almost under them. I pushed my way out a little, that I might see. I did not want to live; but I knew how they would drag the dead—and the dying too—out of the town, and fling them into the ditches beneath the wall. I was afraid of *that*. So I lay very still until night came and all was quiet. Then I managed somehow to get myself free. I crept along slowly, I know not how ; I think I fainted often by the way, but at last I came here, to the place in all the world most like to heaven. And here they will let me stay until I go to heaven itself." The boy's voice was beginning to fail through weakness.

"Don't try to speak any more," Jack said.

"Oh, but I *want* to tell you—Can you give me a drink ?"

Jack saw a pitcher of water cooled with snow, and a cup beside it, not far off. He poured out some and brought it.

"Will you lift my head a little and put it to my lips ?" Gabriel said. "My hands are cut in pieces. Thank you. That is good. I *want* to tell you how God brought home the three who were away from us that day."

"The *three* ?"

"You did not know that our dear grandfather had gone, the night before, to visit his old friends the Nazarians ? And he found them so frightened, with only women there in the house, that he stayed. But in the morning, when we knew what was coming, Kevork went to seek for him, that we might die all together. Neither of them ever came back to us. Only yesterday did we hear

about Kevork. One of the sheiks made his followers bring him all the strong, fine-looking young
men he could find. About a hundred were
brought to him. He had them held down hand
and foot by his followers, while he cut their throats
with his own hand, reciting all the time verses
from the Koran. Kevork was among them."

"And our dear Father Hohannes?"

"He was at the Nazarians, as I said. He
thought that perhaps the Turks, having killed the
men, might be satisfied and go away. So he bade
the women conceal themselves, and sat calmly at
the door reading his Bible. When they saw him
there, they said, 'You are an old man with white
hair; we will spare you, if you will only acknowledge the Prophet. You need not speak; just lift
up one finger.' 'I will not lift up one finger,' said
he. Then they dragged him out into the street
to kill him, and—and—Yon Effendi, I can tell
you no more. Spare me!" He turned his white
face away with a look of agony.

"Dear boy! dear child! tell me no more if it
hurts you so," Jack whispered soothingly. "However dreadful it may have been, it is over now."

"It was not so *very* dreadful," Gabriel said, after
a pause. "It was soon over. But oh, Yon
Effendi, there is *more!* I said *three* were absent
from us." His dark, wistful eyes, so full of pain,

gazed piteously into the wondering face bent over him.

A distant suspicion of who the third might mean dawned for the first time on John Grayson. 'You said three were brought home to Heaven—Hohannes, Kevork, and——"

"*Shushan.*"

In unutterable anguish John Grayson turned his face away. "*No*," he murmured hoarsely, "Shushan is not in Heaven but—*in Hell.*"

Gabriel half raised himself in his intense excitement. "Then you don't know——"

"It is *you* who don't know," Jack interrupted bitterly. "There is no such blessedness as death for her—or for me."

"Oh, but you don't know," Gabriel said again. "Yon Effendi, listen—you *must* listen to me. I have comfort for you."

"What comfort possible for me?"

"The comfort of God; our Shushan is with Him."

Jack turned, and looked again in the face of Gabriel. His own was set and drawn in its anguish of suspense. His lips moved, but only one word would come—"Speak."

"As they were killing my grandfather, zaptiehs passed by with Shushan guarded in their midst. She saw his white hair,—his face,—and broke through them all to throw her arms around him and plead for his life.   They were taken by surprise, and did not stop her in time.   No one knows how it happened, but, in the confusion, a sword meant for him went right through her heart."

John Grayson sprang to his feet, with a cry that made all the wounded round them turn on their mats and look up in wonder.   He never even heard Gabriel's concluding word : "So, as I said, they are all now with Christ."   But in another moment he was on the ground again beside him, his whole frame shaking with a storm of sobs— hoarse, heavy, uncontrollable,—surging up from the very depths of a strong man's soul.   After the sobs came tears—tears again at last !   No longer were the heavens iron and the earth brass ; all the flood-gates were open now, and there was a very great rain.

He knew nothing until Miss Celandine's firm, gentle hand was laid upon his shoulder.

"My friend," she said, "I know not who you are, nor what your grief may be.   But I cannot let you disturb all the others who are here. Especially, you are doing great harm to my patient beside you."

"Don't you know me, Miss Celandine ? " Jack faltered out, struggling for composure.   "Don't you remember John Grayson ?"

"John Grayson! But he was a youth, and your hair is grey."

"With anguish. But now I remember no more my anguish, for God has had mercy upon me. My Shushan is with Him."

"Yes, we know it, and thank God for her."

Chapter XXI

"GOD SATISFIED AND EARTH UNDONE"

JOHN GRAYSON had been directed by Miss Celandine to go to the parlour where Shushan had bidden him farewell, and to wait for her there. It looked as if it had had many occupants since, and as if some of them were still in possession. Yet for the moment he was alone, a thing unusual in that crowded house. His heart was filled with a sense of unspeakable rest ;—and, after rest, came thankfulness ;—and with thankfulness a fresh burst of weeping, his tears growing ever gentler, ever softer and more full of healing.

In those blessed tears he found again his hope and his God. Christ was no dream, but a living, loving Power, strong to save. He had been with his beloved one, and had delivered her. Once more, in the darkness, his hand touched that right Hand, so strong and so tender, which at once upholds the universe, and supports the failing heart of every tried and tempted "wrestler with the Spirit until the breaking of the day."

So already the cross of Christ, laid upon both their heads, had been taken from Shushan's young brow, and she had received instead of it the crown of life! While he—who loved her, who would love her until his life's end—he had to bear it still. But it *was* the cross of Christ, and not the brand of Cain. Not *that*. Never that again! Never more would he wander aimlessly amidst the dying and the dead,—

> "Beating in upon his weary brain,
>   As though it were the burden of a song"

that hideous travesty of the enemy's splendid, unconscious testimony to his crucified Lord : "He saved himself, others he did not save."

Rather perhaps might he be permitted, in some humble way, to follow Him, and help to save others. Of himself, there seemed little left to save now. The traveller whose purse is empty sings before the thieves; and if he has been just relieved of a crushing, killing burden, his song may even be one of thanksgiving.

He did not know how long he had been waiting in that room, when another person came in and sat down, waiting also. She had with her three pale, frightened-looking little children. Had he judged by her dress alone, he would have thought her an Armenian woman of the very poorest class; but one look in her face made him know her as a lady. It was a very sorrowful face—what Armenian face was not sorrowful then?—but it was also very beautiful, and it bore the unmistakable impress of a refined and cultured mind. He felt sure he had seen her somewhere before; she was associated somehow in his mind with a box of sweetmeats, an odd fancy, for which he could find no reason. But his thoughts soon left her, and returned to their own engrossing theme.

"Thomassian Effendi," said one of the children presently, in a wailing voice, "won't you take me up in your lap? I am tired."

Jack looked round in surprise. Could this be indeed the beautiful, luxurious, cherished wife of Muggurditch Thomassian? He spoke his thoughts aloud.

"Madame," he asked, "do I speak to the wife of Baron Thomassian?"

"To his widow," she answered calmly.

So much Jack knew already, and he wondered if the lady knew any more.

"Have you had certain tidings of his——" He paused for an instant, unwilling to voice the word.

"Of his martyrdom?" the widow said proudly. "Yes; he has gone home to God. The way was long and rough, but the end was peace."

"Then you know how nobly he witnessed for his Lord?"

"We know that he was found faithful."

"I was with him almost to the end," Jack said.

Then he told the story of his imprisonment, and of Thomassian's courage and faithfulness. Every word was as balm poured into the bleeding heart of the new-made widow.

"And now, madame," he said at last, "how is it with you in your loneliness?"

"As I suppose you know, we have been robbed of everything. My husband was known to be a rich man, and our house was one which invited plunder. What does it matter? When a scorpion has stung you, you do not feel the prick of a gnat. All I want is a handful of rice to feed these poor little ones."

"Are they—relatives perhaps?" asked Jack. He knew she had no children.

"No; they are poor orphans I found in the street crying for their mothers. It helps me in my desolation to have them to think and work for. That is why I have come to Miss Celandine.

I think she may give me something to do, I care not what. Anything to keep these from starving, and me—in another way."

"Perhaps you can help her in caring for the wounded."

"I fear I have no skill for it. I am not like Anna Hanum, whom you may have seen, and who is to Miss Celandine as another hand."

Jack remembered, with a pang, that he himself owed Baron Thomassian money, which he had no means of repaying. Other people dropped in gradually, to wait for Miss Celandine, and began to comment upon her long delay.

"Amaan! Something fresh must have happened," they said. Of course they meant some fresh calamity. What else could happen there?

At last food was brought in, great dishes of pillav and of soup, with bread—meat there was none.

"I would Miss Celandine were here," Madame Thomassian said to Jack. "She will not have tasted food since the early morning. Only that God gives her strength, for our sakes, she would have been dead long ago."

Presently there was a stir amongst them all.

"Here she comes," passed from lip to lip.

She came, but not alone. Her arm was around the waist of a tall, slender girl, who but for its support might have fallen to the ground. Another girl, much younger, clung to her side, and two boys followed, the elder carrying in his arms his little brother, a child of three.   Her wasted, sorrow-stricken face was lit up with a glow almost of triumph.

"We have got them *all*!" she said.

Those in the room rose up and crowded round. Some said, " Park Derocha!" others wept aloud for joy, for all knew the Pastor's children.

"Oh, if the Badvellie could only look down and see them all safe here!" some one cried.

" He does not want that," Madame Thomassian answered quietly, "for he knows the end of the Lord."

The children were soon seated on the divan. Every one wanted to kiss their lips, their hands, their feet even.   Their clothing was an odd mixture; Elmas wore a dress of Miss Celandine's, the rest, whatever garments had come first to hand, for the Turks had stripped them of almost everything.

" My zaptiehs have just found them in a mosque, and brought them to me," Miss Celandine explained.   " They are starving."

Indeed the lips of little Ozmo were already quite blue ; he seemed unable even to cry.   Some one ran to get milk for him, and in a short time all were being fed and tended by loving hands.

Then everybody ate, in a primitive, informal way. Jack had his handful of rice and his piece of bread with the rest, and no food he had ever tasted seemed to him more wonderful than this. He was eating with Christians again. There sat Miss Celandine, in her frail womanhood, a tower of strength to them all ; there were the dear Pastor's rescued children, pale and changed indeed from the unfathomed depths of suffering they had passed through, but all there, not one lacking from the little flock. There was the sweet face of Elmas, his Shushan's friend. And Shushan was safe too. God had *not* forgotten to be gracious, nor had He in anger shut up His tender mercies from them. Jack went over to Elmas.

"Dear Oriort Elmas," he said, "do you know me? I am John Grayson. My Shushan loved you well. And you will be glad to know that she is—*safe*; so are all the rest, although Gabriel only is with us still."

But now Miss Celandine was clearing the room, that the Pastor's children might have the rest and quiet they so sorely needed. There was not another spot in the crowded mission buildings that could be given up to them. With those who needed her she would speak in the passage outside.

Jack waited patiently for his turn, and it came

at last. It may have been a relief to the lonely woman to use the tongue of her native land again, for she took time to tell him how the Pastor's children had been saved. "The captain of my zaptiehs saw my anguish during the awful days," she said. "He was moved, and asked me was there anything he could do for me. I said, ' Stop these horrors.' He answered that he could not. ' It is the will of Allah,' he said, as they all say. Then I answered, ' Find those children for me, and bring them here. They are mine ; they belong to the Mission.' And I described them all to him. I believe he sought them diligently ; and now here they are at last, after nights and days of cold and hunger and of agonizing fear. Yet God has kept them. Now, as for you, Mr. Grayson, will you come with me ? I have something to give you."

He followed her to another room filled with people, where washing and cooking were going on. Motioning him to stay at the door, she made her way over beds, mats, babies and cooking utensils, to a press, which she opened, took something out, and came back with it. They went to the court together without speaking, and there, under the leafless branches of a fig-tree, John Grayson got back his father's Bible, the Book of his betrothal. "Shushan said to me one day that if her end of the cross was the first lifted off, I was to give this to you. See, there is a bit of silk put in, to mark the place she was reading when she was sent for to receive her father's blessing."

Jack opened the Book, and these were the words his eyes fell upon : " Speak ye comfortably to Jerusalem, and cry unto her that her warfare is accomplished, that her iniquity is pardoned, for she hath received of the Lord's hand double for all her sins."

He pointed them out to Miss Celandine, who only said, " ' *Of the Lord's hand,*'—it is *that* that makes it possible to live. But, Mr. Grayson, what will you do now ? "

" Anything *you* tell me."

" For the present, you will stay here with us, until the way opens for your safe return home."

" Miss Celandine, *you* did not go home."

" The passport, which I asked for more than two months ago, was only sent to me on Saturday, one hour before the massacre began. Then the Pasha was most anxious to get me away; he advised, he even urged me to go. So I knew that evil was determined against this people ; and, of course, I stayed."

" If you had gone, I suppose that not one of them would now be left alive," Jack said.

" Certainly not one of the three hundred that

were in our premises then," Miss Celandine answered quietly. "Mr. Grayson, it is but poor hospitality I have to offer you. Not a room even, only a place to lie down in somewhere, and day by day a morsel of bread."

"*And* safety, *and* peace," Jack said. "If you permit me, Miss Celandine, I might spread a mat in the church, and give a little help, especially at night, to the wounded who are lying there. Then I could be near Gabriel, the only living thing left to me—of my own."

"So you can. Here you *must* work, or you will die. But here also, if you serve Christ in His brethren, you will find Him. Another thing you can do for us: your strength is sorely needed to bring to us our out-door patients, and to help them back again to their homes, or rather to the desolated ruins that were once their homes."

All this John Grayson did faithfully. In body he was never alone, by day and by night he lived in a crowd—a crowd of suffering men. But in spirit he "sat alone, and kept silence," because he bore "upon him the yoke," or rather, the Cross of Christ. He "put his mouth in the dust, if so there might be hope." And there *was* hope for him, though the light was kindled at no earthly shrine.

It was his greatest comfort to wait upon

Gabriel; but Gabriel did not think it well that time and trouble should be spent on him. "It is waste," he said to Jack; "there are so many wanting your help who have hands to work with; better go to them, for what should *I* do, if I live?"

"God will see to that, brother."

"I know; only, if you drop a handful of piastres in the street, you try to pick up the good ones first."

Elmas Stepanian loved well to steal a few moments from the care of her young brothers, to sit by Gabriel and minister to his wants. His eyes used to brighten wonderfully when he saw her.

"You are so good and sweet," he used to say. Once he added, "And, Oriort Elmas, our Kevork loved you so."

Elmas did not blush or turn her face away; she only said quietly, "My dear father liked your brother well." For indeed—

"Death was so near them, life cooled from its heat."

Contrary to every one's expectation, the little babe John Grayson saved took hold of its life with a will. Two or three times it was very near dying, but it always rallied. In spite of tainted air, imperfect nourishment, and other disadvantages, it gave promise of growing into a bright, healthy child. Anna Hanum, Miss Celandine's helper, who had taken it first from John Grayson's arms, brought it one day to show to him with pride and pleasure. But, as she held it up, he was far more struck with her own face than with that of the babe in her arms. It was full of peace, profound and utter, such peace as one may see in the faces of the happy dead, only this was a living face, glowing with some inner light of love and blessedness. When she was gone, he turned to Madame Thomassian, who chanced to be at hand, waiting for some work.

"It does me good to look at that face of Anna Hanum's," he said. "She comes among these suffering, broken-hearted people like a light in the darkness; ever ready to soothe the sorrows of others, because, alone of all here, she seems to have none of her own."

"None of her own! Oh, Mr. Grayson, how little you know! Have you ever heard her story?"

"I have not."

"Her husband was a long time ill—paralysed. The years went on, and she had a weary life of it, waiting on him night and day, and earning bread for both of them. Nor, they say, did he make her toil light by loving gratitude. She never complained, but the neighbours knew that sickness had soured his temper, and things went not easily with her. But she had one great joy, God's good gift to her."

The childless woman who told the tale repressed a little sigh, as she went on,—

" Her bright, beautiful, gifted boy was the pride of all the neighbourhood. She loved him with more than a mother's love ; and she toiled, and slaved, and almost starved herself to give him the learning she set such store by, and he thirsted for so ardently himself. He was the best pupil in the school here, and then he went on to Aintab and to Marash, where every one had the highest hopes of him. You may guess his mother's pride when he came back with all his honours to see her, before beginning active life. He was just in time to receive his father's blessing, and to close his eyes. But he stayed on a little while with her ; and it was God's will that he should still be here when the storm broke upon us. Mr. Grayson, they killed him slowly, with cruel torture, before his mother's eyes. She stood by, strengthening him to the last, and bidding him hold fast to his faith and his God."

" And she has come through *that* !" Jack said, much moved.

" She has come through *that*, and she has come forth on the other side. God has satisfied her with Himself. Now, her own burden gone, she goes about helping and comforting all the rest, with Heaven in her face, and Heaven in her heart."

"'For I have satisfied the weary soul, and I have replenished every sorrowful soul,'" John Grayson repeated to himself. "Yes, *He can do it.* These are the miracles He works now, instead of dividing seas and scattering hostile hosts."

Meanwhile Madame Thomassian gathered up the needlework she had come to fetch—coarse garments for some of the many who needed them —and Jack could not help remembering the soft, luxurious life, surrounded by every indulgence wealth could procure, which had once been hers. Now she toiled on from day to day, content with the pittance which was all Miss Celandine had to give to the poor women who were thus employed, and contriving out of that pittance to feed the little waifs she had taken from the street.

Even as she turned and went her way, he heard her softly singing to herself that favourite hymn of the persecuted Armenians :—

> "Jesus, I my cross have taken
> All to leave and follow Thee ;
> Destitute, despised, forsaken,
> Thou from hence my all shalt be ;
>
> "Perish every fond ambition,
> All I've sought, or hoped, or known,
> Yet how rich is my condition !
> God and Heaven are still my own."

Chapter XXII

GIVEN BACK FROM THE DEAD

"When we can love and pray over all and through all, the battle's past and the victory's come—glory be to God!"
—"*Uncle Tom's Cabin.*"

ONE day Jack roused himself to go to the desolated house of the Vartonians. Very few of the surviving Armenians dared to be seen walking in their own Quarter ; and, it was said by an eye-witness, no man was ever seen to walk upright there. They crept furtively about with bowed heads, slipping from shadow to shadow, afraid of the face of day and the eyes of their fellow men.

Jack's object in going was to find, if possible, his father's note-book, which he had entrusted to Kevork to give Shushan in case of his own death. It was to him a very precious relic, and he thought it might probably be amongst the things that had escaped the plunderers, as there was nothing in its plain appearance and binding to attract them.

It was agony to enter that blood-stained court,

knowing all that had happened there, and to pass through those desolate rooms, associated in his mind with all the pleasant trifles of domestic life, thinking that every voice which he had heard there, save Gabriel's, was now hushed in death: every foot that trod those floors was dust. Even that dust had no quiet resting-place in the shadow of a Christian church. Those horrible trenches outside the gate, those hotbeds of fever and pestilence, told that, if the living were dumb, a cry that " shivered to the tingling stars " was going up from the desecrated dead.

Jack passed sadly through the rooms he knew, yet did *not* know as they looked now, but failed in any of them to find what he sought. At last he came to a chamber upstairs, where he was startled to see a human figure lying at full length on the floor. If it were a dead man, the death must have been very recent. But when he came near he saw at once that this was not death, but quiet, natural sleep. The man's dress was *à la Frank*, good and new ; and his side face, which was all Jack could see, had the look of life, almost of health.

It had a look besides which made Jack cry aloud in amazement, " Kevork !—my brother ! "

The voice aroused the sleeper. He sat up and looked about him. " Who is it ? " he asked. Then, after a moment's astonished gaze, " If Yon Effendi's father were not dead, I would think he had come to look for his son in this charnel house!"

"Brother, I *am* Yon Effendi. How have you come back to us from the dead?"

"What does it matter? Are they not dead, all of them? You too, they told me you perished in the burning church."

"And they told *us* your throat was cut."

Kevork put his hand to his throat, where a red mark still remained. "The work was done, but not well enough," he said. "Would it had been! Why spare this blood, of which no drop flows any more in the veins of any living man?"

"That is not true, Kevork. Gabriel lives."

"Gabriel? How did he escape? Not—not—do not say he denied the faith!—not *Gabriel.*"

"No; he was heroically faithful. He was left for dead, but he lives still. How he will rejoice to see you again, my brother!"

A deeper shade passed over the face of Kevork, and he stretched out his hand to Jack. "My *brother*," he repeated, pausing on the word. At last he went on in a low voice, "I know all—*the worst*;—your anguish and mine are the same. Our Shushan and Oriort Elmas——"

"Are *saved*—SAVED!" Jack cried, pressing his hand in a mighty grasp, and looking in his sorrowful face, his own radiant with thankfulness. "*My* treasure is safe in heaven, yours still on earth—in the Mission House with Miss Celandine. *All* the Pastor's children have been rescued, and are there, thank God!"

Kevork Meneshian bowed his head, and did what John Grayson himself had done in the hour of his blessed relief from an anguish too great for tears. Jack let him weep for a while, then he said gently, "Come, brother, let me bring you to our friends, who will rejoice over you as over one given back to them from the dead."

On the way Kevork told his story. "That morning," he said, "when we knew what was coming, I went to fetch our grandfather, that we might all die together. There was no more danger, and no less, in the street than at home ; but I was soon caught by the Turks."

"Yes," said Jack ; "that we heard ; and your throat was cut."

"There is the mark. But there were a hundred of us, so the sheikh's hand grew weary ere he finished. I was near the end of the long line, and I only got a hasty gash. I did not even lose consciousness ; but I was afraid to stir, so I lay there in my pain, thinking I should bleed to death. By-and-by some soldiers came along, and looked at the bodies. They saw I was not dead, and were going to finish me, when a Turk interposed, and bade them let me alone. He had hard work to protect me from them, nor did he succeed without striking one of them pretty sharply with the butt end of his gun. Then I saw his face, and recognised that Osman we met once or twice—a friend of the Pastor's."

"Osman! He told me he rescued an Armenian, an acquaintance. I wonder he did not name you."

"Where did you meet him?"

"We were together in the prison."

"I suppose he suspected some spy within hearing. Well, he took me to his house, bound up my wound, and hid me in an inner chamber. There he left me, promising soon to return; but for three days and nights I saw him not again, nor any one. You may guess what I suffered shut up there, thinking of all our friends."

"And you must have been nearly starved."

"No; he left me some food, though I was too miserable to care for it. At last he came, and told me he had been imprisoned for assaulting the soldier who wanted to kill me; his relatives, as he suspected, having contrived the thing to keep him out of harm's way, since he knew they thought him lacking in a proper zeal for Islam. But, on my account, and still more on that of the Badvellie's children, whom he wanted to save, he had been very eager to get out, and managed it at last, with large backsheesh. He told me all the terrible news—of those who were dead, and of those who, less happy, were living still."

After a sad pause he went on. "For myself, I am grateful to him. He supplied all my wants, and kept me concealed there many days. At last, yesterday, he came to me and said, 'I can hide you no longer. People are beginning to suspect something. If they find you, they will kill you, and kill me also for giving you shelter.' I said, 'For myself I care not, for what have I left to live for?' but added that I could not bear he should suffer on my account. So he said the best he could do for me was to give me a Frank dress, arranged as Mussulmans wear it, and money enough to keep me for the present. Which he did, and may God reward him, and number him— if it so may be with any Turk—amongst His redeemed!"

"Amen!" Jack said. He did not like to tell Kevork, what Osman evidently had not told him, that the father of Oriort Elmas had fallen by his hand. There was no need for more, for now they were at the gate of the Mission House. "It is best," Jack said, "that I should bring you first to Miss Celandine; she will know what to do. For we must not tell Gabriel too suddenly; he is ill and weak. You must be prepared, Kevork, to see him greatly changed."

Yet the meeting between the brothers seemed to fan the feeble, flickering spark of Gabriel's life into a flame. It was another tie to earth to feel he had one brother there left him still—" No, *two* brothers," as he said, looking lovingly at Jack.

A little while afterwards, Jack was sent for one day by Miss Celandine. "Franks have come to her from Aintab," said the excited messenger.

Delighted to think that Miss Celandine's long loneliness was over, Jack went to her at once. He found her in earnest converse with a grey-haired American missionary, whom, in introducing Jack to him, she called Dr. Sandeman. Then she said to Jack, "I want you very much, Mr. Grayson. Baron Vartonian is in there," glancing at the door of an inner room. " He came with Dr. Sandeman. He has just heard that of all his large family there remains to him now not one. You know more about them than any one else who is living now, save Gabriel. Will you go in and speak to him, and comfort him if you can ? "

Though his heart fainted within him at the thought of such a sorrow, Jack went into the inner room. There were two persons there. Old Baron Vartonian sat on the divan, his head bowed down upon both his hands, his face hidden. Now and then the sound of low, deep moans—such moans as only come from a strong man's deepest heart—broke the stillness.

Beside him stood a young man with a face incredibly pale and worn and wasted, as if with some great agony, though its look was one of past rather than of present suffering.

> "The look of one that had travailed sore,
>   But whose pangs were ended now."

His hand was laid tenderly, and with a caressing touch, on the old man's shoulder ; for that was all the human sympathy he was able to bear just yet. He motioned Jack to sit on the divan. "You were their friend, you loved them," he said.

"And received from them much kindness," Jack answered in a low voice. After a pause he went on, "She that was dearer to me than my life was as a child in their house. It was they who brought her to the Mission School, where such joy and help were given her."

"Why do I live?" the old man broke out suddenly. "It is wrong! It is horrible! It is against nature! No reaper reaps the green and leaves the ripe. No gardener leaves the dry stick in the ground and uproots the flourishing tree. I am alone—alone—alone! I came back, after all those long months of suffering, thinking, ' now I will rest, now I will end my days in my home with my dear ones ; my son—my firstborn—shall close my eyes, and my children, and my children's children, shall lay me in the grave.' And I find all gone—sons and sons' sons, with the mothers and the children, and the children's children—even the little babe I had never seen. Oh, my God ! Oh, my God ! "

Then letting his hands fall and looking at the two who stood beside him : " But I do not believe it. It is not possible. Surely *one* at least is left alive. Let us go and see."

The pale-faced young man rose also. " It were best for us to bring him to his own house," he said to Jack. " Perhaps, when he sees it, he will be able to weep."

So Jack went, for the second time, to the house of the Vartonians. The old man, burdened with a weight of sorrow nature seemed scarce able to bear, asked them after a while to leave him in the family living-room, which had been the centre of his home. While he sat there, alone with his memories and his God, the two young men waited together in the court.

Jack found that his companion was a theological student almost ready for the ministry, to which he had been looking forward with eager hope, when one day he was suddenly seized by zaptiehs and flung into a dungeon. Dr. Sandeman—who was to him as a father, young Mardiros Vahanian said with kindling eyes—had done all in his power to help him, or even to find out of what he was accused. At last it was discovered that another person had been arrested, upon whom there was found an English newspaper containing a notice of the massacre at Sassoun. This man, probably under torture, said that he had it from young Vahanian, —and that was all his crime. On one occasion Dr. Sandeman got leave to visit him, though he only saw him in the presence of Turks, and was only allowed to speak to him in Turkish. As they parted, he ventured to whisper in English just this, " Do not give up hope "—and terrible things had the poor lad suffered afterwards on account of this one word. Not then, and not at any time from his own lips, did Jack hear the true story of that prison year, heaped with agonies, with tortures, and with outrages to us happily inconceivable.

During a short time, towards the end, he had shared the cell of Baron Vartonian, who also had been imprisoned on some futile charge. A strong friendship had grown up between the young man and the old, thus thrown together ; and now, in the old man's utter loneliness and desolation, Vahanian wished to take the place of a son, and to cherish and comfort him.

Jack could not help doubting, when he looked at him, that he would be long left in the world to comfort any one. But not liking to express his doubt, he asked him how it was that in the end he got out of prison.

"I do not very well know," the young man answered. "Dr. Sandeman never ceased to work for me; and I think that, somehow, he got the British Consul interested in my case, and that he interceded for me, as I know he did for Baron Vartonian, against whom indeed there was no charge that the Turks themselves believed in. It was one of those false accusations that any man can get a Turk to bring against a Christian for a couple of medjids, and the hiring of two false witnesses to back him up; and Christians being disqualified from bearing witness in a court of law, the accused of course has no chance of proving his innocence. However, thanks, I suppose, to the Consul, Baron Vartonian was released, and so was I."

Jack asked him if he thought he was recovering his health.

"Oh yes, I grow stronger every day. If you had seen me when I first came out of prison, you would wonder at the change." So he said; but Jack wondered, instead, what he could possibly have looked like then.

" No doubt," he said, "while you were in prison, you often wished to die."

"I did—*sometimes*," he answered, his eyes kindling—"not that I might be away from my pain, but that I might be with my Saviour. But for the most part, I felt Him so near me there, that I thought death itself could scarcely bring us any closer."

Jack's look softened. "In spite of all your suffering, I call you blessed," he said in a low voice. "Still, after all, that was knowing Him by faith. In heaven, it will be sight."

"Which will be different, and *must* be better, though it is hard to see how it can. I thought I knew something before of the mystery of communion with Him, but I felt as if I had never tasted it till then. I did not know there could be such peace, such joy."

"Has it stayed with you since you came out?"

"No, and yes. When a child is hurt, the mother takes it in her arms and fondles it; when it is well, she lets it run by her side. But she does not love it the less."

"Perhaps it seems strange to you now to come back to life? Perhaps you would rather not?"

"I would rather die, you think, and go to Him? Not just yet. There are too many in the world that He wants me to help."

"Like these poor people here who have suffered so much?"

"Yes; but there are those more worthy of our pity than even they."

"*More* worthy? Truly on God's earth it seems to me that there are none. But I know what you mean," Jack added in a lower voice. "You are thinking of those, in harems or elsewhere, — for whom we only dare to ask one thing—*death*."

Vahanian's face grew sad. It was some moments before he spoke again. At last he said, "There are those still more pitiable. No man has compassion—no man cares for the soul of—the Turk."

Jack started, as if he had been shot. "How *could* we?" he asked.

"Yet you say every day, 'Forgive us our trespasses, as we forgive them that trespass against us.'"

"I never thought of it in that way. And I tell you, if I ever get back to England, I will *not* forgive the Turk! I will *not* keep silence about his evil deeds, about the things I have seen and heard of here!"

"Nor should you. To stop them would be to show the very kindness of God even to the Turk himself. But I would it were God's will to stop them, not with His wrath, but with His love."

"How could that be?"

"As he stopped St. Paul's. Do you not believe Christ died for the Turk as well as for the Christian?"

" He died for all," Jack said reverently. "And I know He commands us to forgive. But this thing is not possible—to man. And yet, it is strange, but I remember that when I was led out to die, as I thought, by their hands, I felt no anger against them—indeed I scarcely thought of them at all. Yet afterwards, when I knew *all* they had done, I could have torn them limb from limb."

" Friend, you suffered more than I, because you suffered in others. It is only written 'when they revile *you*,—persecute *you*.' But am I to think God has no better thing for you than what He gave me? Because I have had a few drops of this wine of His, of which He drank Himself, am I to doubt that He can fill the cup for you, even to the brim? It is for our sorest needs that He keeps His best cordials. And now I will go back again to my friend, Baron Vartonian. I think he has been long enough alone."

He went, and Jack looked after him, wondering, —and learning a new lesson of what Christ can do for His suffering servants.

This is no fiction, it is literal truth. Except, indeed, that these poor words fail to convey the depth and intensity of the pitying love, which Divine grace had kindled in that young heart for those at whose hands he had suffered such things.

Chapter XXIII

BETROTHAL

MISS CELANDINE'S thoughtful kindness had screened off a little corner in the crowded Church Hospital, where Gabriel's bed was placed, and there was room for Kevork and John Grayson to sit beside him, when they could. Elmas also came often to see him. When Kevork first returned, he had brightened up so wonderfully, that the restored brother hoped they might be left together. But there was no real return of strength, and the temporary excitement ended in a reaction that meant increased weakness and suffering. Yet neither Jack nor Kevork wished to face the truth : they both, especially Kevork, clung to that frail young life—tenaciously, desperately.

One day, not long after the arrival of Dr. Sandeman, Jack drew aside the curtain, and came in. Kevork was there already, and made room for him to sit down.

A smile passed over the sick boy's wasted face, but it was soon succeeded by an anxious, troubled look. "Yon Effendi," he said, "you are grieved to-day. What is it?"

Jack smiled too. "Oh, Gabriel, those fingers of yours!" he said. "There is no escaping them."

It was a saying amongst them that Gabriel, whose hands were useless, had been given "fingers in his heart," instead; for if there was any special sorrow or need, he always knew it by some instinct, and, figuratively speaking, put his finger on the place. For now, on his own account, he had no more grief, no more fear; his heart was all "at leisure from itself" for the griefs of others. He smiled again in answer, and not sadly at all. "My fingers touch a trouble of yours, which yet is not all a trouble," he said. "You have been talking to the American Badvellie."

"Yes, and to Miss Celandine. And they both advise me to go home."

Kevork turned a startled face to him. "But there is no use in thinking of it," he said quickly. "They would not give you a passport, after what you have done."

"That is just what *I* said. There is no blood upon my conscience, but upon my hand there is blood enough. Were I to apply, as things are now, for a passport, my antecedents would be looked into, and I should never be allowed to leave this land alive."

"They would never kill an Englishman," said Gabriel.

"Not openly in broad daylight, but in one way or another, I should disappear."

"So I think," said Kevork eagerly. "You must run no such risks as that, my brother."

"Dr. Sandeman has a different plan," Jack said. "That fine young fellow, Vahanian, wants to stay here to be with Baron Vartonian, and to help among the wounded. What if I took his passport, and went to Aleppo in his place?"

"You would be found out."

"The doctor thinks not. He almost undertakes to put me safely through. I can dye my hair and stain my face a little. Not much will be needed, so well your suns have browned me."

"Then, Yon Effendi, your mind is to leave us," Kevork said sorrowfully, almost bitterly.

"My mind is *not* to leave you," Jack answered. "Only I want to know which thing is right to do." He looked tenderly at Gabriel as he added, " A while ago, I could not have gone. I could not have left you alone, Gabriel—but now you have Kevork. God has given him back to you from the dead."

"God has given Kevork to me," Gabriel said ;

"but what is He going to give Kevork? For, you know, I cannot stay with him!"

"Don't speak that way," Jack said hastily.

Kevork was more visibly overcome. "I cannot go on alone," he said. "I *cannot*. Gabriel,—you must not go."

Gabriel was much worse that night; and early in the morning Jack went for Kevork, whose sleeping place was in another part of the crowded Mission premises.

"Come quickly," he said. "I think he is going from us."

Kevork sprang up from his mat, threw a jacket over his zeboun, and, choking down a sob, followed his friend in silence. The sweet morning air, which had the touch and thrill of the springtime in it, fanned their brows as they crossed over to the church, where Gabriel lay.

"Who is with him?" Kevork asked.

"Anna Hanum."

She was kneeling beside the dying boy, and as they entered looked up with her calm, sweet face.

"He is easier now," she said.

"You will try to be glad for me, will you not?" Gabriel whispered; "you know it is best."

"You will soon be with them all—your father and mother, and my Shushan," Jack answered.

"I shall be—with Christ," Gabriel said.

"For whom you have given your life."

"Who gave His life for me."

But his dark, wistful eyes turned away, even from the beloved Yon Effendi, to rest upon his brother's face.

"There is some one else I want to see," he murmured. "Stoop down, Anna Hanum."

He whispered a name into her ear.

She said, "Yes, dear," and glided softly away.

"It is Miss Celandine he wants," both the young men thought. Jack took the place beside him. He lay still, with closed eyes, resting. Only once he opened them, when a moan from the crowded space outside was heard through the curtain.

"Some one is suffering, Yon Effendi," he said. "Please go and help."

Kevork was left with him alone, his tears falling without restraint.

"*Don't*, Kevork," he whispered ; "there is comfort coming, for you."

Jack returned presently. Miss Celandine, who had *not* been sent for, came in also, and with her —Elmas Stepanian.

At the sight of the beloved teacher, Gabriel tried to raise himself; but it was more than he could do. He looked at her appealingly. "The hand—that has saved us all—to my lips—once more," he prayed.

Instead of giving him her hand, she stooped down and kissed him, lip to lip, and motioned to Elmas to do the same. In *her* face he looked earnestly, while he gathered all his remaining strength to speak.

'Oriort Elmas, Kevork has loved you ever since he was at school in Aintab. All the rest are gone from him; I am going now. It is too hard for him to stay here alone. Will *you* comfort him, Oriort Elmas?"

"If I can," she answered soothingly, as one speaks to the dying.

"But I want to hear the Promise—on the Book —before I go."

She drew back, her face flushing crimson, and looked at Miss Celandine in perplexity.

Kevork drew a step nearer and spoke. "Oriort Elmas, it is quite true. Though I would not have dared to say it *now*, had not he said it for me; for we stand together in the shadow of the grave. But if this dear lady, who is a mother to us all, will allow it, and you will give me your promise, there is nothing man may do."—(his voice quivered and thrilled with suppressed feeling)—"nothing man may do that I will not do for you, and find my joy in it, for I love you more than life."

Elmas Stepanian's character, strong by nature, had been annealed in the furnace of affliction. That furnace had burned away the bonds of those timid conventions that usually held the daughters of her race. In a low but firm voice she answered, "If Miss Celandine approves, I will give it."

Jack was standing beside Miss Celandine. He took out his father's Bible, which he always kept with him, and put it in her hand, with a significant look from her to Kevork. She understood the mute appeal. If she gave the Book to Kevork for the purpose they all knew, it would be her act of sanction to this strange betrothal.

She paused a moment: then she said, "The God of your fathers, and your God, bless you both," and laid the Book in the outstretched hand of Kevork.

Kevork gave it to Elmas. "So I plight my troth to thee, for good days and evil, for health and sickness, for life and death, and for that which is beyond," he said.

"And I also to thee," Elmas answered.

"Now it is all right," Gabriel said, with a look of infinite relief. "I will tell them."

"But you are very tired," Jack interposed, noting a rapid change in his face, and turning to get a cordial he was accustomed to give him.

"Kevork," he whispered, "take Oriort Elmas away. There are too many here."

"*No*," said Miss Celandine ; "I think you had better stay. Mr. Grayson, never mind that cup ; he cannot take it."

There followed a few minutes of struggle and suffering ; a brief conflict of the spirit with the failing flesh. It was soon over. Once more the look of peace settled down on the wasted face, and now it was for ever. Gabriel looked around, and recognised them all. Then, in that action so common to the dying, he slowly raised his right arm, and waved the bandaged, helpless hand. "With His own right hand, and with His holy arm, hath He gotten Himself the victory," he said with his parting breath.

His brother closed his eyes, and the others mingled their tears with his, until at last Miss Celandine said gently,—

" My children, he needs our care no more ; and there are many waiting without who still need it sorely."

" I will go with you and help," Jack answered.

So they went, leaving Kevork and Elmas kneeling together beside their dead.

Chapter XXIV

UNDER THE FLAG OF ENGLAND

"Whose flag has braved a thousand years
The battle and the breeze."
—*T. Campbell.*

"MR. GRAYSON, you are young yet," said the venerable missionary, Dr. Sandeman to the grey-haired, toil-worn man before him.

"Do I *look* young?" John Grayson answered. "No, I am old—old. The last year has done for me the work of other men's three score and ten."

"I know what you have seen and suffered."

"It has not been *all* suffering," Jack said. "I have *lived*. I have tasted the wine of life as well as the poison. I have loved, and been beloved."

"I know," the missionary said again; and he spoke the truth—*he knew*. "But there are many years before you yet. For them all, that love will be a memory."

"It cannot be a memory," Jack interrupted, "for it is myself."

It was far from Dr. Sandeman's thought to

blaspheme that creed of youth which stamps the signet of eternity upon its love, its joy, its suffering, its despair.   Old as he was, his own heart had kept too young for that.   He said, "When you return to your own land, you will find waiting for you interests and pursuits, cares and duties also, which will engross your energies, and fill your life."

"Not my life," Jack answered.   "When I wedded Shushan, I wedded her race."

"If indeed God calls you to help in drying the tears of this 'Niobe of nations,' I can think of no higher calling," Dr. Sandeman answered with emotion.

"But for that hope," said Jack, "do you think I could leave this place?   Do you think I could abandon all these helpless sufferers, and that heroic woman, whose name a thousand times over deserves the 'Saint' before it, if only we Protestants had a calendar of our own, as we ought?"

"But we never could," said the missionary with a smile; "it would need a page for every day. However, Miss Celandine herself is urging your departure."

"And things for the present seem quieter," Jack added.   "*Safe* can nothing be, in this miserable land.   I am glad Vahanian is staying; he will be a great help."

"Yes," said the missionary, "and he is glad to work here for the present, though he still keeps the dream and longing of his heart ; and he thinks God will fulfil it one day, and allow him to make known the gospel of His grace to the Turks. Miss Celandine is beginning to gather in the orphans, a few of them—poor, destitute, starving little ones ! Did you hear that Baron Vartonian has lent his house to give them shelter ? "

"No ; I am glad to think of the home I knew being used for such a purpose. And it will comfort his own desolate heart."

"But now for yourself, Mr. Grayson. Are you ready for the journey ? "

"Yes," returned Jack, with a rather mournful smile. "You see, I have no packing to do."

"Right ; the less you carry the better."

"Here is the one treasure I bring back from Armenia ; and I have learned here, as perhaps I should never have learned elsewhere, what a treasure it is," Jack said, producing his father's Bible. "By right," he added, "it should belong to Oriort Elmas, for it is the book of her betrothal ; but she and Kevork both say I must take it back, on account of its memories. I wish, Doctor, those two could come to England with me."

"With you they cannot come. But I wish they could follow you ; for Kevork seems to have taken an active share in resisting the Turks at the time of the first massacre, and such things are not forgotten."

"The Turks forget nothing—except their promises," said Jack. "But, Dr. Sandeman, there is another matter which causes me some embarrassment. I am absolutely without money. The fact is, I have been living upon these poor people, and latterly upon Miss Celandine."

Dr. Sandeman smiled. "I think she would say your services have been worth more than your morsel of .bread. And as for your journey, we can take you on without expense as far as Aleppo. I am going there."

"You are very good ; and the cost at least I can repay you afterwards, but the kindness—never. But I shall have to get somehow from Aleppo to Alexandretta, and there to take a passage in the first steamer I can find. How can all that be managed ? "

"When you come to Aleppo, you shall tell your story to the English Consul. I have little doubt he will provide for your safe conveyance to Alexandretta, and lend you the passage money."

"How shall I get him to believe me ? I should not mind so much if he were the same I knew when I passed through Aleppo with my father, five years ago. But this is another man."

"He will believe you," the missionary said quietly. He would not speak of his own influence for a double reason—it would be boastful, and it might be dangerous. "Your story bears all the impress of truth, and you can prove it in a hundred ways."

"Then my course is plain," Jack said. "And the first step," he added with a sigh, "is to say farewell to the dear friends here." He rose to go, but turned back to ask, with a little hesitation, "Dr. Sandeman, have you seen the Cathedral?"

"*Yes*," said the missionary with a shudder. "After all this time, it is still the most sickening sight I have ever beheld. Not sight alone; every sense is outraged. Do not go near it, Mr. Grayson."

"And yet," Jack answered, "Christ's martyrs went to Him from thence."

John Grayson's journey, in the company of Dr. Sandeman, proved as little eventful as any journey at that time and in those regions could possibly be. One sad episode indeed there was. As usual, they halted at Biridjik. They found the town a wreck and the houses in ruins, many of them burned, others plundered and defaced. The streets were almost impassable with rubbish, broken glass, fragments of furniture, and other far more ghastly memorials of the massacre.

The remaining inhabitants had been forced to become Moslems to save their lives. They kept themselves shut up in their houses, or moved about—pale, attenuated shadows, with fear and horror stamped upon their countenances. No intercourse was permitted between them and the missionary's party; only a few of them dared to look at the travellers with eyes of piteous appeal and recognition, and to make furtively, with rapid fingers, the sign of the cross. Jack longed to give them Gabriel's word of comfort, "Christ will forgive you; only you have lost a grand opportunity." He said this to Dr. Sandeman, who answered, "*You* have a right to say that; so had he; but it seems to me that no man who has not been tried thus can estimate the trial, the opportunity, or the loss."

"But oh, the sadness of it all!" Jack said. And then these two brave, strong men of Anglo-Saxon race did just what the exiles of Israel did so many ages ago, "By the waters of Babylon they sat down and wept."

Before they quitted Biridjik John Grayson went, in the early morning, to visit his father's grave. He was greatly relieved to find it had been left undisturbed, for he knew that horrible outrages had been committed elsewhere upon the graves of the Christians. Kneeling on the hallowed spot, he thanked God for his father's noble life and bright example, and for sustaining and preserving himself through so many perils.

Then the thought came to him, as it had done so many times before, though never perhaps with such poignancy, that other dust, most precious, had *no* resting-place in sacred ground. Over the grave of Shushan none might ever weep, nor could any find it, until that day when all that are in the graves shall hear the voice of the Son of Man. Bitter it seemed to John Grayson that this solace, the right of the humblest mourner, was denied to him.

But presently he rose from his knees with the thrill of another thought—a new one—in his heart. He looked around him. Not far could his eye reach as he stood there; but the eyes of his mind were ranging over the whole beautiful, sorrow-stricken, desolated land, from Trebizond by the northern sea to the rice plains of Adana in the south. "My Shushan has a royal resting-place," he said. "For me, all Armenia is her grave. And, as holding that sacred dust, I will love, and live for, and cherish that land all my life long, God helping me."

Throughout their whole route the travellers found heart-rending tokens of the ruin of the country and the misery of the people. Some sights they saw are absolutely beyond description, and would haunt them both until the end of their days. "How long, O Lord, how long!" was the word oftenest on Dr. Sandeman's lips.

Still, no man molested *them*, or hindered them in any way. Aintab was first reached, then in due time Aleppo, and John Grayson found himself once more amongst Englishmen. He felt as if he had been dead and buried, and brought to life again in a new world, which he had forgotten, and which had forgotten him. He met however at the Consulate, some who remembered his father, and once he came to know these, his past began to revive within him. At once upon his arrival he wrote to his friends in England ; but he did not think there would be time for an answer to come before he left.

The Consul, although personally a stranger, was very kind, which did him the more credit since he thought at first there was something curious and unusual about this young Englishman with the grey hair and the sad face. Indeed, he asked Dr. Sandeman privately if Mr. Grayson was entirely in his right mind. Once reassured on this point, he gave him most efficient help. He got him a passport, advanced him the necessary money, and sent a competent and faithful dragoman, and a couple of kavasses, with · him to Alexandretta, with orders not to leave him until they saw him safely on board a vessel going to England.

With a sense of almost bewildering strangeness and wonder, Jack stood at last on the deck of the great steamship *Semaphore*, bound for Southampton. He watched the crowds about him—sailors preparing for the start, passengers getting on board with much stir and bustle. They had to come in boats, and there was quite a little fleet of these about the companion ladder, the rowers shouting and screaming as each tried to get his own craft in first. The dragoman had told Jack that all the Franks stopped at this place and went on shore, to visit the spot where a battle was fought long ago by Alexander the Great—the battle of Issus, that was what they called it.

An official stood at the ship's side, examining the passport of every passenger who came on board. Near him stood the captain, a rough, hearty-looking British seaman. There was great hurry, crowding, and confusion, and it was very evident the passport business was not done as thoroughly as it might have been. It was not difficult for a passportless person, or even two or three, to slip in " unbeknownst," as he heard the under-steward, an Irishman, remarking casually to a friend. Jack edged himself out of the crowd, and watched. Presently he saw a boat filled with zaptiehs—well he knew their hateful uniform—put off from the shore, and make for the ships in the bay. It might be the *Semaphore* they meant, it might be one of the others. Jack knew his passport was all in order, still he did not like that sight. He could not realize yet that he was out of Turkey, that he stood on the deck of a British ship, and that the glorious flag of old England was waving above his head.

So he went quietly downstairs to the cabin, resolved to stay there until the good ship *Semaphore* should be actually on her way.

Meanwhile, the Turkish boat came on apace, and before it, faster still, flew another little boat. A young man, standing up in it, sprang on the companion ladder just about to be withdrawn, and ran up, leaving a girl and a boy in the boat.

"Too late, my man," said the captain, waving him back.

"Oh, sir, take us!" the young man cried. He was trembling, and his face white with terror. "Take us!—we will pay!"

"I can't. We have no more room."

"We will pay you well—ten pounds a-piece."

"No; our second cabin is full. And we are off now."

"Fifteen pounds a-piece."

"No, not for twenty pounds."

"For pity's sake! We are Armenians, fleeing for our lives."

"You Armenians are all rogues," said the captain. "No is no," and he turned away.

"For CHRIST'S sake, then!" cried the young man in an agony.

The captain turned back again.

"Why did you not say that before?" he asked, in an altered voice. "I am a Christian man, and I cannot refuse *that* plea."

"Thank God!" the young man almost sobbed. —"*My sister.*"

In less than a minute more the boy and girl were helped up the ladder by willing hands, and all three stood together on the deck—*safe*.

Then the great heart of the ship began to throb, and she was soon steaming merrily out of the harbour.

John Grayson came on deck again, and seeing three Armenians standing by the side of the vessel, drew near, laid his hand on the young man's shoulder, and looked him in the face.

"Kaspar Hohanian!" he exclaimed in surprise. "Is it possible this is you?"

Kaspar seemed scarcely able to speak even yet. But he drew a long breath, tried to compose himself, and returned Jack's look of inquiry.

"Who are you?" he asked.

"Do you not know me?   Do you not remember our awful week together in the prison at Urfa, expecting death.   I am John Grayson."

"With that white hair!   I thought you were dead."

"So I thought of you, and with more reason. I thought all the band who watched and prayed together through those sad days were gone to God—save me."

For a moment both were silent.   Jack did not care, until he knew more, to look again in the face of his friend.   He could not but remember there was only *one* way of escape for any of that devoted group.   Kaspar divined his thought, and said,—

"No; I have not denied the faith.   Though, if the same trial came again, I dare not answer for myself.   Strangely enough, Mr. Grayson, it was through you my life was saved."

"How could that be?"

"I will tell you when I find my sister a place to rest in."

"The young lady is your sister?   May I——"

But the captain came up just then, interrupting them.

"Come along," he said to Kaspar, with rough kindliness, "I will find a place to stow you in. Don't be afraid, young lady."   Then to the boy,

" Run along, my boy, to that ladder you see leading down below."

But the lad stood motionless, his large brown
eyes staring vaguely in the direction of the voice.

" He is blind, sir," Kaspar explained. " During
the massacre he hid in a dry well. He was there
several hours, and came out stone blind from the
terror."

" Poor boy! Well, come along with me, all of
you. The ladies will make room for your sister
among them."

" And, Captain," Jack interposed, " the boy can
have my berth. This young man and I, who are
old friends, can sleep on the deck together."

The captain agreed. He was heard to remark
afterwards that he " thought Armenians were all
savages, but these people seemed just like ourselves."

At night, under the stars, Jack and Kaspar
resumed their conversation. They were very comfortable ; the Irish steward brought them rugs and
cushions, and lingered to say he was glad the
gentlemen and the young lady had got away from
" thim murtherin' brutes of Turks. I was in Constantinople last September," said he, " and, by the
Powers, Oliver Cromwell himself was a thrifle to
thim ! "

" And I wish we had Oliver Cromwell here to

deal with them now!" Jack said, with juster views of history.

The great ship was ploughing easily and steadily through calm waters. All around and all about them reigned sleep and rest. It was a good time to talk of past perils and to enjoy present security.

"How could you say your life was saved through me?" John Grayson asked.

"I must tell you first why I was not killed with the rest," answered Kaspar. "That was horrible. All the rest were dead, even Thomassian; but they took me back again to the prison. There they brought me a paper to sign, setting forth that the men who had been executed were convicted of a plot to attack the mosques and murder the Moslems at their Service on Friday. If I signed, they promised me life, and without the condition of renouncing my faith."

"And you?"

"Was I going to take the crown from the heads of the martyrs of God, and fling it down to the dust to be trampled on like that? They urged me, arguing that these men were all dead, so that nothing I could say or sign could do them any harm, whereas, if I refused, they—the Turks— could do me a great deal of harm, which was certainly true."

"And then?"

"Then I *went down into hell.* Do not ask me more. I was praying every hour for death, when, to my amazement, they came to me, not with fresh tortures, but with meat and drink, good clothes *à la Frank*, and the offer of a bath. I was wondering what strange form of mockery or torture their imaginations had got hold of to which this might be the prelude, when they explained to me that you—the Englishman—had made your escape; and that, just after they discovered this, the Pasha had sent orders for you to be brought to him, and would be very angry, and accuse them of great negligence, when he found you were not forthcoming. They knew I spoke English, and they offered me my pardon if I would personate you for the time; thinking, I suppose, that being rather tall and of fairer complexion than most of us, I would look the part tolerably well. So I was brought into a light, comfortable room, and for three or four days very well treated. It was during that time I heard of the massacre. At last I was set free. How it came about I do not quite understand, and I suppose I never shall. I suspect however that the Pasha never sent for me, having so much else at that time to occupy him, but that, instead, he sent orders that the Englishman was to be quietly set free without noise or stir.   And he may have directed his messenger to see the orders carried out, else might they not have let me go so easily."

"Did you try to go back to your home?"

He bowed his head.   "My two elder brothers and my little sister—all dead.   Artin hid in the well in our yard, to come out blind, as you see, and to wander about in darkness and misery, escaping death by a miracle.   I found him starving, and almost out of his mind."

"And your sister?"

"Markeret?   Through the brave kindness of two aged women, friends of our family, she was saved.   If any had a chance of escape, it was such old women, who were thought neither worth the killing nor the taking.   They spread a rug over her, and actually *sat* upon her all through the killing time.   The Turks came in often, searched the house, and stole or destroyed what they found. But happily they did no worse.   You can imagine the distress of body and the agony of mind of those endless hours.   When things seemed a little safer they took her out, half dead, and concealed her in their store-room.   But I do not think the look of fear will ever leave her face.   It is stamped there."

Jack thought it was on his own as well.

"But to have made your way down here from

Urfa, with those two, was a perfect wonder," he said. "How did you do it?"

"I had help. I told you of the Turk, our acquaintance, who tried to save me before? I went to him with my tale of misery. He promised to help me, and he did. He took into counsel a friend of his, one Osman Effendi, whom you know. Together they managed matters so well for us, that, after many difficulties too long to tell of, we came safely to Alexandretta. There we mingled with the crowds who were making holiday in the plain of Issus, and tried to slip with them on board the steamer. But the zaptiehs were after us."

"Can I help you when we come to England?" Jack asked.

"No doubt, by-and-by; and I shall be thankful. But at first we have friends to go to. A brother of my mother's went long ago to a place they call Man-jester, to trade in Turkish goods. He will receive us, I am sure. The gold coins Markeret has about her will pay our passage, and *may* leave something over, to bring us there."

"Come to me for whatever you want," John Grayson said cordially.

Kaspar thanked him, and dropped into silence. His face showed excessive weariness, and all the more plainly because of the reaction from extreme terror. However, he roused himself to say: "I want to tell you something rather odd. One day Osman shut me up for safety in his private room. I saw a book lying there, and noticing that the characters were Arabic, I took it up to look. It was a Bible in Turkish. He came in and found me reading it. He said to me, with a kind of carelessness that I think hid some real feeling, 'Yes, I got a loan of that. I wanted to find out the secret of your people's patience under all that has come upon them.' I asked if he had found it. He answered me, 'I think I have. It is the spirit of Hesoos, your Prophet. He was like that.'—Oh, I am very tired!"

"Well, then, my friend, lie down here under the stars, and *sleep*. Think that now no enemy's hand can touch you, or your brother, or your sister any more. Sleep safe under the flag of England, the dear old 'Union Jack.'"

Chapter XXV

AT HOME

"How soon a smile of God can change the world !
How we are made for happiness—how work
Grows play, adversity a winning fight !"
—*R. Browning.*

IT was a bright July morning. After a prosperous voyage, the *Semaphore* was steaming in to Southampton Pier. John Grayson stood on the deck, looking at the shores of the native land he had never hoped to see again. Near him, though not speaking, stood Kaspar Hohanian; and a little behind them Artin and Markeret sat together, the sister telling her blind brother all she saw. The three had just been thanking the captain, with full hearts, for many kindnesses shown them during the voyage.

Presently the throbbing pulses of the ocean monster sank into stillness; the double gangway was laid across; and then ensued a frantic rush of eager passengers, laden with every description of the luggage called by courtesy "light." Others stood on guard beside their boxes, or shouted to the porters, who were rushing still more frantically the other way.

Along with the porters came a tall athletic young parson, in a soft felt hat and clerical undress. With alert and cheerful aspect, he went about among the groups, looking earnestly at all the men, in evident search for some one. He bestowed a rapid glance upon Kaspar Hohanian, but turned away disappointed. Then he almost flung himself upon John Grayson—only to draw off again instantly, much disconcerted. "I beg your pardon," he said.

Jack looked him in the face. It was a good face, and a strong face too—frank, manly, trustful and trustworthy. The young man's complexion, naturally fair, was well bronzed by air and exercise, his eyes were English blue, his hair and beard light brown.

"I beg your pardon," he said to Jack, with the slight, respectful inflection of tone a well-bred young man uses to an elder. "I mistook you for a cousin, who is on board, and whom I have come to meet."

"May I ask the name?"

"Mr. John Grayson. We have not met since we were both schoolboys. So, you see, I am a little puzzled."

"Fred—Fred Pangbourne, don't you know me?" cried Jack, springing forward and seizing both his hands.

"I—I could not have believed it!" Fred ejaculated, horror-stricken. "My poor Jack, what have they done with you?"

That question could not be answered in a breath. "How is your father? How is every one?" Jack queried, evading it.

"Ah! so you did not get our letters, and have heard nothing. My father went from us years ago. The rest of us are quite well. Now you are coming with me, right away, to Gladescourt."

"To where?"

"My Curacy. At present indeed I may call it my Rectory; since, in the Rector's absence, I live in his house. Where is your luggage?"

"In this handbag."

Fred looked surprised, but only said, "Let us come at once then."

"Stay, Fred; I must look after my friends." He turned to them and spoke in Armenian. "Kaspar, take care of your sister; I will look after Artin."

Fred wondered who these people could be, but was too courteous not to offer his services. He thought the dark-eyed girl remarkably pretty, but felt provoked at the boy's passivity and want of interest in everything, until Jack whispered, "He is blind."

A few words in the strange tongue were exchanged with them; then Jack enquired, "Do you know about the trains to Manchester, Fred? Can my friends get there to-night?"

"Oh, I dare say. I will find out. But come on shore now. I have ordered breakfast at the Hotel; and," he added, in the warmth of his heart, "will you ask your friends to come with us?"

"You can ask them yourself," said Jack, smiling. "They speak English,—Kaspar very well, the others a little." Then he duly introduced his friend Baron Kaspar Hohanian to his cousin the Rev. Frederick Pangbourne.

A couple of hours later, the three Armenians were safely deposited in the train for London, with full instructions how to change, when they got there, to the Northern Line, while Jack and his cousin were rolling swiftly in a different direction. Conversation, as usual in such cases, was intermittent, incoherent, dealing with trifles near at hand, rather than with the great things each had to tell the other. "Those Armenians astonish me," Fred remarked. "Their manners are perfect. They might take their places, with credit, in any London drawing-room. But then, I suppose, they are of the highest rank in their own country. You called the young man ‘ Baron.’ ”

“ Oh, that is nothing ! Baron only means ‘ Mr.’ But I really think, Fred, from what I heard on board, that the English fancy the Armenians are a kind of savages. They are a highly refined and intellectual race, with a civilization older than our own, and a very copious and interesting literature.”

“ But what a wreck your friend looks ! Has he just come out of a great illness ? ”

“ He has come out of what is infinitely worse —a Turkish prison. But, Fred, there are a thousand things I want to know. My poor uncle ? ”

Frederick Pangbourne told him in many words what may here be compressed into very few. When the tidings of the death of the two Graysons came to their friends at home, Ralph Pangbourne was just dead, and his eldest son was lying dangerously ill in typhoid fever. Young and experienced, and beset by many cares and troubles, the new squire, on his recovery, was quite unable to investigate the story sent to him by the Consul from Aleppo. Indeed, no one thought of doubting it ; though all sincerely regretted these near relatives, left to lie in unknown graves in that distant land—

“ With none to tell ‘ *them* ’ where we sleep.”

Had one of the young Pangbournes been free to do it, he would gladly have made a pilgrimage (attractive, besides, for the adventure's sake) to the far East, to find the resting-place of his uncle and his cousin. But young Ralph, the squire, was overwhelmed with business; Tom, the second son, was in India, doing well in the Civil Service; and Fred was at Cambridge, preparing for the ministry.

There was another question. What of "the Grayson money," as it was called in the family? It was no secret that, before leaving England, John Grayson had made his will, bequeathing the bulk of his fortune, in case of his son's death without issue, to his nephew and namesake, John Frederick Pangbourne. But though they assumed, as a certain fact, the death of both the father and the son, the Pangbournes felt it would be a difficult matter to prove it in a court of law. Fred, the person principally concerned, entreated his brothers to let the matter rest, at least until the termination of the seven years of absence and silence which the law accepts as equivalent to a proof of death. He had, inwardly, an intense repugnance—a repugnance he could not account for to himself—to the thought of touching the Grayson money. In secret, and unknown to all the rest, he cherished a fancy that his cousin might still be found among the living. When Jack's letter arrived from Aleppo, he exulted openly and heartily. A post-card which followed it having informed him that Jack was to sail in the *Semaphore*, he watched daily for news of the vessel; and it was with joy and gladness that he hastened down to Southampton, to be the first to welcome him on English ground. He had set his heart upon carrying him off at once to the sweet Surrey rectory, where his favourite sister, Lucy, kept house for him, and shared the pleasant labours of the rural parish. But he was not prepared to find, instead of a lad five years his junior, a worn, broken, grey-haired man.

He did not tell all, or nearly all, this to Jack, though he told a great many other things. The only reference indeed that he made to money matters was to say, "You must run up to town on Monday, and see Penn & Stamper. They will tell you all about my uncle's affairs. You know, Jack, you are a rich man. Won't they just have a balance worth looking at to hand over to you, after all these years?"

They got out at a little road-side station, and walked over sunny fields to a private door opening into a well-kept pleasure ground. Another minute brought them to the Rectory porch, over which climbed a beautiful wisteria. The whole scene looked the very picture of peace, of "quietness and assurance for ever." Fred stopped a moment, to point out the spire of "our Church," which was seen above the trees at the far side of the house. As they looked at it, a fair girl came running down to the door to welcome her brother. Blue eyes, golden hair, cheeks like a tinted sea-shell, coral lips and the sweetest of smiles, made up for Jack a vision of beauty bewilderingly new and strange. Yet he only felt it touch the surface of his soul.

After dinner, which was early, the two young men walked about together; Fred joyously and proudly showing his cousin the beauties of his home, which, he said, might be his for long enough, as his Rector, for special reasons, was residing abroad.

"It is a home of peace," Jack said. Old, old memories were coming to life every moment. The sound of rooks cawing in the elms, the velvet lawn, the flowers in the trim parterre, the very feel of the air and hue of the sunshine, brought back those old days when his little feet had trotted over just such velvet turf, his little hand clinging to his mother's gown. Ah, if *she* were here! And his father — the father who had been also his hero, brother, comrade, friend. Then a sweet thought brought sudden tears to his eyes. Surely the angels would see to it that Shushan found them out! His heart, bruised and sore with longings for what might have been, grew still. His Lily had a fairer home than this—

"Over the river, where the fields are green."

The cousins went back to the house. Lucy poured out tea for them, and asked Jack, lightly and prettily, many questions about the strange places he had been in, and the strange things he must have seen. He answered evasively, with a reserve of manner which she thought very odd, until she hit upon the explanation that this new cousin—who was so young and looked so old— had been so long amongst wild, barbarous people, that on his return to civilization he was actually feeling—*shy*.

She was not sorry when Fred took him off to his "den," as he called his very comfortable and commodious study. But she said, with a pretty monitorial air, and a careful eye to the sermon for to-morrow—"Remember, Fred, this is Saturday night."

Then the real talk began. Jack, in writing from Aleppo, had simply told of his father's death, and added that he himself had endured *and seen* much suffering, and that he was coming home to tell the rest. Now he poured forth the whole story into willing and sympathizing ears.

Lucy went up to bed that night wondering if

Fred and the new cousin would ever stop talking, and full of anxious thoughts about the neglected sermon. As long as she stayed awake she heard their voices in the room underneath her own ; and at last she dropped asleep, with the sermon still upon her mind.

Waking in the early summer morning, she heard steps in the passage outside her door, and words spoken that seemed to echo her thoughts.

"But your sermon ? "

"I have got it. Good night—or rather, good morning."

Chapter XXVI

A SERMON

" Thy Father hears the mighty cry of anguish,
And gives His answering messages to thee."
                                        —*C. Pennefather.*

BRIEF sleep, if any, had John Grayson that Sunday morning. As so often heretofore he could not sleep for pain or sorrow, now he could not sleep *for rest.* The sense of the peace that was all around him was too new, too wonderful. He soon arose from that fair, snow-white English bed, with its pure linen smelling of lavender, to wander out over the dewy lawn, where the morning sun touched everything with glory. The birds sang aloud to welcome the new day—the long, long day—every hour of it to be filled with their innocent joy. One sweet-voiced blackbird lighted on a rose-bush close to him, and sang. They seemed to have no fear. In this happy land fear did not reign. No doubt it was there—often —for England, after all, was earth and not heaven; but it was a shadow lurking in dark places, not an eclipse blotting out the sun, a presence darkening all the joy of life.

But this blessed peace only stamped deeper upon Jack's heart the memory of that far land of agony and blood. " If I forget thee, O Armenia," he said aloud, " let my right hand forget her cunning. If I do not remember thee, let my tongue cleave to the roof of my mouth, if I prefer not thee above my chief joy. My chief joy," he thought again, " lies buried there, and can never live for me upon this earth. But, by that grave, by that dead love, or rather by that love that can never die, I am pledged not to rest in happy England, but to work for sad Armenia, and to wait for my Sabbath keeping until we keep it all together in the Home above."

He did not know how long it was before his cousin came out to summon him to their early Sunday breakfast. Fred's voice had lost the joyful ring it had at their first meeting. He looked like a strong man who had just heard of a great bereavement. Lucy, waiting to receive him in her fresh Sunday dress, with her look of peace and purity, felt vaguely that there was sadness in the air, but her mind was too full of her Sunday-school class to dwell upon that subject.

" Will you come with us to church ? " Fred asked his cousin.

Jack looked surprised at the question. "Certainly," he said. "Why not?"

"Because I have to say that which will give you pain—yet I cannot forbear. You have given me my sermon for to-day."

Nevertheless John Grayson joined the stream of church-goers: fathers, and mothers, and little children, old men and old women coming in together, while the rosy-cheeked Sunday scholars took their appointed places. He looked round with strangely mingled feelings on the old country church, which was without elaborate ornament, although seemly and reverent in all its appointments, as befitted a house of God. But what most arrested him was the "fair white cloth" on the Holy Table, showing that the Feast of the Lord was spread that day. He had never yet partaken of it in the Church of his fathers; but he no more doubted his right to come than the child doubts his right to sit down at his father's table, because it is spread in a strange room. It was a joy to look forward to that; it was a joy meanwhile to join once more, though with trembling lips, in the dear, familiar prayers—those prayers "that sound like church bells in the ears of the English child."

And now his cousin stood in the pulpit. In his aspect and bearing there was a deep solemnity, which, young though he was, made him look in truth "as one that pleaded with men." He read his text, "*A name which is above every name*," and began with an exposition of the context, lucid, thoughtful, and evincing careful study.

Jack's thoughts wandered from the words to the speaker, and from the speaker to the surroundings, once so familiar, now so unwonted and strange to him. Presently however a word arrested him.

"My brethren," said the preacher, leaning over the pulpit in his earnestness, "have you ever thought what a wonderful thing is the love of Christ?"

"Surely," Jack said to himself, "if we have ever thought of Him at all, we have thought of that."

"I do not mean now," the preacher went on, "the love of Christ for us. I use 'love of Christ' as I use 'love of country,' 'love of friends,' to mean—not theirs for us, but ours for them. And I say, that the love of Humanity for Christ is a mystery only less than the grand, supreme mystery of all—the love of Christ for man. And the greater mystery is proved and illustrated by the less. As we may look, in its reflection, on some object too bright to gaze upon directly,—as we may measure a mountain by its shadow, so may we gain some faint conception of *how* 'He

first loved us,' by the wondering contemplation of
how men in all ages have loved Him.

"Consider.   The Man called Christ Jesus lived,
for three and thirty years, or less, in a little corner
of the world, which He never left.   Of those years
thirty were spent in silence and obscurity; only for
two or three did He flash into sudden fame, soon
cut short by a violent death.   He did not write,
He did not organize, He did not rule; He only
taught, and lived, and loved.   Yet what has His
name been in the world ever since?   What is it in
the world to-day?

"You will say, 'It is the Name of the Founder
of our religion, through Whom we approach the
Divine Majesty, and as such we hold it in reverence.'   It is that; but to thousands upon thousands it is something infinitely more.   It is the
name of their dearest, most beloved, and most
trusted personal Friend—the Name of Him whom
it is their deepest joy in life to serve, their sweetest
hope in death to see.   It was the poet gift of voic-
ing the deepest longings of humanity that inspired
the dying song we know so well,—

> "'I hope to see my Pilot face to face,
>   When I have crossed the bar.'

"There is one test of love, usually accounted
supreme. 'Greater love hath no man than this,

that a man lay down his life for his friends.' Freely and joyfully has Humanity poured forth her best blood for the Name of Christ. Those who have given Him this supreme proof of love we call His martyrs, or His witnesses. Other names, other religions, other causes, have had their martyrs too. Indeed, I think the word is true that all great causes have their martyrs. And I dare to think too that the wine of self-sacrificing love, though we may count it vainly spilled, cannot sink into the earth beyond His power to gather up who takes care of lost things. But I think also—nay, I know—that the martyrs of Christ stand apart from all the rest, in their immense multitude, in the joy and peace they had in suffering and in death, and in the sustaining, animating power of their love to Him for whom they died.

" I have spoken to you, sometimes, of the martyrs of past days. I could not help it; their memory is very dear to me, and the records of their faith and their patience have touched and thrilled my own heart since childhood. But I never dreamed or guessed that even while I spoke, —now, in the end of this nineteenth century, this age of science and enlightenment, this age of pity and compassion, a new legion was marching on, through blood and fire, to join the noble army of martyrs before the throne of God."

Here the grey head, which had rested bowed and motionless in that seat below the pulpit, was raised up suddenly, and the eyes that had witnessed so much agony sent a look into the preacher's face that almost stopped his words. But, after a scarcely perceptible pause, he went on,—

"It has been, to some of us, a pain all the greater because of our utter helplessness to read even the meagre accounts that have come to us of the massacres in Armenia. Now that I have heard from the lips of an eye-witness, who is here present amongst you this day, the details of *one* such massacre, I am bound to tell you solemnly that the pain should have been greater still. The most awful, the most lurid accounts we have had, fall short of the terrible reality. The half has not been told us."

Then he gave briefly, and as calmly as he could, the story of the massacre of Urfa, and of the burning of the cathedral, as John Grayson had told it to him.

" I refrain," he continued, " from recounting horrors which would needlessly wring your hearts. I speak of death ; I do not speak of torture. I tell you a little of what men, our brothers, have suffered. But oh, my brothers,—oh, my sisters, and theirs !—I have no words to tell the worse agonies of your helpless sisters. I dare not tell —I dare not even hint at the things I know—and which they have had to suffer ! Only, thank God on your knees to-night that He has made you Englishwomen !

" And, remember, I have told of Urfa, but Urfa is only one town of many in Armenia. Like things have been done in Sassoun, in Marash, in Diarbekir, in Melatia, in Kharpoot, in Van, in Erzeroum,—in hundreds of towns and villages with strange names we have never heard. The land, which for fertility and for beauty might be a very Garden of Eden, is fast becoming a desolate wilderness.

" But, you will say, all this agony does not make martyrs. For that is needed, not suffering only, but witness-bearing. True ; though in a loose, general fashion all those who lose their lives in any way on account of their religion are often called martyrs. But even the most stringent application of this name of honour must include all those who have, *voluntarily*, so laid down their lives. He who has been offered life on the condition of apostasy, and has refused it, has won his crown, and no man may take it from him. Armenians without number have stood the test, and made the grand refusal. In some places the utterance of the Moslem symbol of faith, in others

the lifting up of one finger, was all that was re-
quired, yet men and women, and children even,
have endured death and torture rather than say
those words or make that sign. Shall I give you
instances? Shall I tell you of the venerable
archbishop of the ancient Armenian Church, who
had first his hands, and then his arms hewn
off, but no agony could separate him from his
Saviour, and at last he died repeating the creed?
Shall I tell you of the student of theology, who
answered his tempters with a steadfast ' No, for
I have come to this hour in God's will and appointment, and I will not change,' and was slowly
cut in pieces? Shall I tell you of the little girl,
the child of twelve, who said to the Moslem,
I believe in Jesus Christ. He is my Saviour. I
love Him. I cannot do as you wish even if
you kill me'? Shall I tell you of another girl
and her young brother who, when the murderers came, embraced one another, their faces
radiant with joy? 'We are going to Christ!'
they said. 'We shall see Him just now.' Time
would fail me indeed to tell of these, and of the
many like them in faith and patience. But one
thing is as true of those who suffer for the Name
of Christ to-day as of those who suffered for that
Name in the first century, or the sixteenth, or any
century between—there walks with them in the
furnace One like unto the Son of God."

There was a pause, and then the preacher resumed. "But there are two questions our hearts are asking, in the face of all this suffering: 'What is Christ doing?' and 'What shall we do?' There is no use in saying that the first of these questions is one which we ought not to ask at all. There are times when there is little use even in telling our passionate, aching human hearts that we ought to be satisfied with what we know and believe of His spiritual presence with His faithful people. Thank God, He did not forbid the questionings of His tried servant the prophet, who flung himself at His feet with the half-despairing cry, 'Righteous art Thou, O Lord, when I plead with Thee: yet let me talk with Thee of Thy judgments.' Nor of that other who pleaded, 'Thou art of purer eyes than to behold evil, and canst not look on iniquity: wherefore lookest Thou upon them that deal treacherously, and holdest Thy tongue when the wicked devoureth the man that is more righteous than he?' Indeed, I dare to think that, if we *do* throw ourselves at His feet—the feet pierced for us—there is no question we may not ask Him there.

"What then *is* Christ doing? He sits in His glory at the right hand of the Father; He sees all this agony, and He *lets it still go on.* He sustains the sufferers; He strengthens and comforts them often ; but—He *lets it still go on.* 'How can He bear it?' our hearts cry out sometimes. I think the answer is, that He *is* bearing it. He suffered for the sufferers ; that is not all—He suffers *with* them. That is yet not all ; He suffers *in* them. They are not His people only, but His members ; of His flesh and of His bones. For reasons inscrutable to us, His agony must go on still in them—still He cries to the oppressor, 'Why persecutest thou Me?' But one day He and they, and we also, shall see the end. Then shall we know the secret of the Lord ; then shall the mystery of God be finished.

"Meanwhile, with the martyrs it is well. 'Therefore are they before the throne of God, and serve Him day and night in His temple, and He that sitteth on the throne shall dwell among them.' But *all* are not yet there, beyond the agony. For the thousands upon thousands of sufferers, bereaved, tortured, famine-stricken, dying slowly in Turkish prisons, or, deepest horror of all, in Turkish harems, what shall we say? Is the burden laid on our hearts for them too heavy to be borne? Remember, Christ bears it *with us*, as, in a deeper sense than we can fathom, Christ bears it *in them.*

"I think this answers our second question, What shall we do?

'It is MY SAVIOUR struggling there in those poor limbs
    I see.'

Friends, if He is there indeed, in His members,
what sacrifice would we not make, what treasure
would we not pour out with joy, to come to His
help?

"But perhaps you say, 'What *can* we do?' I
am not speaking to those who can influence the
councils of our rulers, except by prayer, and by
the formation and expression of that intelligent
opinion which does, in the end, make its power
felt. Therefore it is beside the question to ask
what they should have done, or what they should
do now. We have to find out what *we* should
do, each one of *us*.

"There are thousands of little children, father-
less and motherless because their fathers and
mothers have gone to God, often through the gate
of martyrdom. They are wandering in the streets,
homeless and destitute. They die, or haply they
are taken by Moslems, and taught to hate the
faith their parents died for. *We can rescue these.*

"There are thousands of widows, desolate in
heart and home, each with her tale of anguish,
longing, it may be, to lay down her weary head
and join her loved ones in the grave, yet forced
to struggle on for the daily bread of those still
dependent on her. *We can succour these.*

"There are thousands of ruined men, who have lost home, occupation, health, and whose hearts are well-nigh desperate with the things they have seen and suffered. *We can give back hope to these.*

"One word more, brethren. We have spoken of the power of the name of Christ. That Name, which we teach our little ones to lisp,—that Name, which sanctifies our daily prayers,—that Name, which our beloved ones whispered to us with failing breath as their feet drew near the dark valley, that Name, which yet—oh, strange mystery!—is dearer to our hearts than even theirs,—that Name was on the lips of each one of the slaughtered multitude whose blood is crying to heaven—that Name is still on the lips of the suffering remnant that are left. It is in that Name that they ask our sympathy, our help.

"I have spoken of our dead, our dear dead who lie out yonder, where God's blessed sun is shining on the graves in which we laid them to their rest. We turned sadly away; we thought our hearts were breaking because we *had* to lay them there. What of our brothers and our sisters, to whom it is joy past telling, the only joy they can look for now, to know their beloved ones are dead—and safe? In that land of sorrow they weep not for the dead, neither bemoan them; it is for the living that they weep. Nor are there graves to weep over, even if they fain would do it. The dead—and, remember, they are the Christian dead, —lie unburied in the open fields, or are heaped together in trenches which the earth can scarcely cover.

" Known unto God the Father, known unto Christ the Redeemer, is each atom of this undistinguished dust. Into His keeping He has taken the dead, but to us He leaves the remnants that survive, and that it is possible still to save. Will you take them to your hearts, for His NAME's sake ? "

The preacher gave the usual benediction, descended from the pulpit, and began in due course to read the beautiful prayer " for the whole state of Christ's Church militant here in earth." Very solemnly, in a voice of suppressed emotion, he read on, till he came to the words, " And we most humbly beseech Thee of Thy goodness, O Lord, to comfort and succour all them who in this transitory life are in trouble, sorrow, need, sickness, or any other adversity." Here his voice faltered, but he went resolutely on, " And we also bless Thy holy name for all Thy servants departed this life in Thy faith and fear." Then the rush of feeling overwhelmed him, and he did that fatal thing to do in an assembly charged with emotion —he stopped. A sob broke from one, then from another, and yet another still, until a wave of weeping passed over the whole, like the wind over a field of corn.

It was but a few moments; the reader recovered himself, and continued the Service. Nearly all the congregation remained, and gathered round the Table of their Lord that day; and it may be they felt, as they had never done before, the bond of communion with the scattered and suffering members of the Lord Christ.

That evening John Grayson said to his cousin, "Of course you know that I am going back again,—with only a change of name."

"I am going with you," Frederick Pangbourne answered quietly.

"You!" Jack's heart gave a sudden leap.

"Why not? There are plenty to work here, and I have often thought of the mission field. Is there any field more urgent than this?"

Jack was silent, grave with a solemn joy. What might not they two accomplish, shoulder to shoulder, the fortune he had already resolved to share with Fred all consecrated to the work!

Fred continued, "Do you remember that cry that rose from ten thousand hearts, when Peter the Hermit called upon all Christendom to rescue the sepulchre of Christ from the hands of the Moslem—'Dieu le veut?'—'God wills it'? Is it not as much a war of the Cross to rescue from them, not His empty sepulchre, but even a few of His living, suffering members? We can say— you and I to-day—' God wills it.' "

APPENDIX

THE greatest care has been taken to make the foregoing pages absolutely true to fact. All that has been told of the massacres and their attendant circumstances has been taken either from thoroughly reliable published sources, or from the narratives of trustworthy eye-witnesses. In the story of the massacre of Urfa and the burning of the Cathedral the official report of Vice-Consul Fitzmaurice has been largely used, and only supplemented by the additional details furnished by those on the spot.

In one respect particularly the truth has been strictly adhered to. Every instance given of *martyrdom*, properly so-called, or of courage, faith, patience, or devotion, is entirely authentic. The stories of Stepanian, of Thomassian and his wife, of the Selferians, of Anna Hanum, of Gabriel, of Vahanian, etc., are all perfectly true, the names only have been altered.

This alteration of names was rendered necessary by the circumstances of the case. But every one at all acquainted with the subject will recognise the heroic lady I have ventured to call Miss Celandine. To the very remarkable character of the martyred Pastor Stepanian I have, I fear, done imperfect justice. The particulars of his death and of the fate of his children are given quite accurately, and the ideas attributed to him, and even the illustrations used, are really his own. The only slight departure from known fact has been the assumption that the quick and painless death —for which those who loved him thanked God—(to one such it brought the *first tears* she was able to shed) came from the hand of a friendly Turk.

For one other departure from fact I have to apologise. I have ignored the existence in Biridjik, during the time embraced by the story, of a Protestant Church and pastor; and this although the sufferings of the pastor and his family in the massacre there would form, in themselves, a thrilling narrative. But I desired to show something of the Gregorian Church and the Armenian people, as they existed apart from any contact with foreigners. Throughout I have tried to give the impression, which is the true one, that Gregorians and Protestants have suffered and died, with equal heroism and equal willingness, for the náme of Christ.

There is, nevertheless, one important sense in which facts have *not* been truly represented. It has been absolutely impossible to depict the worst features of these horrible crimes. To tell *all* we know would be simply to defeat the end for which we write—no one would read the pages. It has been necessary to cover tortures—the most ingenious, the most hideous, and the most excruciating—with a veil of general expressions, and outrages yet more terrible than any torture with a still denser veil of reticence. Of what has been endured by unnumbered multitudes of our helpless sisters, it is agony to speak; but is it not also sin and cowardice to keep silence?

An attempt has been made in the foregoing pages so to speak and so to keep silence, and especially so to subordinate the horror of cruelty to the glory of martyrdom, that the most sensitive and tender heart may not be too painfully wrung. There is indeed much excuse for the tender-hearted when they say, as they often do, "We will not read about this subject; we will not think of it. It is too horrible. Our lives are full already of cares and duties, perhaps even of Christian work. We cannot take up this burden in addition to the rest. It would sink us."

That is intelligible and natural, sometimes even right. But it is *not* right that those who thus decline to examine the case should at the same time prejudge it, should dismiss with scorn, or incredulity, or carelessness, the testimony of those who, having gone down into that depth of horror, have come back burdened with an anguish which can only find relief in the effort to help the surviving sufferers. One of two things people surely ought to do—they ought to examine the evidence for themselves ; or, declining this, and possibly with good reason, they ought to accept the conclusions of those who have.

In the earlier stages of the tragedy many were misled, and not inexcusably, by reports that came from official sources in Turkey. Here is a specimen—a message sent by the Sultan to the Ambassador of England, in February, 1896, when the unprovoked slaughter of the unarmed and defenceless thousands of Urfa was still reeking to Heaven:— " That the Armenians have everywhere and always been the aggressors, that the Mussulmans have been attacked in their mosques during their prayers, that they have suffered nameless atrocities from the Armenians, for the latter had Martini guns, dynamite, and bombs, while, to defend themselves, the Mussulmans had only old, superseded fire-arms."

Were Pascal amongst us now, he would scarcely devote to the confusion of the Jesuits his celebrated " *Mentiris Impudentissime !* "

Happily, the truth is known now. It may be briefly summed up in the words of Victor Bérard, an eminent Frenchman well acquainted with the East, who has devoted himself to the careful investigation of the whole question, and published the results in " *La Politique du Sultan.*" " In the opinion and the language of all, Christians and Mussulmans, 'young' and 'old Turks,' Greeks and Bulgarians, natives and strangers, he (the Sultan) remains the promoter and arranger of all that has been done within the last two years.

Every one knows and every one says, 'He has wished it, he has ordained it. The Master has permitted us to kill the Armenians.' This permission has cost the lives of more than *Three Hundred Thousand* human beings. For, besides the public butcheries, the 'fusillades en masse,' and the massacres with spear and sword, how many stabbings with knives, assassinations, and private murders! Besides those who were murdered, how many women, children, and old people perishing in the fields left uncultivated, in the villages infested with the odour of corpses, in that epidemic of plague and cholera which, since 1895, has desolated Turkish Armenia! Putting all exaggeration aside, we may make the following calculation. Since the 1st of July, 1894, more than 500 Armenian communities have been stricken or suppressed. Some, like those of Constantinople or Sassoun, have had more than 5,000 dead. The figure of 3,000, as at Malatia, Diarbekr, Arabkir, has often been reached. That of 1,000 is common, and the minimum of 300 has been everywhere exceeded. Van, with 10,000, seems to hold the first rank. Taking then an average of 500 dead, we remain much under the truth, and this average, for the 500 communities stricken, gives 250,000 corpses. How, in a time of unbroken peace, could a man conceive such an enterprise, and how, under the eyes of Europe, could he bring it to pass?"

It need only be added, that those on the spot consider the above figures indeed *much under the truth.*

A common way of dismissing the subject with a phrase is to say "The Armenians are as bad as the Turks." This may be understood in either of two senses : the first originators probably meaning it in one, while those who repeat it commonly take it in the other. It may mean, "The Turk at bottom is as good as the Armenian,—The Armenian at bottom is as bad as the Turk." Whether this be true or no, it does not affect the present question. If we see a man being murdered, we do not stay to enquire into his character and antecedents before coming to his aid. Were the Armenians the most degraded race in the world, and the Turks (originally) the noblest, that is no reason why humanity should allow the Turks to torture and outrage and slay the Armenians.

But, if the meaning is that the Armenians are as much to blame for these troubles, as much in fault with respect to them, as the Turks, it might be relevant, if it were true. True, however, it emphatically is not. Hear the testimony of Dr. Lepsius, who has made an exhaustive study of the whole question. "The Armenians are not to blame. It would certainly have been no wonder if the Armenian people, who for years, by a systematic policy of annihilation on the part of the Porte, had been given over defenceless to every kind of injustice at the hands of Turkish officials, to every sort of violence on the part of their Kourdish lords, to extortion by the commissioners of taxes, and to the utter illegality of the law courts, had risen up in a last desperate struggle against the iron yoke of tyranny. But as a matter of fact it was impossible to think of a national rising. To begin with, the Armenians, though large districts are thickly populated with them, are by no means everywhere in a majority in the provinces in question, and by the law which forbids Christians to carry arms, while allowing them to Mahometans, they are absolutely defenceless. In fact, no one in Armenia has ever thought of demanding anything like autonomy. All that was hoped for was that the Reforms should be carried out which eighteen years before had been guaranteed by the Christian Powers, and which seemed to promise to the Armenians an existence at least bearable. Through the entire district of the massacre we have not been able to discover, notwithstanding the fulness of our information, any movement (except that in Zeitoun) which could be considered to be of the nature of a revolt. The commissioners in their report were not even able to establish any act of provocation on the part of the Armenians ; and when such were alleged by the Turkish authorities, the official report has proved it to be untrue. This is what occurred in Zeitoun. The Armenian mountaineers of the Anti-Taurus, being terrified by the news of the massacres in the neighbouring provinces, fled in thousands for protection to Zeitoun, a natural fortress among the mountains. In the neighbourhood of this town there are more than a hundred villages inhabited exclusively by Armenians, who also pressed into Zeitoun. Near the town there was a Turkish citadel, with a garrison of about 600 men. The Armenians received news that this garrison was about to be considerably reinforced, and that an attack was designed on the defenceless people in Zeitoun. The Armenians decided to forestall it ; they armed themselves as well as they could,[1] stormed the citadel, and forced the garrison to surrender before reinforcements arrived. They then fortified themselves in Zeitoun, and held it the whole winter against an army of 80,000 men, who, from time to time, were sent against them. The result of the struggle has justified the Armenians of Zeitoun, if indeed we are prepared to recognise the right of self-defence." For the European Consuls intervened, and obtained for the brave Zeitounlis honourable terms of peace, and an amnesty. It ought to be added, however, that the promises made by the Turks were shamelessly violated, and 3,720 of the Zeitounlis put to the sword.

But are there not Armenian Revolutionary Committees, and Armenian Revolutionaries, who elaborate dark designs in secret, and throw bombs, and do other desperate things ? "Certainly there were some Revolutionaries," Dr. Lepsius says again, "and in some foreign towns there are still

---

[1] The Turks had never succeeded in depriving the mountaineers of this district of all their firearms. Besides, they contrived in some fashion to make arms for themselves.

Revolutionary Committees. Human nature must have changed if there are not, and one can only wonder that their number is so small and their action so unimportant. At any rate the Turkish Government is under obligation to them for existing, and is satisfied that they should not die out ; for who would then supply the sparrows to be shot at with the cannon prepared? The editor of the *Christliche Welt*, Dr. Rade, has already shown up the nonsense that is put into European newspapers about Armenian " Revolutionary Committees," etc., and has passed a just judgment on the boundless credulity of our newspapers and their readers." (It must be remembered that Dr. Lepsius writes in German and for Germans.)

In fact, the Armenians and their friends would be glad to know what course of action they could possibly pursue which would commend them to the sympathies of Europe ? If people are attacked, they must either submit, or resist, or run away. Run away the Armenians cannot, they are strictly forbidden to leave the country ; and those who have succeeded in doing so have done it in spite of the Government. If they resist, they are rebels, revolutionaries, and the Sultan in killing them is only " exercising his undoubted right of punishing his revolted subjects." If they submit, which is what, except in the case of the Zeitounlis, they have almost always done, they are cowards, unworthy on that account of our sympathies. *Cowards!* The sands of the Colisseum and the gardens of Nero in old Rome were strewn with the bones or the ashes of just such cowards, but that is not the name by which we call them now.

" Still," it is sometimes said, " the Armenians did not suffer as Christians, but as Armenians. Other Christians, subjects of the Porte, have not been molested." That, even if true, is but half the truth. Christians who were not Armenians were not killed ; Armenians who were not Christians (that is to say, who renounced Christianity) were not killed. Therefore the Armenians suffered, not as Armenians alone, and not as Christians alone, but as *Armenian Christians*. And those Armenians who need not have suffered if they would have ceased to be Christians, suffered definitely *as Christians*.

But how did the Armenians concentrate upon themselves all this furious hatred? Why should they be massacred rather than Greeks or Syrians? There are several reasons. The Greeks enjoy the protection of a foreign Government, somewhat in the same way as do the Americans and the English. The Syrians, besides being less numerous, are much more under the observation and the patronage of foreigners. "The Armenians happen to be the most numerous of the Christian races in Turkey; therefore they bear the brunt of the Crusade. The Jacobites, the Chaldeans and the Nestorians have their proportionate share."

But some say the Armenians have made themselves particularly obnoxious to the Mussulmans as money lenders and usurers; that they have shown themselves rapacious and exacting, and greedy of dishonest gain. The same accusations were brought against the Jews in the Middle Ages, and against the Russian Jews in our own day. There is, perhaps, the same amount of truth in them. Put a clever, industrious, ambitious race under the heel of an indolent, unprogressive one, and the former is sure to seize eagerly, and not to use too scrupulously, the only power within its reach, the power of the purse. As for usury, was not 33 per cent. considered a fair demand in the Dark Ages, in view of the lender's standing an even chance of getting nothing at all, or of getting something very undesirable in the shape of the rack or the dungeon? Insecurity is the parent of usury.

But, granted that the Armenians in other parts of the Turkish Empire, and even occasionally in Armenia itself, may have earned some popular hatred in this or in other ways, the vast majority of the victims have been,—not usurers, not wealthy merchants,—but industrious artisans, small shop-keepers, cultivators of the soil, with an admixture of the more educated classes, the most envenomed hatred being directed against those in any way connected with religion, whether as Gregorian priests or as Protestant pastors. Skilled craftsmen, who abounded amongst the Armenians, have been so nearly exterminated that some towns are left without a mason, a carpenter, or a shoemaker ; in others the Turks have saved a few of these artificers alive, to supply them with the conveniences which they are unable or unwilling to make for themselves.

The Armenian character cannot be dismissed with a few hasty generalities. It is doubtful that *any* national charac-ter can be so dismissed ; and the higher we rise in the scale of organic development, the more variety we find. "*Ab uno disce omnes*" is an indifferent rule even for the Fijian or the Samoan, but who would apply it to the English-man or the Frenchman? The Armenian, heir of an old civilization, stands on a plane with the latter, not with the former. The worst Armenians—and naturally they are those oftenest found in foreign countries—show just the faults sure to be engendered in any race, and especially in an astute, intelligent, enterprising race, by centuries of oppression. These are, want of truthfulness and honesty, and greediness of gain. Against these, which may be called the national faults, there are great national virtues to set off—moral purity, sobriety, strong domestic affections, gratitude, fidelity to conviction, industry, and a very remarkable love of learn-ing. The best Armenians —men like Pastor Stepanian— who have cast off the national faults and retain the national virtues, develop a very noble and singularly attractive charac-ter ; and are besides, in the fullest sense of the word, *gentle-men*. "The wood is fine in grain, and takes the polish easily."

This deeply suffering race is not faultless—what race ever

was, or is, or will be ?—but it is emphatically *worth saving*. And it is STILL in our power to save very many,—starving men,—desolate and hopeless women,—and helpless little children. Should any reader of the foregoing pages desire to bear a hand in this good work—and even those who have little to give may save, or help to save, *one* woman or *one* child—they may learn how to do it by communicating with the Association of " Friends of Armenia," 47, Victoria Street, Westminster.

Butler & Tanner, The Selwood Printing Works, Frome, and London.

www.ingramcontent.com/pod-product-compliance
Lightning Source LLC
Chambersburg PA
CBHW021539110726
47902CB00004B/946